TELL THEM TO BE QUIET AND WAIT

TELL THEM TO BE QUIET AND WAIT

CAROLINE COOK

atmosphere press

For Hannah Croasdale, Goldie Cook, and the women whose stories we don't know.

I am here; we are all here, because of you.

Based on true stories.

PROLOGUE

BEVERLY
1935

. . .

These men were carnivores. She could smell beef on their breath. She could see it in the way looked at her, like they could've cut her open, like they could already picture how she would bleed.

The sunlight slanted into the dark conference room, catching all the dust swirling in the air above the mahogany table.

"Why do you think you can do this job?" said Dr. Bell. They had all introduced themselves in a flurry at the start of the interview, but Bell was the one with the hooked nose and bowtie askew.

"Well, sir, I have a Ph.D." Beverly Conner shuffled the papers in front of her, the thin kind they make Bibles out of that you can almost see your fingers through. The pink silhouette of her hand looked strange with black type floating above it. "I believe that makes me overqualified for this position." She ran her finger down the job description. "A lab technician."

The room was dark and imposing, the air faintly rancid

with burnt coffee and the post-luncheon breath of six professors.

"Miss Conner."

Dr. Conner. She wanted to correct him, but not as much as she wanted to fix his bowtie.

"Miss Conner, can I be frank?" He was not asking her for permission, but he seemed like the kind of man who felt it best to frame things as a question, even when he had already arrived at an answer. "We've never had one of you before." He coughed. "A woman, that is, in the department."

"Or at Marsden, here, at all," Dr. Ballard, who might have even been younger than Beverly, added without looking up from the tabletop. He was picking off flecks of lacquer with his thumb.

"May I ask what you study?" She turned back to Bell.

"Ornithology, ma'am." He knit his sausage fingers together. His wedding band looked like it was cutting off circulation. "I'm quite close, I think, ma'am, to proving I've discovered a new species of woodpecker." His cheeks briefly flushed with pride. "Ma'am."

"Then you and I both see the value in new things, Dr. Bell."

BEVERLY

1935

. . .

Beverly Conner's mother wasn't right about everything, but perhaps Beverly could agree this once: sage was a good color on her. She studied herself in the mirror. It pulled out the flecks of green in her hazel eyes and cast flattering shadows across her broad chest and nearly nonexistent breasts, which was the kind of thing women like Beverly's mother lost sleep over. Beverly didn't mind much either way.

The cautious sputtering of a motor down the street meant the town was waking up. She needed to hurry.

Beverly normally wore pants, something with pockets that let her long legs move the way God intended, but this morning, she put on the green dress from the back of her closet. Her only dress. It smelled of lavender sachets and mothballs. She did the little buttons up carefully, she looked herself over in the mirror. And then it was off to work. Her first day, in fact.

Riding her rusty bike — a sort of going-away present from her brother Scooter, the only thing he could find in his garage that would be of use to her all the way up north in New Hampshire — was much harder in a dress. She wasn't the sort of woman who cared much about skirt lengths at dinner, but she did want to make a good impression on the people of this town. It was a small one, and if they didn't like her now, they might not ever.

The road was filled with potholes. Marsden was too poor to fix them, and with the snow they got this far north, they'd have to fix them again every year. A shuttered diner on the corner had been closed since she'd moved in, the sign that read "Uncle Lucky's" still swinging from its post. Through the frosted windows still sat linoleum booth tables edged in bands of silver and a row of vinyl barstools at the counter. She heard they used to have the best waffles and homemade New Hampshire maple syrup, but when the Depression hit, waffles seemed less important. Uncle Lucky might have left town. Her stomach growled, and she wondered how long it had been since she'd eaten a meal someone else had cooked.

Beverly's rubber wheels glided across sidewalk cracks and gravel paths. Though austere campuses like this weren't really Beverly's thing, she had to admit Marsden was beautiful. She'd never really appreciated the architecture at the University of Pennsylvania, but that was more because half of the buildings there were still closed to women. Maybe they were beautiful inside. Marsden College was more brick and less stone. Bricks are warmer and, often, imperfect. Beverly liked things like that, things that preserved the fingerprints of the people who'd made them.

Two boys in cable-knit sweaters chucked a football across the dewy grass. It was only in places like this that it was acceptable to sweat in collared shirts and cover wool slacks in grass stains before breakfast, where shouts and playful curses hung suspended in the morning fog, where life was dictated by bells that meant mealtime or class. The line between formal and informal was blurry, if it existed at all. She smiled at the display as she rode past. Beverly could remember those mornings, when the world seemed to fall at your feet, the day was ripe. The sun poked above the bell tower and she squinted.

It was a sweet-smelling September morning, the air heavy with leaves just about ready to fall. Cold morning mist, burnt coffee, bright sunshine, cinnamon. It was warm still, but Beverly was the only woman within spitting distance who wasn't wearing a sweater. Actually, there weren't many women within spitting distance at all, and Beverly could spit pretty far, having grown up in that rowdy house full of boys.

Marsden College was a school for young men — most of them from New England, nearly all of them wealthy, and none of them having ever called a woman "Professor" before. But that was something Beverly could only brace herself for, because the fact of the matter was that her mother needed money for hip surgery, and Scooter had enlisted in the army. He'd always been her favorite, the only one in the whole flock who was younger than her, and she promised she'd send him whatever she could. Sometimes when things got tough, she'd see his gap-toothed smile and press on. Their father had died years ago, and that was all there was.

Beverly would've kept teaching at Woods Hole Marine Laboratory until she died in her sleep or was swept out to sea, but she needed the money. She knew what she was getting herself into, leaving Woods Hole behind. It was time, as her mother said, *to get a real job.* Her mother would've preferred a marriage, but Beverly was already in love.

Beverly made it all the way to Carlisle Hall, home of the Botany and Zoology departments, without showing off too much mid-calf. She chained up her bike and paused outside the imposing door. Vines crawled around it. Beverly inspected one of the leaves of ivy that clung to the precarious cracks in the bricks, no food and no water to speak of. Just the promise of sunshine.

She studied plants for a living, but they never ceased to amaze her. They could grow in the most uninhabitable places.

LENA

2015

. . .

The letter in the fat, glossy packet had read, "Welcome to Marsden College, Class of 2019." The folder had barely fit in her mailbox, and she had flipped through it dozens of times. The brochure was full of pictures of smiling students, reading under an oak tree with a single, perfect beam of light illuminating their page; laughing over spaghetti in a not-too-crowded dining hall with exactly three meatballs on their plate; sitting in a dorm room on beds jacked up on risers, eye-level with a stunning view of campus blanketed in white snow.

Lena Rivera had assumed that was what every day at the College would be like. She was seven hours from Virginia and everything it held: the public pool where she'd learned to swim and decided that she preferred not to; the summer camp where she'd gotten mono at thirteen and swore up and down she hadn't kissed any boys, and she hadn't; the community college where she'd brought eight sharpened pencils to take the SAT, just in case seven of them broke. All the places she'd felt like she'd outgrown and simply could not wait to leave behind. But she'd never left anything behind before, so she didn't know what it would feel like.

Lena was unloading her father's station wagon in front of a building that looked decidedly more ominous and decidedly less warm than the pictures in the brochure. It was a squat, four-story brick cube with a now-illegible plaque by the front door dedicating it to a donor that had died. A cracked gutter was threatening to fall off the roof. One large flower bed by the heavy aluminum front door cradled the corpses of yellow mums, shriveled and brown in the sun. Everything was cleaned, but not clean. Front steps swept of leaves and debris, but crumbling.

Through the thin window in the door, the kind with fine wires latticing the glass, Lena saw a row of bulletin boards stapled with construction paper, advocating for safe sex. It looked dark in there.

Lena lifted another box from the trunk and felt her bangs finally stick to her slick forehead. This box had sweaters and boots and scarves, and as she glanced at them, she almost couldn't remember what it felt like to be cold. Her new classmates carried their boxes inside and didn't seem as nervous or as exhausted as she did. Had she packed too much? Had she not brought enough?

Lena hadn't expected her palms to be so sweaty; the kids in the brochure were never sweaty, they simply glowed. In the brochures, the weather was always perfect, the sun was always golden but not too hot. Hair did not stick to foreheads. Hands were not awkward. No one had sweat stains or anxiety attacks. Everyone was happy and knew where they were going and had friends.

"You got that?" her father asked with a chuckle as he followed her inside, carrying the low coffee table she'd gotten hand-me-down from her older brother. It had a few bumper stickers from the local bars in his college town, and had traveled a few hundred miles to its new home in New Hampshire. In high school, it hadn't bothered her that most of the things she owned were previously loved by her brothers. It didn't make sense to spend money on new things when older things worked well enough. New things were for impressing people, and Lena had never cared much about that. Until today, that is, when suddenly she cared very much.

"Fine." She stuck to single syllables because she wasn't certain she had enough oxygen for more. They shuffled through the hallway to her room, 211, which was, thankfully, a single room all to herself. She couldn't handle a roommate today. Dormitory, from the Latin *dormire,* "to sleep." All this useless information rattling around in her head.

The building smelled of mildew, something stale and sweet, dry and humid at once.

All the people in the hallway were carrying new fridges, gleaming white drawers and milk crates. Lena didn't want to care about whether or not her furniture was old enough to remember Y2K. She wanted to care about registering for classes and buying all of her textbooks. Perfect students, the perfect clones of their equally perfect parents. Lena's stepmother hadn't been able to come; she'd gotten an overtime shift dropped on her at the last minute. So it was just Lena and her dad. She twisted the class ring on her finger. In high school, it hadn't mattered, really, if she'd fit in. She hadn't had energy left to care about those things; there was only a stream of flashcards and standardized test scores. But now the things that flashed before her eyes were the laser stares of classmates in the hall. Everyone here looked older than her.

Her father closed the door to her room and looked around with a smile. "Home sweet home?"

"Sure, Dad."

Lena clenched and unclenched her fists, spinning around slowly, taking in the room. It looked especially grim with no belongings in it, just a striped mattress and desk with graffiti carved into it by one persistent ballpoint pen. There was a wide window, like in the brochure. Shadows of tape peeled the paint off the cinder block walls. The mattress was dappled in questionable oblong stains. She bit back her germaphobia and pressed one hand into the mattress. Springs snapped. "Looks great." Her voice betrayed the smile.

He dropped the beat-up table on the thin carpet squares between her bed and the desk. "Yeah. This'll work. I think this will work quite well, Lena." He said it like maybe he could convince them both. She could hear the doubt in his voice. And she was doing this for him, sort of — she was doing this for both of them. She was going to college. He had never gotten the chance. She watched him spin and take in the room slowly, locking his hands behind his neck and stretching from carrying more than his share of Lena's belongings up the stairs. "Just like the movies."

Lena's throat tightened the way it always did when she knew she was about to cry. This was ridiculous. She couldn't believe she'd finally made it to Marsden, where her fifteen-year-old self had been dreaming of, and the only thing she could think about was how much she wanted to go home. Virginia. Where everything smelled like sunscreen and sweat and cherry popsicles and no one cared what kind of mini fridge she had.

All of the orientation materials were in the Student Center. Her father stayed behind in the dorm, cutting the tape off of her boxes and duct-taping her extension cord to the floor "so it would be out of the way." Lena opened the large glass door and was hit with a wall of sound, layered conversations and laughter. It was ten degrees warmer in here, the vaulted ceiling punctured with skylights that were acting like a sort of greenhouse. There was a café on this floor, a billiards hall in the basement, and some meeting rooms upstairs. Someone bumped into her. "Sorry," she said, to no one in particular. It looked like everyone was lining up at a few card tables at the far side of the entryway.

A girl in a Marsden t-shirt was handing out packets from behind the table. Lena got in line. On the left were a bunch of bulletin boards advertising for last year's fraternity chili cook-off and for club volleyball tryouts. On the right, a series of plaques and glass cases with gold trophies and silver bowls inside. One single bronze bust. The bust was labeled after Marsden's first president. Lena didn't stop to read any of the other inscriptions.

"Welcome to Marsden!" the girl at the table said with a painfully wide smile. "What's your name?"

"Lena Rivera." The girl scanned her list. "R-i-v-e-r-a," she added.

"Got it!" She crossed Lena's name off of the list. Lena looked and saw six other Riveras on the sheet. She'd been the only Rivera in her high school. The girl handed Lena a packet with a map of campus, her card for the laundry room and her key for her mailbox, and a lot of other things that she'd eventually throw out without reading.

She pushed open the doors to the Student Center. It was hot outside, but not as hot as it had been in there. She wondered if she'd remember the way back to her dorm without the map.

BEVERLY

1935

. . .

"This is your... office." Dr. Bell kicked open the door. He didn't bother using his hands. Swollen and pink, they were smooth on the palms and hung dumbly at his sides.

"This... is a closet," she retorted, dropping her papers on the shelf in front of her. "With respect, Dr. Bell, I can touch all the walls at once." At Woods Hole, she'd had an office with a window and wood-paneled walls she'd stuck thumbtacks in to hang her samples as they'd dried. There had been space for her students and colleagues to gather in the doorway, at her desk, leaning against the overflowing bookshelves. The chair she'd used had been molded to the shape of her back.

"We don't have much space, *Miss* Conner."

Dr. Conner. She swallowed the words the way you do a hiccup; it hurts all the way down and for a moment you wonder if your chest might burst open. She was getting used to the feeling.

"There's a lot of people who work here," His eyes swept around the cinder block cell with a panic, like perhaps whatever it was that made it so grim in here was contagious. "And they all need their offices, you know. And their labs," he said, already looking back into the hallway.

Bell left, his cedarwood cologne still hanging in the air. He was a person who cared about such things, like the way he smelled and whether or not his shoes shone. The only scientists Beverly had met before who smelled like cedarwood had been working with real cedar trees. At Woods Hole, she had waded through stagnant water with her students in tow, rain or shine. It was the best part of the job.

The door to the closet marked it, No. 21. So it wasn't an office, but it had a number. The closet had no windows. From her desk at Woods Hole, she had been able to see the ocean.

A wooden shelf stretched from end-to-end of the cinder block walls. A chair was pulled up to it; it seemed someone had thought that shelf would suffice for a desk. It held the employee handbook and an off-white telephone, hard Bakelite that would yellow over time, with a wheel dial that was missing the three. When Beverly would finally get around to reading the handbook, she would discover that all the pronouns of the hypothetical professors in question were male. That made sense to Beverly. In the official paperwork at the back of the handbook, she'd filled in her address and her emergency contacts and had simply left the box for "wife" blank.

The Zoologists and the Botanists were nice enough, though upset they were lumped into one department. Ignoring someone didn't make you unpleasant or hostile. No one spoke to her besides Dr. Bell, who only deigned a few awkward words because he'd been asked to give her the tour. There was no women's restroom in the building, he noted as they passed the third men's room on her floor, so she'd have to go next door. It wasn't a question.

Dr. Bell told her that the professors all ate lunch together in the lounge. When noontime rolled around, Beverly walked past the door three times before summoning the nerve to push it open. Clustered around three tables and swirling in cigar smoke, all the smartly dressed men looked up to see her enter. One froze mid-bite of his sandwich and Beverly could hear the squeak of the lettuce between his molars. Another didn't lower the coffee cup raised to his mustache. There was only one open chair, between two white-haired men in tweed jackets, the kind with pads on the elbows. She approached slowly, holding her brown bag in a fist clenched so tight the paper started to dissolve in sweat. "Is this seat taken?"

The men at the table looked at each other, expressionless. One took a long drag on his cigar as his eyes swept up and down Beverly's body, brushing her jawline, her collarbone, her wrists that poked from her sleeves and even her ankles as they disappeared into her shoes. After his examination was complete, he spat the cigar from his mouth and said, "Yes. The seat's taken."

"Oh. Well." She smoothed her skirt and opened and closed her mouth a few times. "That's alright, actually, I have a... meeting. So. I should be going." Beverly didn't look behind her as she slowly stalked back out of the lounge. She wondered why they kept it so dark in here. Her eyes skimmed the countertop with a row of smart steel coffee pots. She wondered who filled the pots each morning, and she wondered if it was something these men had ever thought about.

She didn't breathe until she was out of the lounge, and then she ran, her quick footsteps echoing on the tile, down the stairs and out the front doors of Carlisle Hall. In every direction, from every building, spilled men in collars and sweaters. They climbed over the backs of the benches on the sidewalks, tackled each other even if they were carrying books, whooped at the players of an impromptu baseball game on the quad. They all knew where they were headed: anywhere. Every surface conquerable, like ants. Beverly's palms were slick at her sides.

There. An oak tree — ignored in the sunshine. Beverly sat down awkwardly, never sure how to sit in a skirt, and felt the mulch prick her bare skin. It was cooler in the shady jagged halo under the canopy. The bell tower rang and rang, and she sank into the trunk.

It was why she'd become a biologist, really. Plants were much easier to talk to than people. This would become a ritual of hers, eating lunch beneath the tree, sometimes doing a crossword puzzle to keep her mind occupied — her mother had always told her that a rambling mind can run away from you. But as she listened to the birds and the din of the lunch-time campus roar, she didn't know if this would be a place she'd return or not. It didn't matter today. She didn't know how long the men in that building could play the silent game. Today, she knew that she had earned her turkey sandwich for lunch, and white bread and American cheese had never tasted more decadent. She was a real employee of this College. Employees get lunch breaks. She chewed and watched the clouds. One of them might have been a bird.

LENA

2015

. . .

For the first time in her life, Lena Rivera was not paying attention in class. And this, her first class of college, really wasn't the time to be slipping up. Her first biology class, no less. Surely, her performance in Bio 101 would make or break her entire career, and she wasn't paying attention — but it wasn't her fault.

It was a big lecture hall; the kind shaped like a Roman amphitheater, all the drama and none of the polish. The back wall held an old oil portrait of an ancient college President. There were rows of blue folding chairs, indistinguishable from the kind in a movie theater except for their wooden desks, all facing the front wall which was latticed with white boards. The professor slid them up and down while she was talking, sending them gently rolling towards two skylights and a clock that Lena assumed was broken. It couldn't have been 11:02 for that long.

"There will be six quizzes." The professor was reviewing the syllabus, the first syllabus she'd get at Marsden, and Lena's mind wasn't even in the clouds, it was fully in outer space. She could not stop staring at this guy with black hair at the front of the room. Black Hair Guy, like everyone else in the lecture hall, was paying attention to the professor. He was the TA, in the seat of honor in the front row. It was probably frowned upon to be ogling the TA.

"The book for this course will be *Miracles of Biology* by Beverly Conner and Henry Nightingale. Do you all have the text?" She did have the text, she had all of them. She'd emptied out her savings on shiny hard-covers at the college bookstore. Lena brushed a sesame seed off of her folding desk. She'd bought an everything bagel this morning, a first-day-of-school tradition between her and her father since preschool. She'd been running late, though, because the line at the dining hall was longer than she was expecting. She wolfed the bagel down at her seat before her professor came in, since she wasn't sure if you could eat in class. She still didn't know. The sesame seed landed on the floor, and she wondered if her dad had had an everything bagel that morning without her.

Black Hair Guy was taking notes in the margins of the syllabus with a pen that must have cost a few hundred. She wondered if he'd be leading the study groups, if his hands would be grading her quizzes. He kept sweeping his bangs out of his eyes with his left hand, which had a tiny tattoo on the wrist that Lena could not distinguish.

"My office hours are from 2:30 to 4:30 on Wednesday afternoons."

Lena had worked her whole life to get to college. And for the past few years, since she'd had that first piece of mail from Marsden pinned to her bulletin board, she'd been working to take classes here in Carlisle Hall. She clicked her pen. Focus, focus. Black Hair Guy was focused, and he'd already taken this class before.

"I think that's everything on the syllabus. Shall we start on Chapter One?" Hundreds of textbook spines cracked like an orchestra. There were a lot of people in this lecture hall. In high school, she was valedictorian out of a few hundred. Now, she was one of a few hundred valedictorians. And she couldn't focus. Lena snapped from her trance and hefted the massive volume from her bag. Chapter One. Chapter One.

"I'm sure most of you took AP Biology in high school, so we're going to breeze through the basics." The slide changed to an image taken from a microscope slide. "Who can tell me what this is?" A sea of confident hands shot into the air. Lena's did not. The image looked familiar, but she couldn't place the word. Her eyes blurred out of focus, the close-up on the microscope fading into a green pattern. Her foot bounced under the desk. Behind her, someone coughed. She wondered if the chairs in every lecture hall were like this one; they weren't very comfortable. Maybe some of the lecture halls were better. Maybe this one was very old. For a moment, Lena wondered how many generations of Marsden students had sat in these rows and struggled to focus. Maybe it was just her.

Class was over before Lena had floated back down to Earth.

The air outside was sticky with the dregs of summer, but it was a welcome change after the still, recycled air in the lecture hall. Lena had always thought stepping outside after class was like stepping into the parking lot of a movie theater — a rude reintroduction to reality, the rough embrace of harsh sun and humid air.

Lena focused on putting one foot in front of the other. She didn't yet know her way around campus. She had just finished her first class: she was doing this, really doing this thing she'd been dreaming of for years. But the daydream always began and ended in the lecture hall; she had no idea what to do when she left.

In the distance, an oak tree cast a turquoise shadow on the grass. There was nothing more inviting than shade in the right moment. A heap of mulch was piled around the trunk and a little bronze plaque that named someone from another time, when everything was in crackling black and white. Lena threw herself to the ground, relieved to have a place she was supposed to be for one moment. Around her, even the other chatty freshmen had already separated themselves into confident twos and threes and were pouring out onto campus. Two women walked past her.

"Was that your first class, too?"

"Yeah. Ugh, we did it."

The first failure — if you could even call it that — stung a little. She'd barely paid attention in class, and she had a lot of catching up to do if she was going to get a spot in a lab, get an internship, get into a good grad program, secure the best postdoc, conquer the world, leave fire in her wake, retire. When she was a little kid, she and her father would set up lines of dominoes all over the first floor of the house, stretching across the kitchen countertops and the windowsills. When you knocked over the first one, they all fell. She had always thought school, her career, was like that.

A leaf fell, slowly. Lena cracked her textbook, which folded its thin, glossy pages over to Chapter One. She settled into the rough bark of the oak tree and thought, perhaps, this could be her first friend at Marsden. Trees don't ask too many questions. They don't have newer clothes than you and they don't judge if you stammer when you're nervous.

She would deal with real people tomorrow. Today, she was reading her textbook in the shade, as the most beautiful campus spread out from her in every direction. She could do this, she could do this. And if she said it to herself one more time, she almost might start to believe it. Then again, Lena Rivera had never been a very good liar.

BEVERLY

1935

. . .

The clock on the wall was three minutes slow. It was the big kind, with a flat glass face that wasn't even shiny anymore, so that it could be read from here, at the front of the lecture hall, without a glare. The silence was almost peaceful. She looked up the rows of chairs — hundreds of identical, empty seats, blue cloth upholstery — to the back wall, paneled in dark wood and bearing the weight of an oil painting of the college President. For now, it was just Beverly and her firm grip on the podium and the stack of notes in front of her. No judging eyes, indignant stares, or expectant blank notebook paper.

Dr. Bell was out for the week. His wife was having a baby, and while he wouldn't be a part of the birth or present for any of what happened after, going home, at least at first, was customary. Or so it had been explained to her. This was the only class he needed covered; the rest were exams and labs that proctors could fill in for. But there was one lecture that the rest of the department simply couldn't find time to give. And that's how Beverly gave her first lecture in Carlisle Hall, or was about to — in four minutes.

The doors at the top of the stairs swung open and a few

boys filed in, near clones of each other in earth-colored sweaters and creased pants their mothers had pressed. The first boy, the perky blonde one with rosy cheeks, bounded down the stairs with a confidence in his step Beverly was certain she'd never had. He walked right up to the podium where she shuffled her notes. "You must be Miss Conner. Dr. Bell told us we'd have a... *guest* lecturer."

She leaned forward, her hands skimming the edge of the pulpit. "Dr. Conner, yes. And you are?"

"Kenneth Wilford. I'm a Botany major," he said, glancing at a spot just above her head for only a moment, as if reminding her he was taller. "So, you let me know if you need someone to call on." His eyes fell to her hands for a moment, resting on the podium. "I'll be right here," he gestured at the front row.

"Well, this is an intro class, so I think I can handle it," she tilted her head and smiled, "but I'll be glad to have at least one enthusiastic student. *Mr. Wilford.*"

He didn't falter.

"Mr. Wilford, please take your seat."

He looked down at his hands, which she couldn't see from behind the podium. Kenneth produced a shiny red apple, polished it on his button-down, and set it on the lip of the desk. "For the teacher." His eyes flashed and he sat down in the front row, challenging her, but it wasn't clear yet to what.

The other boys who filed in behind him filled the lecture hall with the hum of conversations. The red-headed boy who'd come in after Kenneth nodded at him and set another apple on the table. Each one, with slicked hair and amused smirks, carried an apple and set it with the others. At first it was two and then a few more, and Beverly decided that acknowledging the joke would make it more real. She would keep the upper hand as long as she bit her tongue. The hollow echo of apple flesh sounded each time another was added to the pile. She wasn't sure what they were doing, why they found it funny, until suddenly there wasn't room for all the apples, and fifty red faces were staring back at her from their seats, barely containing their glee. One lone apple bounced from the top of the pile, thumping each apple all the way down until it landed on the thin carpet and rolled to a stop at her shoe.

The hum of conversation died as they watched Beverly pick up her notes from the podium, sweep her eyes across the mountain of apples as if they weren't even there, and begin. "Welcome to Botany 200. As you know, Dr. Bell is out and I'm —"

Kenneth stood, his chair squeaking against the floor. Clutching his chest, he warbled, "An apple for the teacher, that seems the thing to do —"

Another stood behind him and continued, "Because I want to learn about romance from you." They sprung up from the back row, the sides, and the middle. *"An apple for the teacher, to show I'm meek and mild/If you insist on saying that I'm just a problem child."*

The entire lecture hall was standing, some clutching their chests dramatically. One in the front row fell to his knees. They were hardly singing, more shouting. It must've been heard in the hallway, surely.

"You'll get all my attention! Your wish will be my rule! And maybe you'll be good to me and keep me after school!" They finished, collapsing into whooping laughter. Beverly gripped the podium with white knuckles and did not raise her eyes from the lecture notes in front of her. Her own neat handwriting was sliding together as her vision blurred.

"*Miss* Conner," Kenneth said as their hollering died down, "we just wanted to welcome you to Marsden the best way we knew how. With a little help from Mr. Bing Crosby, of course." He fell back into his chair and winked at her. "Please, ma'am, your lecture."

She scanned the room, suddenly feeling very hot and hoping it wasn't showing on her face. She thought she might pass out. She'd read that if you locked your knees that could happen, and she wasn't sure how to tell if her knees were locked or not.

The boys' shiny, expectant faces glinted back at her. Their eyes sparkled with uncontainable delight, looking down at her from their arena of seats. The silence was too much. Beverly began to clap, slowly, then louder. At first, they seemed to like this. After a moment, though, unease flashed in some eyes. "*Bravo.*" Her eyes swept across the room, afraid to land on one of their faces for more than a moment. Her clammy palms slapped together, hollow. "Or, I suppose, *bravi*, if you're," she swallowed hard, "the kind of person who," she sighed, "knows Italian." It was a silly question. They probably were.

Kenneth audibly sighed, his lips quirked into a pitying smile. He made a big show of crossing his arms and leaning forward on his desk, feigning interest. "Is that so, *Professoressa?*" A perfect accent.

Beverly had tried to enroll in language courses at Penn, but women couldn't enroll in classes outside of their major. She'd even snuck into the back of a French classroom once, but the professor had thrown her out. Her Italian, like her Latin, was self-taught.

They were still waiting for a lecture. "Right," she began, without any idea where she was headed. Beverly lifted the notes again, keeping them low enough to the desk so that the boys couldn't see her shaking hands. "Right. Well. As you know, Dr. Bell is out and I'm going to be giving you all the lecture on algae today. Fortunately, I have a Ph.D. in phycology from Penn," she glanced up from her notes and saw blank stares. She turned to the chalkboard, filmed with fine dust, and wrote "phycology" in her perfect scrawl.

"For those of you Botany majors," she called over her

shoulder so that it would stick Kenneth between the beady blue eyes, "Phycology is the study of algae. You should probably know it." She wondered if he could hear her voice shake.

The chalk fell to its metal tray with a satisfying clink. She turned back to their pale expectant faces, shimmering like the scales of a fish. "Perhaps you're wondering why anyone would study pond scum. Who can tell me what makes algae different from others in the plant kingdom?"

No one moved. "Now's really not the time for shyness." She felt confidence ebb back. "After all, boys, I've already heard you sing."

Kenneth's eyes dropped to the floor.

"Alright. It seems I've got some teaching to do. Algae generally lacks vascular tissue, and often roots and leaves and all the things that probably come to mind when you think of the word 'plant.'"

The door at the top of the stairs swung open. The Dean's face appeared, one she only recognized from passing in the hallway and from a portrait hung in the administration building when she'd interviewed for the job. She kept talking but slowed a little as she watched his eyes settle on the mountain of gleaming apples she was teaching beside. "Why is this important? Perhaps one of you Botany majors might see where I'm headed with this." The Dean took a step further and the door gently rested on his back. "Kenneth. Why don't you have a go."

"Plants photosynthesize," he said with a sweet smile. "And they need leaves to do that, y'know, because of the surface area." He leaned back into his chair, satisfied, until he noticed her still staring at him expectantly. The confidence on his face flickered only for a moment. "And, uh, also sunlight. As well."

"Kenneth is right. You've probably been taught that plants are shaped the way they are to make photosynthesis the most efficient it can be. But algae, then, goes against all those ideas. So what do we think is happening here?" Beverly dropped her notes. She wouldn't be needing them. She paced around the chalkboard, liking the way her shoes echoed in the lecture hall. "Boys. I just told you to throw everything you thought you knew about plants out the window. Why aren't you writing this down?"

A cacophony of notebooks being opened snapped them from their stunned daze. She caught Kenneth's eye and held his gaze. Beverly let herself sneak a glance to the back of the lecture hall. The Dean was shaking his head, but he was too far away for Beverly to tell if he was smiling or not. And then he was gone, leaving the door swinging in the frame.

Beverly picked up an apple off the top of the stack while they were writing. Kenneth looked up from his notes, his face still confused by what he'd been writing, to see Beverly take a large bite. Her chewing made the others look up. "It's bitter," she said towards the blonde mop of hair as she set the apple down on the desk next to his. Juice pooled in the wood grain.

. . .

She was always thankful for the bike ride after work, but especially today. The waves of adrenaline were still hitting her, and she sucked in deep breaths of dusk all the way home. She'd worn pants; no skirt to get caught in the bike chain. She wove between two boys carrying their textbooks against their chests. She cut down by the library, where the only women on campus, the librarians, were smoking by the imposing front doors in neat little clusters. Their girlish laughter rang across the sunset like the bells in the clock tower. On the quad, the Marsden ROTC was practicing drills. Crisp, neat lines of men wearing crisp, neat uniforms. Rifles slung over their shoulders, pointing toward the sky. Men in uniform always made her think of Scooter.

She thought of her brother and the way he would eat chicken and biscuits, and tried to focus on happy memories of crumbs on the kitchen table for the rest of her ride. Her mother swatting him with a damp dish towel, sitting down to dinner without even taking off her sauce-splattered apron. There were no more thoughts of Kenneth, at least until she tossed her bike in the bushes outside of her house.

The screen door tried to slam behind her, but it bounced off the door frame the way screen doors do. It hung in the breeze for a moment, like it was expecting someone else to come in after her. But it was just Beverly, and the occasional creak of the floorboards, and the many drafts of her most recent scientific paper scattered on every flat surface.

Between the salt and pepper shakers, the ceramic ones her mother had sent from Macy's and were probably the nicest thing in the house, sat a rapidly accumulating stack of bills — made out in her father's name even though he was dead. In total, she owed ten dollars. Her monthly salary wouldn't cover all that, plus the house and food. Beverly opened the refrigerator. A jar of jam and a jar of pickles sat side by side, a repulsive pair that reflected light from the one lone bulb in dark reds and bright olives. There was one particularly hard block of cheese. She wondered if cheese ever went bad, really.

She sat down at the kitchen table and was glad, actually, to have so many apples. Beverly pulled out a waxy one and took a loud crunch. White flesh and clear juice ran down her chin and for a moment, it didn't even bother her that there wasn't anyone to tell about her day.

LENA

2015

· · ·

The music in the basement was so loud that Lena could feel her molars vibrating. She had never noticed that when music is loud, it almost tastes metallic. Her throat and chest were rattling from the music, something with a lot of bass and indecipherable lyrics, and she kept getting jostled by sweaty, writhing partygoers. People turn red when they're drunk. They're warm and lose all sense of where their limbs go. Like baby deer, Lena noted, only with deer, we expect them to be able to stand up on their own immediately.

She wasn't sure why she'd come to this party. Lena had never liked parties in high school. It hadn't even been peer-pressure. No one had asked her to go with them. In fact, she'd come alone. After the first mysterious liquid, an inexplicably blue one, had splashed onto her canvas sneakers, she decided she'd made the wrong decision. This was her only pair of sneakers, and she'd somehow kept them white enough for the past two years. Thirty seconds in a frat basement and all that hard work was gone. She was still scrubbing at the stain with the rubber tip of the other shoe when she was jostled, again, by a blonde man dripping with sweat in a Lakers jersey. He shouted an apology that Lena could not hear over the music. She felt the bass in her temples and wondered for a moment if she might die.

There was a stop sign in the corner, hanging on the wall. Lena was pretty sure that stealing street signs was illegal. She wondered if you needed to bring a drill with you to remove the sign from its post, or if you took the whole post with you.

Someone bumped into her left side, someone who wasn't wearing a shirt. Their slick skin slid against hers. Maybe she only came to see if she would like the way it felt when people looked at her. She hadn't liked it much in high school, though few people had. Lena wouldn't have admitted it if anyone asked, which they wouldn't, but she dug out some old drugstore mascara and had put on a shirt she knew was a little too small for her. She felt like a fraud, but what mattered was if anyone else could tell. That little part of her that glowed with pride when the girl complimented her nails in line at the dining hall or the boy in her study group asked her to get coffee sometime — that part that she swore up and down didn't exist — that part wanted to go to a party. Unfortunately, the rest of her was the vocal majority, and it desperately wanted to go home.

"Sarah?" Basketball Jersey shouted in her ear.

"Oh, no, sorry," Lena said. Her shoe squeaked on something sticky. He thought he knew her. She couldn't decide if he was attractive or not, but she felt like she should want to talk to him.

"I know you from somewhere! Are you in my 8 a.m. Spanish?" His sour breath smelled of yeast and tobacco. The only person Lena had ever met who smoked cigarettes was her Aunt Lisa, and she quit years ago. Did people still smoke? She recoiled at first but realized that she'd need to be close to him if she wanted him to keep talking to her, which she thought she did, maybe. That was why people went to parties, to be looked at and spoken to. Maybe his breath wasn't that bad. He wasn't bad looking, though it was dark in here. Lena wondered if that's why it's always dark at parties, so you can't tell if the people there are attractive. Was she attractive?

"No, sorry." She elbowed away from him in the crowd, but he grabbed her bare shoulder. His fingers, wet from the beer in his hand, slipped on her skin.

"Are you sure?"

"Not possible, I take French." Her eyes swept the crowd, expecting, for a moment, to see a familiar face, but it was too dark to tell if she knew anyone. The whole room was lit by a few strings of flashing Christmas lights and one lightbulb over the makeshift bar in the corner, built out of cases of beer and a few two-by-fours that leaned dangerously to one side. It looked just like it did in the movies. An overflowing trash can spilled crushed cups onto the floor, and the few dancers around it kicked them. They all seemed to be having more fun than she was. Of course, she was having fun. This was fun. Music. And the drink-and-a-half was starting to make her head spin. That wasn't a lot, she didn't think, but she didn't know. Maybe it was. It was hot in here.

"What?" He was shouting over the music and used it as an excuse to move closer to her again. Someone bumped into her from behind and she was thrown into his chest. She didn't like that he reached up to catch her. She didn't like that his sweat was on her shirt. She didn't like that he was still looking at her. But this was the kind of thing she was supposed to like. This, being thrown against a senior, probably one of the brothers in this fraternity. An accident, so neither of them had to invent a scenario to brush against each other. That was what she should want. But she felt something rising in her chest.

"I'm gonna go home," she said, loudly enough, hopefully. Lena pushed herself off of his chest and looked around for the stairs. It was easy to get disoriented in the dark. Had she come downstairs? She was pretty sure this was the basement.

"Let me walk you!" Basketball Jersey grabbed another beer from the bar and guided her towards the stairs.

"I'm really fine, you should stay. Seems fun."

It was strange to hear her own voice as they emerged from the cloud of people. She started up the stairs to get away from him, watching her body come into the dim lighting of the stairwell like she'd been separated from it for the whole evening. He followed her up the stairs. Basketball Jersey shotgunned the beer on the stair behind her, pausing only for a moment before tossing the frothing can to the ground. She stopped to watch him, almost hypnotized. Everything was a little more viscous tonight. Her body moved through the humid basement air like it was resisting her. Maybe this was what being drunk was.

"Where d'ya live?" he asked. She couldn't meet his eyes; the foam at the corners of his mouth was distracting. And disgusting. She wondered if he was going to try to kiss her and if tasting the beer on his lips that he didn't know was there still would make her throw up. She'd never kissed anyone before, something she'd deny if anyone asked her, but she thought that throwing up would not be good. "Where?" he asked again.

"Oh. Uh. The dorms."

He laughed. "No shit." It was brighter up here, on the first floor. A fraternity house came into view, something made of stained pine and sagging in all the corners. She blinked in the light and panicked at the sight of only a few people nursing cups and talking in quiet twos and threes to be away from the noise. Not one she recognized. "You're a freshman, aren't you?" He licked his lips and ran his fingers through his hair.

"Um," Lena wondered if it would be helpful to lie, but doubted it would be convincing. She'd never been particularly good at it, and the one-and-a-half drinks in her system would make it even worse. "Right."

"So you live on the s-south side of campus," he slurred, running his hand along the wood paneling. Lena wondered if he was going to fall, and how many of her bones would break if he fell on her. She pictured it, for a moment, his briefly-unconscious, pink flesh pinning her to the sticky floorboards striped with years' worth of black grime. She wondered if she'd hit her head, what she'd do with a concussion in the first month of school. Would her student insurance cover a trip to the hospital? What would she tell her father?

The door to the foyer was opening and closing, letting in gasps of cold midnight air. It was only when she sucked in breaths of untainted air that she realized how intensely sour the house smelled, beer mixed with sweat and something else she really hoped wasn't urine. Women in leather miniskirts and much more comfortably dressed men came and left. That was the exit. She could just run. "Really" — she realized she still didn't know Basketball Jersey's name, and didn't want to — "I know my way home. I'm basically sober at this point. I'm fine."

He slung his arm over her shoulder, his fingertips bouncing on her collarbone as they walked. Her chest tightened. "Come onnn," he said, like finishing the word was too much effort, so he let it spill from his mouth. "I gotta take care of the freshie!" She wriggled her shoulder under the weight of his arm, like maybe it would slip off of her on its own, but he was heavy.

Basketball Jersey pushed the front door open by slamming into it with his side, a motion that nearly tipped the two of them over. Lena took the chance to slip out from under him and tried to outpace him down the front walk. Black sky stretched above them in all directions, and the landscape was dark and punctured by streetlights. She thought if she ran now, she could make it home. She didn't want to know what would happen if he came all the way back to her dorm. She didn't want his fingers to brush her skin ever again.

He remained a few feet behind her, his shoes scuffing the sidewalk. An occasional car raced past them, and he cursed at the bright headlights but otherwise was cheerfully whistling to himself or asking her questions she dodged answering.

There was a stoplight up ahead, a four-way intersection with so much open pavement that his voice carried even farther. The light glowed a red that mocked her, and even though it was after midnight and no cars were coming, Lena was the sort of person who waited for a green light every time. He caught up to her then, oblivious to her trying to outrun him. "How do you say pretty in Spanish?" he slurred, but his eyes were focused, creased at the edges with the lines eyes get when you smile. "*B-bonito.* You're *bo-ni-to.*" He laughed.

"*Bonita,*" Lena corrected under her breath.

He smiled shakily, his pink lips curling up at the edges, slowly, the way a cat's do when they lick their lips before a meal. Lena could tell he'd never had braces. She hadn't either, but suddenly his crooked teeth were repulsive, and she could feel her heartbeat in her palms. She wondered if he was going to kiss her. This couldn't be the way it happened; this didn't happen in movies.

Lena glanced at the sky for a moment and wondered why she couldn't see any stars. The admissions packets had said you could see the stars in New Hampshire.

"You're really pretty, for a freshman." He reached for her face with a bloated pink hand and missed, resting on the bare patch of her stomach, exposed from her shirt riding up. He squeezed the fleshy white part of her that had barely seen the sun. Never another person's hand. It looked like he might say something else, then, he suddenly doubled over and vomited into the bush right next to them.

"Oh my god, are you okay?" Her voice didn't sound like her own in the night air.

Basketball Jersey fell over into his puddle, face-first. The stoplight turned green.

For a moment, she wondered if she should leave him there. He repulsed her that much, and her body was shaking, and she wasn't sure why. But a decade of flashcards kicked in, and she knew he needed to be upright to keep his windpipe clear, and that he could drown on his own vomit, and that was perhaps the worst way to die. She was struggling to lift his limp body when a few men started crossing the street and saw her in the glow of the green light, turning yellow. Then red.

"Do you two need help?" Someone shouted. Lena looked up and recognized the beautiful bangs and dark eyes. Black Hair Guy, the TA.

"He does. *I'm* fine, but I think he might need to go to the hospital."

"Oh my, alright." Lena's TA knelt down on the sidewalk beside him and lifted him to a seated position easily, not even worrying for a moment that Basketball Jersey might crush him and break all of his bones. "What's his name?"

"I don't know. I've never met him before. I was trying to get away from him, actually, but I mean, I don't want him to die." The TA's friends nodded, like that made perfect sense, and called for campus security. Lena wasn't even sure Marsden had one of those. "I'm Lena," she offered, and wasn't sure why. She wanted Black Hair Guy to know her name. Basketball Jersey could think she was Sarah.

"Peter," Black Hair Guy said. He met her eyes for a moment, looking up at her from the grass. His eyes were warm, being held in his gaze was warm, somehow. "Why don't you go home? We got this." Lena didn't even say thank you before she broke into a run. Her buckling knees couldn't keep her there a moment longer. The midnight dew on the grass in the quad soaked through her sneakers. The cold air filled her lungs until they couldn't stretch any more. She didn't stop until she got to her dorm, taking the stairs three at a time, and just praying she'd make it to her room before the tears started. She wasn't even sure what she was upset about, really, but she knew she didn't want anyone to see her. It could have been worse, she kept telling herself. He barely touched her. Best case scenario. It could have been worse.

Lena didn't cry when she got back to her room. She fell into bed, buried her face so far into the pillow she could almost taste the smell of stale linen and sweat, and tried to will herself to fall asleep. There's a certain numbness that comes with discomfort, when your brain refuses to accept that what just happened to you was horrible and that you might still have a stranger's vomit on your shoe. Lena didn't know what that numbness felt like. She pulled out her phone and searched for Peter, the TA. There were a few dozen Peters at Marsden. Lena wanted to focus on Peter, the Good Guy. Everything could be classified in Lena's mind. She was hard-wired for exams and flashcards. Peter. Good Guy. And she wouldn't let herself think about the others.

Lena could still feel his wet fingers and everywhere his skin had touched hers. After a few moments, the disgust at those patches on her shoulders and collarbone and stomach — the contamination — outweighed her desire to melt into the bed and never come out of it. She grabbed her shower caddy and her flip flops and towel and went down the hallway, careful not to look at her face in the mirror, in case she didn't recognize it. That was a silly thing to think, of course. Lena turned the shower on and scrubbed and scrubbed at her skin until she could be sure his smell was completely gone. Her fingernails left red stripes across her arms and stomach. She watched as iridescent bubbles clumped together on her skin and chased each other over her kneecap, down her shin and onto the tile floor. They circled the drain a few times before disappearing.

She remembered a lecture from a science class in middle school. Her teacher had said every cell in your body is replaced after seven years. At the time, twelve-year-old Lena had thought the fact terrifying: would she still be the same person if all of her cells were different then? She'd stayed after class to grill the teacher, who desperately wanted to go home, on what exactly that meant, even the cells in her brain? Now, the thought was comforting. Maybe in seven years she wouldn't remember this night. In seven years, she'd be 25 and everything would be different. She wondered if there was something wrong with her for not liking the way it had felt when he'd touched her. It didn't matter. As the water slid over her body, she reminded herself over and over again that she only had to wait seven more years for his memory to be completely gone.

BEVERLY

1935

. . .

The Dean of the Faculty was knocking on Beverly Conner's door, and she didn't know why.

"Miss Conner?" She recognized his polite, husky voice in the hall. Panic jolted through her body.

Her hands flew around the shelf she'd been using as a desk, but there wasn't much to straighten. A postcard Scooter had sent her after finding her new faculty mailbox, a glossy picture from his latest travels which she tucked between the pages of her notebook. It was just a postcard, but it still felt like something that was only meant for her eyes. All she'd brought to furnish the office was a single pen, brought to a sharp right angle against the corner of her legal pad. The microscope, her greatest treasure, sat dumbly awaiting more samples. And there was nothing to be done about the beat-up telephone; it would outlive them all.

"Come in."

Dean Peabody had been a physicist before he became an administrator. He'd worked in the U.S. Army, was more comfortable around telescopes than his own six children, and was one of Marsden College's most engaging lecturers before he was promoted to Dean. All of this is to say that Dean Peabody knew acceleration when he saw it, and when his eyes crinkled at the sight of Beverly Conner standing there, chin held high in her dark closet office, he knew he was looking at a shooting star.

"Pardon the interruption, Miss Conner." There was just enough space for two chairs, and he helped himself to one of them. He was a broad-shouldered man, still boasting a thick head of salt-and-pepper hair. He took up the whole room, and Beverly was confident that the air that remained was slowly being squeezed out. "I wanted to pay you a visit. I've heard good things."

"I can't imagine from whom," she quipped quietly as she ran her fingers along the edges of the notebook. "Not that people haven't been very nice!"

It was dangerous to appear ungrateful — she had a job, didn't she, when President Roosevelt had to make them out of thin air? — and she stammered her recovery. "I just meant, of course, Dean Peabody, that I've been trying to stay out of everybody's hair. It's a busy place, our Carlisle Hall." Growing up in that house full of boys, she'd never been nervous around men. But Dr. Peabody wasn't a man, he was a Dean. And, unfortunately, there weren't any of those around growing up.

Leslie Peabody sighed. His breath was soured by the distant memory of tobacco and sweetened by the fresh one of coffee, and his blue eyes searched her face for a moment before he responded. His face was grooved by years of experience, not just age, and you could almost see the muscles in his cheeks twinge as he bit back his smile. "Miss Conner—"

"Beverly. Please, if you would."

"Beverly." And the smile burst through, in spite of himself. "I wanted to find out how you were getting on. You've got yourself a Ph.D., I saw."

"From Penn, sir. The University of Pennsylvania." She

kicked herself. He knew Penn.

The Dean weighed his words on his tongue, rolling them around like a toffee. "I don't really know how to ask this." Physicists were not trained on how to speed up a moving particle; the protons in the lab had never needed encouragement. In his whole career, the Dean had just been around to observe, to document, but Beverly Conner needed an ally, not a lab tech or a scribe. And it seemed like he knew it. "Beverly, how are you finding things? I mean, you're overqualified for your job — I understand you're... *prepping slides* for the department courses. The Chair tells me you stepped in to lecture when Dr. Bell was out —" His face must have been redder than hers, and she wondered if it was at the memory of the mountain of apples. He did not mention it. "You like teaching? You've taught before?"

"Sir, I was an instructor at Woods Hole for a few summers. It's the greatest place in the world." Her cheeks burned at her own honesty. Everything had been simpler there.

"I had the pleasure, once, while I was in college. A friend of mine took a class there, and a few of us went to visit. He took us out in the boats for a nighttime sail. Fond memories of those waters."

"Me too. A couple girls and I — well, *other teachers*, and I — finally saved up enough to buy our own sloop." A glittering fog clouded her eyes for a moment. She caught Leslie looking at her, surprised, like he hadn't expected her to dispense with her shyness. "And the damn thing crashed on her maiden voyage!" Her laugh was sheepish and bittersweet. "The coast guard had to rescue us!"

"You're kidding!" He leaned back in his seat and matched her grin.

"Made all the local papers, as far as Boston. Everyone loved the idea of these shipwrecked women, soaked to the bone. It was funny because we were all fine, of course, but we lost our boat."

They settled into the silence of content reminiscence, even if they were both reminiscing about different things. It was Beverly's turn to be surprised at how casually she'd been speaking to the Dean. He was the first man here who'd talked to her like she might have something to say. She'd been so starved for conversation.

"I've heard good reports from the boys you've lectured."

Beverly looked down at her hands in her lap and pressed her lips together to smother the smile. "I am glad to hear that, sir."

"If you don't mind me saying, you've got to give a sharp lecture to make those animals interested in anything, let alone algae."

"I assure you, Dean Peabody, algae is much more interesting than it appears. There's hundreds — gosh, maybe thousands — of types, many still being discovered. All sizes, all colors, all ecosystems. They can live anywhere, places you or I could never survive. They're the backbone of a good —"

Leslie Peabody was laughing. And it was not clear to Beverly if he was laughing at her, or happened to be laughing about something else in this tiny room. The phone perhaps. There was much she found amusing.

"Dr. Conner, I am not attempting to pass judgment on your life's work."

"Are you a man of science?"

The corners of his eyes were still folded, still gripped by amusement. "Yes ma'am. Physics is my weapon of choice."

"Then you understand the allure, Dr. Peabody. Because most of those boys find Newton about as dry as you find algae. You watch an apple fall to the Earth and call it a discovery. I probe black water and find something no one has seen before."

They stared at each other in delighted silence. It might have been the first time in weeks either of them had sparred with a true peer. And it felt good for Beverly to speak as quickly as words popped into her head. Carlisle was attempting to clip her wings, and it had sharp scissors. But Leslie Peabody had seen a worthy opponent.

"Well, Miss Conner, uh — Dr. Conner. I'd like to see you promoted. Assistant Professor."

The particles were hurtling faster and faster. And an object in motion will stay in motion. That is, unless something gets in its way.

"Will the department allow that, Dr. Peabody?" All she could manage was a whisper.

"Honestly, ma'am, I don't know. I'm not sure we've ever had..." he folded his hands in his lap. "I'm thinking you'd probably be the first. You know, the first woman. I'm not sure I can get the President on board."

She nodded. "Of course."

"But Beverly. Dr. Conner. I'd really like to try."

Perhaps she had been wrong — perhaps physics had never been about apples for Peabody. As he stood and glanced at her from the doorway, he said softly, "I'm reminded why *some* of those boys do like studying physics." She was afraid to meet his eyes, embarrassed, suddenly. "You get to see how far things can go if you simply let them."

LENA

2015

. . .

The hallways in Carlisle Hall echoed. Ajar office doors let out the hums of phone conversations, an overheating printer, water-cooler gossip. Lena stopped in front of the mahogany door on the left. No. 22, next to an unmarked supply closet. She'd passed it once before she'd found it, and twice more before she summoned the nerve.

"Professor Knowles?" Lena knocked on the door, which was slightly open but so heavy it barely moved, like she thought it would shatter her hand.

Professor Knowles hadn't heard her. The clattering of the keyboard carried into the hallway like bad music. Uneven and loud.

Harder this time. "Uh — Professor Knowles?"

"Come in." Her voice did not sound thrilled.

Lena didn't know why her hand was shaking. She had every right to go to her Professor's office. But Lena still felt like she was taking up everyone's time, especially Bella Knowles. They'd never met, but she'd read three papers of hers already. Some girls had vintage movie posters in their rooms; Lena would've hung Professor Knowles' picture, if one existed and it wouldn't have gotten her expelled for stalking.

Perhaps because of that — it being inappropriate to hang photos of scientists you idolized — Lena had never realized until right then, when Professor Knowles stood up, that she looked just like her. Knowles' brown hair was the same shade as Lena's, and a curly mess, too, but on the professor it looked mature and windswept. They had the same tortoiseshell glasses, but Lena only wore hers for class. And, as an unfortunate coincidence, they happened to be wearing the same blue sweater.

The office was smaller than Lena thought it might be from the outside. The tile floor from the hallway crept in here, too, but Knowles had covered it with overlapping rugs. There were two chairs behind the Professor's desk, facing each other around a small coffee table. Science magazines were fanned across it, but that was the only part of the room in neat order.

"Hello," Professor Knowles' eyes softened only a little when they settled on the spitting image of herself, shaking in the doorway under the weight of a backpack that might as well have been full of bricks. "What can I do for you?" She cocked one eyebrow over the rim of her glasses.

"I'm Lena," she stuck her hand out awkwardly. There really was no smooth way to do this. "I'm Lena. I'm a freshman, Biology major. I got your name from the Chair." It was a lie, but it was better than "I've read all of your papers." Lena swallowed. "I'd like to work with you this summer."

The Professor just kept staring at Lena, a smile creeping into the corners of her mouth and eyes. She smashed her lips flat and sat back down. It suddenly occurred to Lena that she still had her hand hanging awkwardly before her. She put it by her side and tried to find a subtle way to dry her clammy palm off on her jean skirt. Such subtlety does not exist.

"Sit, Lena." Knowles gestured to the seat in front of her. "Tell me about yourself."

"Oh, sure. I'm a freshman." Lena sat down, her backpack falling to the floor with a crash. She cringed, but didn't stop talking. "I'm majoring in Biology and might do a minor in psychology if I have time, just for fun, you know, since it's related but not —"

"Lena. Where are you from?"

"Virginia."

"That's nice. What brought you to Marsden?"

"Oh." Lena paused. "It's one of the best biology programs in the country."

Knowles smiled. "I know that. But what about the beautiful New Hampshire fall? The community? You go apple picking with your...*sorority* or something yet?" She said the word "sorority" like it was a disease.

"Oh, I'm not in a sorority."

"I wasn't either, in college. My mother swears I'll regret it someday." Her eyes swept around the room before settling sharply back on Lena's face. "So, do you do *anything,* then?"

Lena had never been asked that before. Relatives, teachers, coaches, even her dentist — had always been impressed with the honors student, taking extra classes at the local community college, just for a challenge. She was always told she was doing more than enough. "I-I'm a biology major."

Professor Knowles was polite enough to look down at her folded hands before she started laughing. "Well, Lena, clearly you're very driven. I do have some openings in my lab. I suppose you can join us, maybe in a term or two, when you've gotten some more exper —"

"Oh, thank you! I won't let you dow —"

"There's one condition."

"Ma'am?"

"Join a club. Audition for something, go on a date when you're asked. I thought the only way I'd get to where I am is by doing nothing else." She paused to look around her office.

Pinned to the bulletin board and overflowing around the edges, there were photos of her with young kids making a sandcastle on the beach, her getting engaged in front of the Eiffel Tower, crossing the finish line of a half marathon. A lopsided pinch-pot, likely made by one of the sandcastle children, held all the pens and pencils on her desk. Unlike the other professors' offices she'd visited, Lena realized she didn't see a framed parade of advanced degrees. This was something else entirely.

Lena wondered what she would fill her office with one day.

She realized she hadn't responded. "O-okay. But how is auditioning for something going to make me a better scientist? I mean, I won't even pass Bio 101 if I don't spend Fridays studying."

Knowles spun back to her computer and started typing. "You're right, Lena. I'm sure you know best."

Lena's cheeks burned. This was not going the way she wanted. In fact, this was not going the way it was in her head, where she'd started to realize what kinds of things she wanted to fill her office with and perhaps if there was some way to explain that to Professor Knowles before she'd ruined everything —

"You have a beautiful family."

"What?" The Professor swiveled her chair back to Lena with an amused smirk. Lena, determined, waved at the photos.

"You have a beautiful family. And it's nice to see I could have both. You know, a career and, well —"

"Anything else, anything you want," Knowles finished with a satisfied nod. She raked her fingers through her curls. "That's my point."

Lena lingered on the photos for a moment, thinking of her own family vacations when she was young and wondering if her father had ever hung photos of her in his cubicle at the telemarketer's office, the only time he'd had a desk at work.

Then she wondered if staring at a stranger's children for more than a moment was inappropriate, and she didn't want to cross a line and there was no way to tell her that for a second she'd been transported back to the Virginia beaches. For a second she'd been seven years old again.

"Well. I should probably let you get back to work." Lena said to the back of the Professor's head. She was already back to her keyboard.

"Lena," she said without turning around, once Lena was already through the door.

"Yes?"

"I look forward to working together."

BEVERLY

1936

. . .

The woman on the bike was new in town. It was an overcast day, with a periwinkle haze that muted the sunlight. This woman and her red hair gleamed as she sped across the quad. Beverly would have remembered seeing such a woman before. She would have remembered any woman in this town of testosterone and what seemed to be six approved haircuts. This woman stuck out the way algae did in the lakes. Maybe most people wouldn't have noticed, but Beverly did. And she was certain that the woman on the bike was new to Marsden.

She didn't know why she was drawn to her. Beverly had never really been a person *drawn* to anyone. Perhaps it was more so after a few months of working at Marsden, where silence was expected. But in all the time she'd lived here, Beverly hadn't approached anyone. Suddenly, she was running through the grass, overwhelmed by the idea that this woman on the bike would ride away and never be seen again.

"Excuse me," Beverly was out of breath when she caught up to the woman with the red curls cascading down her back. Her hair was tied up with a shiny satin kerchief, roughly, like she needed it out of her face. Her cardigan sleeves were pushed up to her elbows, and her Peter-Pan collar was wrin-kled on one side. She had dirt on her knees and a leather bag around her back that had papers nearly falling out of it. She had all the trappings of a woman who had been told how to dress, but insisted on living her life anyway, hemline be damned. She was a kindred soul, of that Beverly was sure. They were easy to recognize. Bats had their echolocation and whales had their sonar, and all of that was to say that Beverly was pretty sure that you can just feel it when someone vibrates in the same wavelengths as you.

The woman stopped pedaling and her curls bounced as they hit her back. "Yes?"

"New. Er — you're new. Here. I mean." Beverly hadn't considered what she'd say to the woman when she stopped.

Her laugh was like bells. "Yes, ma'am. Moved here last week. Working in the library."

"I'm in biology. Uh, well, they're Botany and Zoology at Marsden, they tell me."

"You a professor, then?"

"Not yet."

The woman laughed, like the word "yet" had been a good joke.

"I'm Rachel Poole."

"Beverly Conner."

"It's a pleasure, Bev. Can I call you Bev? You don't seem like a particularly formal girl."

Beverly blushed. "Not formal, no. I used to think that they beat all formality out of anyone wanting to be a scientist," she rambled, "y'know, because you have to get your hands dirty. But here it seems they're the most formal of all them. The scientists, I mean, they're the most buttoned-up of everyone here." She glanced up from her feet and saw that this woman was still laughing. She was embarrassed, but even if it was because she was stumbling over her own words, Beverly wanted to keep Rachel laughing. She decided she'd like it very much if Rachel never stopped laughing. "So, to answer your question. Not formal."

"You did just chase me across the quad." Her voice was flat, teasing.

"Oh, er, I got a little excited. I don't see many women around here."

"I don't suppose you do." Rachel looked around. Men in sweaters roved in bands, like hyenas or lions or something else with sharp canines. They carried books tucked under their arms and gestured around themselves like even they — young men, children — knew the air around them was theirs to fill with their words or suck into their lungs. Rachel issued a dramatic shudder, and it was Beverly's turn to laugh. "How have you been finding it? Marsden, I mean. Are they too much for you?" She lowered her voice. "I couldn't believe it when I moved in and someone asked me to join the Faculty Wives Women's Club for dinner. They say they look out for the librarians and all. I mean, Faculty Wives Club? I had never heard of such a thing."

The Faculty Wives had never extended such an offer to Beverly.

"It's been...an *adjustment*." Neither of them cared much about the opinions of others — that much was clear by the fact that they'd both moved to a town like this, unmarried with no plans to change that. But neither of them wanted to lose their job, and they became aware that they were discussing the pros and cons of their employer here, in its most public heart. "I came from Woods Hole Marine Lab, where there were as many women as there were men, and everybody'd get in the water just the same." For a moment, she could almost taste the salt in the air. "So I'm still getting used to only seeing boys in the hallway."

"Do you miss it?"

"Every day," Beverly said without hesitation. "But it was time to move on, I think." She felt like she was trying to convince herself more than Rachel, who didn't seem convinced.

A pack of seniors was chasing a freshman across the quad. After such a short time, Beverly already recognized the infraction. The freshman was not wearing his beanie, the knit cap that identified him as a member of the freshman class. It was a sort of uniform, it was required. To keep the young and foolish remembering their place. The women's gaze followed the boys in their gleeful, terrifying brawl.

"It's been a bit of a shock for me, too. And I'm still staying with the woman who hired me, my sister-in-law's cousin. I'm sure flying the nest will be a real treat."

"Throwing you into the deep end, are we?"

Rachel laughed and something in Beverly's chest began to glow. "Well, I'd be happy to hear any more advice you have, if anything comes to you."

"Gladly. I suppose I'll have to figure some things out for myself, then, first."

"You could start by telling me where to look for an apartment. Not sure what parts of town are affordable, or willing to rent to a single girl."

The seniors caught the freshman and tackled him to the ground. The young one yelped as his shoulders were pinned back in the grass. Even from this far away, the hollow thump in the grass made them both wince. Freshmen scurried by, straightening their own beanies and avoiding eye contact with the red-cheeked seniors. His head hit the grass repeatedly, his protests echoing across the field and growing quieter. It was worse, somehow, when he stopped screaming. This wasn't like anything Beverly had seen between brothers. It was something else entirely.

She glanced for a moment at Rachel. Her glassy eyes, wide with some triggered maternal rage, were fixed on the boys.

"Christ Almighty," Rachel whispered to herself.

Beverly turned back around in time to see the seniors wander off, the only memory of the incident the verdant stains on their knees. The freshman in the grass still hadn't moved, and the others were already striding away from him.

She smoothed her cardigan as they ripped their eyes from the carnage. "As it so happens," Beverly said, "I need a room-mate."

LENA

2015

. . .

Lena first noticed it was missing in the dining hall. Her class ring. The nicest thing she owned — she wasn't sure if nine karats was a lot for gold, but it sounded like a lot. Her father had thought it was important she have one when she graduated, and he'd shelled out some of their savings on the memento. At the time it seemed like a waste of money. Since she'd come to Marsden, it had become her only daily tie to home.

There weren't many places it could be, because there weren't many places that Lena had had the nerve to explore yet. It was only the second week of classes. That morning, she'd gone to class in Carlisle Hall. She'd eaten lunch under the oak tree outside, then she'd had a group project meeting for her calculus class in the library. When she left the library, Lena got lost on her way to an improv troupe audition, which had been a cheek-burning, excruciating experience that she'd only forced herself to stomach through so she could tell Professor Knowles she'd tried *something* besides her coursework. They had played several "warm-up games," as the troupe's veterans had called them, which involved adopting foreign accents as suggested by the audience. A pink-faced freshman had pointed at her and shouted, "Scottish!" and Lena had stood in silence for several moments, the only thing that surfaced in her mind was Banquo's monologue from *Macbeth*, which she couldn't do in an accent and she barely remembered anyway. She did not get a callback, and though Lena hated failure, it seemed she hated improv more.

Dinner was where she'd noticed the ring was missing. She reached for her middle finger to twist the ring — she always fidgeted with it when she was nervous, and the crowded dining hall was over-saturated with things to be nervous about.

Lena broke into a run as soon as she tumbled down the brick steps. The sun was starting to dip behind the trees. If she ever stopped to notice that kind of thing, Lena might have realized how beautiful the campus looked when it was dipped in honey.

She was hot and panting by the time she reached Carlisle Hall. There was someone at the oak tree, her tree, eclipsed in silhouette. Approaching and disturbing a stranger reading a book in peace did not rank high on Lena's favorite activities. Maybe, hopefully, the doors to Carlisle would still be unlocked and the ring would be under her seat in the lecture hall and an uncomfortable conversation about something as silly as her class ring would be avoided tonight.

Lena kept picturing the sound of her father's voice if she had to call him and tell him it was gone. He'd be positive, like he always was, and make a joke about how they'd have to buy her another one. And Lena would strain to hear him over the screaming of her younger sister and her stepmother's sewing machine in the background. And then he would say that he had to go, because he always had to go to the night shift at the grocery store right when Lena got a free moment to call him. Maybe he would worry about the ring the whole time he was shelving grape juice. Lena was crushed at the thought, and she hadn't even told him yet.

The doors were locked, and they issued an achy protest as Lena yanked on the handles. She turned back towards the tree, where the figure had looked up from his book, brushing his bangs out of his eyes and squinting in the sunlight. Her stomach sank. It was Peter The TA, the one who had saved her from Basketball Jersey and his clammy hands. She still hadn't had the nerve to thank him. Peter Mitchell. She'd found him online and her finger had hovered above the "Friend Request" button that she'd never had the nerve to press. She wasn't sure if she wanted to be "friend," official and labeled and public like that. But still, she'd pulled up his profile, a picture that was a few years dated from a family vacation to Narragansett. Peter.

Lena didn't know that this moment would be one she would think about often. You never know when you're living through a memory. No one ever grabs you by the shoulders and asks, "Are you paying attention? You're going to want to remember every detail of what's about to happen. You're going to be frustrated when you can no longer remember, exactly, the way your skin felt in the shade or the way your own laugh sounded as it tumbled from your lips." And no one told her those things. And she didn't pay attention to them. The Very Important Moment started happening before her and she wasn't ready, not even a little bit.

"I think the building's locked," Peter said with a laugh, closing his book in his lap and pushing himself to his feet. He brushed the mulch off his pants. "You looking for something?"

"No. No. I, er, I think I left something behind in the lecture hall. But don't worry about it, I'll get it tomorrow when they open up the building." She started to walk away, trying to catch her shaky breath as soon as her back was turned so his beautiful eyes wouldn't have to watch her try not to choke on her own tongue.

"If you're sure," he called after her, his voice the color of the sunset that was starting to bloom across the sky. It was exactly what his voice should sound like. Lena hesitated. She wondered how long is too long to pause and then decide you're going to speak again. Now was her chance to talk to Peter, the kind of chances that happened to other people and not to her, and the ring was still missing, and he might have found it and she didn't know what she would tell her father if she'd really lost it for good.

Lena could feel Peter's eyes on her.

"Well," she turned around, accepting defeat. "I might have left it...there. Where you're sitting." It took effort to unclench the fists that fought to form at her sides.

"It's not a class ring, by any chance?" A smile pushed its way to his eyes. He was respectful and clearly felt the embarrassment radiating off of her. He looked like he was trying not to laugh, though Lena often assumed that.

"How'd you know?"

"I found one when I sat down here to study."

He plucked it from the mulch and held it out to her. "I'm Peter."

"I remember." She blushed and wondered if that was the wrong thing to say. "I'm Lena." She slipped the ring back onto her finger. It felt so good to have one thing be exactly where it belonged, one thing that wasn't constantly changing and whose weight stayed the same. "I never got a chance to thank you for the other night. I was pretty shaken up, I guess, and I'm not sure why, but anyway, you really saved me."

"That guy was in pretty bad shape, happy to help." He raked his fingers through his bangs. "But for what it's worth, you should probably find friends who don't vomit on you." He laughed, then looked up at her. His eyelashes were impossibly long. "Do I know you from somewhere else?"

"I-I think you're my TA. For Bio?"

The smile finally broke through. "Lena! I thought that name sounded familiar. I've been grading your homework." He gestured behind him to the textbook and open notebook of papers lying in the mulch. The tree was almost in silhouette now, glowing orange as it eclipsed the setting sun.

"Oh, god, I'm so sorry! I promise I'm smarter than it seems." He laughed, and she liked that it was because of her. "You're sitting at my tree." She hadn't meant to say it, and she certainly hadn't meant to sound accusatory. "I mean, it's not *mine*. I just work here sometimes. I mean, it can be yours too." Her cheeks were hot, the way your skin dances when you're standing too close to fire.

Peter laughed and his dark eyes flashed. "Funny. I've always thought of it as my tree. But it can be yours too."

They stared at each other for what might have been a moment, or maybe it was longer. Lena wracked her brain for something intelligent to say, or for something natural to do with her hands. She looked down at the ring; it glinted the last rays of sunlight back at her and she squinted. When the world blinked back into focus, Peter was still staring at her. She couldn't decipher his expression.

BEVERLY

1936

. . .

Beverly smelled them coming before she saw them. The professors in the department — who viewed themselves as exponentially more important than the assistant professors and the associate professors — traveled as a pack, trapped in a cloud of cigar smoke, burnt coffee from the lounge, and the same cologne, the only kind sold at the only store in town. They stalked down the hallway in patent penny loafers and sweater vests that their wives had ordered from the Sears catalog. It wasn't hunting gear, but the feeling in Beverly's stomach was what she imagined a rabbit felt just before it sprang to safety.

There was nowhere to run, though. The halls in Carlisle Hall were narrow, whitewashed walls and low-hanging lights that cast yellow halos on the ceiling. Her office wasn't even on this floor; she'd made the trek upstairs to get some staples. As the men neared closer, chattering their polite but biting rapport about golf on Sundays and Frank's wife's pot roast, Beverly braced for impact. They would go for the silence first, pretending she wasn't there. That worked when one of them was alone. But as a group, she couldn't sidle past them as easily. Instead, she would be shoulder-checked like a Marsden hockey player on the pond. "Sorry ma'am," they would chuckle under their breath as she'd try to collect herself. And they'd call her ma'am, as though they didn't know her name and had never been introduced. As though she wasn't the only woman working in the building and as though that was the type of thing men like these could forget.

But none of that happened. As the muscles in her body tensed to prepare herself, the posse slowed. "'Scuse me, ma'am." The leader, Dr. Croasdale, nodded at her. The air swirling around him smelled like cigars and money. "I need some slides prepped for my lecture Tuesday. Can you come by my office in a few minutes and get those materials from me?"

Dr. Bell stood behind him, finding his own shoes quite fascinating, so shiny he could see his reflection in them. And this man called himself a scientist. Beverly's mouth fluttered open and closed. She had her own work to do. And there was no way that Dr. Croasdale had earned himself a Ph.D. and had never been taught how to prepare slides.

The truth was that Beverly quite enjoyed making slides. She liked every part of research, she liked that she could work with her hands and her mind and both at the same time. She liked gluing samples to matboard and preserving a perfect specimen. And she really liked preparing materials for classes. The rocks in her throat and the metal she tasted at the back of her mouth weren't because she didn't like making slides or because she wasn't going to. It was because he'd called her ma'am. Dr. Croasdale should've known who she was.

"I don't mean to be rude, sir, but surely you do know how to fix your own slides?"

"Ma'am," he said with a darkened face, "I'm far too busy for that...stuff." He exchanged a glance with the Professor next to him. "Isn't that why we hired you?"

"I don't believe so —" she began, wiping her clammy hands on her skirt.

"Perhaps," Croasdale interrupted sharply, "I wasn't clear. Ma'am."

"Sir." She bit her cheek so hard she drew blood. "I'll be by in a few minutes. I'm just fetching some staples."

Croasdale smiled and clapped her on the shoulder, and her skin tingled beneath her sweater. "My name," she said as if by accident as his fingers left her, "is Dr. Conner." His mouth opened and then slammed shut, sharply. It twisted into a frigid smile, like he'd just learned how to make one and was showing it off.

"Of course." Croasdale nodded, a real gentleman. The men, satisfied, stalked on, surveying their territory and returning, once again, to their small talk of their stock investments and if Tom's wife has the new Kelvinator Washer-Wringer. In the wild, it's important to know one's habitat — who is alpha, and who omega.

Beverly hurried the last few feet to the supply closet door and threw herself into the comforting darkness. When the door was firmly shut, she let out a sigh she hadn't known she was holding in. Her fingers smoothed her sweater and absently ran themselves through her hair. It smelled sweet in here, the musk of old paper that's turning yellow, wooden shelves slowly turning stale. The metallic smell of ballpoint pens. It choked with the kind of comforting humidity that little back corners and forgotten spaces have, the places that are too close to the pipes and warm you when you get close so you hadn't even realized you were cold before. If you weren't careful, you might find yourself making excuses to go to the supply closet, just so you could shut the door behind yourself and be warm and swallowed in the darkness. That would be silly, of course, but it would be tempting all the same.

Beverly let her eyes run over the sagging shelves. There were no staples.

There was, however, a green book that did not belong

here. It was flipped open on top of a sheaf of onionskin paper, the kind for the typewriters. The glossy pages had black-and-white photos of smiling Men of Marsden, slicked hair and cable-knit sweaters. She lifted the cover with one finger like it was radioactive. *Marsden College, Freshmen Green Book, 1934.*

The inside page was a note from the senior class, offering their advice and mischievous welcome to the dear darling college. She couldn't look away, even though she could have guessed what was inside. Sometimes you have to check just to be sure.

The first few pages were permissible, jokes about the cafeteria or a tongue-in-cheek ranking of the fraternities on campus. Apparently last year, they'd had a campus-wide toboggan race. These weren't the kinds of things Beverly had anyone to tell her. She read on.

A photo. A broad-chested man in his class sweater, hoisting a freshman — identifiable from his felt beanie — into the air by the scruff of his neck, like a mother lion and her cub. His shoes dangled in the air.

Last year's Theater Department had staged a musical and, with the college's regrettable dearth of women actors, had cast faculty wives to play opposite the strapping male leads. The seniors' notes to the freshmen suggested avoiding joining this year's cast if they intended to take a class with the actresses' husbands in the future. The photo, grainy and dark, showed one of the actresses in question during a raucous curtain call, hands clasped over her blushing cheeks, as her husband playfully slapped the student actor across his face.

Education seemed to mean quite a different thing at this place than it had at Woods Hole. There was no slapping at Woods Hole.

The next section was titled "Local Girls." Beverly nearly dropped the book. It went on for pages and pages — local women's colleges, directions of how to drive there, even the phone numbers listed for each floor of their dorms. "What sort of woman is a Smith girl?" Beverly ran her shaking finger across the raised type. "If you're looking for a fun date, go instead to Holyoke, where the girls know how to have a good time." Beverly thought of the girls from her high school who went to Holyoke and wondered if that was true. There was a blonde girl who'd been top of their class, even ahead of Beverly. "Northampton isn't worth the drive. Smith girls have a stick up their —"

Beverly slammed the volume shut, brought suddenly out of the hole she'd fallen into and rudely, roughly, back into the supply closet. She couldn't shake the image of the girls from her high school, peering out the windows of their dorms at Holyoke and seeing cars of Marsden Men gliding up the drive, ready to take them to dinner. She wondered if anyone she knew had ever gone on a blind date with a Marsden Man who never called her back. Beverly remembered her mother giving one of their mothers a tuna casserole. She wondered what that girl's mother would have said, watching her daughter getting into a car with one of those boys. The boys in her lecture, the very same. She pictured Kenneth's self-assured smirk and something in her sank.

Beverly clutched the green leather to her chest and then tucked it into her cardigan to hide it during the trip back downstairs, in case anyone saw. They wouldn't have cared, of course, because they were the ones who wrote the book. But she didn't know why she wanted to keep it, so she wouldn't have known what to say if someone asked.

Thankfully, she wasn't often spoken to in hallways.

Beverly placed the Green Book on the shelf, next to the employee handbook and her microscope. The kind of thing that should be in an office, something embossed and in the school's colors. The kind of thing that Dr. Bell and Dr. Croasdale had in theirs.

LENA

2015

. . .

Peter the TA was texting Lena. She could barely concentrate on her canned peaches or the small talk of her acquaintance sitting across from her — it was strange to think of any of these new faces as "friends." She'd silenced the din of the dining hall; all her attention was trained on the little glowing screen balanced on her thigh under the table.

It had been six days since she'd summoned the nerve to send a friend request. He'd responded after midnight that night and they had been going back and forth ever since, their conversations only pausing when one of them had a class or one of them finally caught a few fitful hours of sleep before an 8 a.m. lecture. Her phone had been dead weight before, just the source of her morning alarm and another thing she needed to keep maintained and charged. Now, she was checking for texts from him during class, under the desk, at the gym, everywhere. The little thrill that ran from her scalp to the soles of her feet every time his name flashed on her screen was dizzying. She wasn't sure she would ever tire of it. Lena wondered if this was what it felt like to do drugs. Probably. Love — not that that's what this was — and drugs both give off dopamine. Everything was just science.

"Earth to Lena." Alex waved her hand in front of Lena's face. "You were in the middle of telling me about this boy, then you started drooling and totally spaced."

"Did not," Lena said, but swiped at her lips just in case. They were sitting in the middle of the dining hall, far louder and less private than Lena would have preferred. But she needed to talk to *someone* about this. Was she reading too much into things? Was it wrong to assume Peter was in love with her if he told her a story about when he first realized he was allergic to shellfish? Was she crazy for barely sleeping so she could talk to Peter, even if it was going to affect her grade on this upcoming quiz? This gnawing feeling demanded that she grab anyone — even these two girls she barely knew — and quite rudely commandeer the entire conversation. She needed answers.

Lena's knee was bouncing up and down under the table. If she'd ever gone to those therapy appointments when she was a kid, maybe she would have better coping mechanisms for whatever it was that was coursing through her veins. But she hadn't. Therapy was expensive, and she didn't have time for it. Lena wiped her sweaty palm on her jeans.

Quinn sat down at the table with a precarious tray full of food. "Is that chocolate milk? In your cereal?" Alex asked, though she barely glanced up from her notebook, thousands of straight lines of her impossibly small handwriting, glitter gel pen. She blew her black bangs out of her face with a huff. She was effortlessly pretty; she had the kind of hair that listened when she brushed it in the mornings and asked it to behave. Lena was certain Alex was prettier than her, and maybe one of the prettiest people she'd ever met.

"They have, like, a dozen kinds of milk. I can put whatever kind of milk in my cereal that I want. I mean, that's adulthood, right?" Quinn said as she unloaded the tray, nearly spilling some of the milk on her t-shirt, one of the ones they'd gotten at orientation that said "Marsden College" in big block letters. Lena wasn't sure anyone wore those, but Quinn had worn a different free t-shirt every day that week. "Like. There's oat milk. Almond milk. Chocolate milk." Quinn loudly slurped her spoon. "I mean, how do you even milk an almond?"

Alex considered this, carefully capping her pen.

Lena had met Quinn earlier that week. She and Alex were both in Lena's Bio class. Lena hadn't told them that the TA in question was also their TA. Three identical biology textbooks were open on the table, taking up the remaining empty seats. They were sitting in a booth, with vinyl cushions that were vaguely sticky from industrial cleaners and probably yesterday's ketchup.

"Sorry, what were you guys talking about before?" Quinn said through a mouthful of corn flakes.

"*Romeo*, the TA," Alex said with disgust, averting her eyes from Quinn's balanced meal of Mexican food and chocolate cereal.

"Ah, young love," Quinn said, distracted. She spooned more puffed rice into her mouth and traced a paragraph in her book with her fingertip. "I think, yeah, uh, go for it. Lena. I know we've only known each other for like, a week," she said, not sarcastically, "so I don't really know, I guess, but I think you seem like you want to do this. So. Do it."

"And then we can get back to studying!" Alex teased.

"Can I borrow your pens with the glitter?" Quinn asked. "What if the sparkles are giving you some kind of edge?"

"I actually read a study that said your brain stores information you write by hand like ten times more than information you type," Alex unzipped a pencil case with a neat row of gel pens, "so I invested in some pens I'd actually use."

"Quite an investment," Quinn muttered and returned to her notebook.

Lena glanced down at her phone, trying to suffocate the panic rising in her throat. She needed advice, and she'd chosen two workaholics who couldn't tear themselves from their textbooks, even at the temptation of scandalous gossip — potentially-academic-probation gossip. Did people get suspended for dating their TA? Lena couldn't afford to get suspended.

Carpet tiles were a strange choice, Lena thought, for a dining hall. Difficult to clean. Alex's burrito was raining overcooked rice and only some of it was landing on her plate. Lena felt sick. "Guys," Lena said as her phone vibrated again, "can we focus for a second?"

"Right," Quinn said, tearing her eyes from her bowl of cereal and back to her textbook, "Well, the quiz is on chapter two. Alex, what's the —"

"Not the *books!* Can we focus on my, um, problem?" Lena dropped her voice and glanced around. There were a lot of ears in the dining hall. Most of them were trained on their own conversations, but she still felt exposed. On stage.

"Right, right," Quinn waved her spoon. "The *boy.*"

It was strange to be talking about a boy with her friends. Though Peter the TA was 20 — a *sophomore* — so perhaps he was a *man*. Lena had no idea how to talk to him, how to even talk about him. These were the sort of things you were supposed to have gotten good at in middle school, or at least high school, and here she was in college and giggling every time her phone screen lit up. There hadn't been a class on whatever this was.

"The TA," Alex said, scanning the room. "Is he here? Oh my gosh, Lena, what if he's here?" If she was honest, Lena didn't really want their advice. She just wanted to know how big of a deal it would be if she went to coffee with her TA. She really wanted to go to coffee with her TA.

"I don't see how this will help us on the quiz," Quinn grumbled, and took another bite. "You *said* we were going to study for the quiz."

"Is it against some sort of rule? You know?"

"Dating your TA?"

"*Talking* to your TA," Lena corrected. "Or, uh, getting coffee. Coffee with your TA."

"I think it's okay, as long as he doesn't pay for your coffee. Or, I guess, if you pay for his, that would be worse. That would be like accepting a gift, which I think is illegal if you work for the government and he basically does, um, if the students of a college are viewed as citizens of a country," Alex said definitively.

"No, that's usually gifts of twenty dollars or more. There's nothing wrong with coffee," Quinn said without looking up from her textbook. She'd spilled a ring of chocolate milk across the table that was clearly making Alex's blood pressure rise.

"My mom works for the government, so I think I'd know," Alex said. Quinn didn't even glance up. Lena doubted they would ever get lunch again.

"Okay. Thanks. Really clears things up." Lena raked her fingers through her wavy hair, making it even frizzier. The thought of breaking a rule made her stomach tie itself in knots. Rules were good; they told you what you should do and what you shouldn't do, and that kept you from getting hurt. Getting a totally non-romantic very platonic coffee with your TA might not be breaking a rule — Alex and Quinn had not cleared that up at all, though she knew what she would do if she was a federal employee — but it was certainly a Gray Area. Lena had spent eighteen years avoiding Gray Areas. The cafeteria Mexican food on her plate stared up at her.

She looked down and saw Peter's name flash on the screen she was hiding under the table. Her eyes scanned the message: *I'm going to grab some lunch in a few. No chance you're free?*

This was really happening. Lena read it six times, just to be sure.

"Alex," Quinn said, "Pass me that highlighter?"

Sure. Lena typed with shaking fingers. *Where were you thinking?*

Alex rolled the yellow marker nearest her in Quinn's direction.

Lena's phone buzzed again. *I'm a few minutes away from the dining hall. That work?*

Someone jostled into the back of the booth. *I'm already here. Come find me!*

"I'm gonna go," Lena said, shoving her books back into her bag and fumbling with the zipper. She piled up all of her dishes on the tray. Quinn and Alex hadn't heard her, or they didn't care. "Bye, guys."

"Mmm," Alex nodded as she turned the page.

Her palms were sweating. Lena dashed across the dining room and returned her tray. She threw her bag onto an empty table, hoping that was enough to reserve it and not even caring if it meant someone stole her laptop. This was more important, for some reason.

She ran to the bathroom and tried not to seem startled when she nearly collided with the girl already inside. Lena waited until she was gone, leaning awkwardly by the paper towel dispenser. It was one of those motion-activated ones, and it released a strip of paper towels as loudly as possible while the two stood in uncomfortable silence. The girl left after an eternity.

Lena dug through her pockets and found only one cherry Chapstick. It would have to do. She wasn't sure why she couldn't let anyone see her primping. She swiped some Chapstick on her lips and wondered why she'd ever bought it, since it tasted like cough syrup, and suddenly she was nauseous again. Lena had always thought if she stared at her own face for too long, she would find things she'd hate. She was pretty sure that was true of anyone. But it just dawned on her now, in the dining hall bathroom, that Peter was going to have to look at her. It wouldn't just be a phone anymore. She wondered for a moment if Alex and her perfect hair ever had that thought. Then she pushed it out of her mind. No use.

Lena skittered back to the table where she'd left her bag. *I'm in the left dining room,* she sent, and then wondered if that was silly and she should've just let him find her.

"Lena, this was the lamest treasure hunt ever." Peter's smooth voice appeared behind her shoulder. Lena whipped her head around to see him. His black hair was slicked out of his eyes. "You gave me too many hints. No fun at all." He smiled, so she knew he was joking, which was an affirmation she very much needed, and tossed his bag onto the empty seat across from her.

"But the prize at the end is great!" she offered, then stammered quickly, "T-the food, I mean." Peter laughed, the honest kind, where a husky chuckle spilled from him like he couldn't control it, or he hadn't tried. It was nice when Peter laughed.

"You're funny." He said it like he meant it. Lena had been called a lot of things, but funny was usually absent from that list. For a moment, he just stood there and looked at the wall. The clatter of plastic bowls and cups roared behind them. Peter dug his hands in his pockets. "Oh," he brightened, like he was glad to have something to say, "by the way, I looked it up, and we were both right." He peeled his jacket off and dropped it on top of his bag.

"How's that?" She wrung her hands under the table.

"There are two editions of *Frankenstein*," he said. "We read different ones in high school. Mine, obviously, was the *right* one." His eyes sparkled.

"I'll be sure to read both and get back to you."

"I'm gonna go get some food. You want anything?"

Lena glanced up and met his dark eyes. "Yeah. Um, surprise me?"

"I don't know what you like!"

"That's part of the fun." Peter nodded like that made sense.

As he turned and headed into the food court, Alex and Quinn walked past, shouldering their heavy bags. "Is that him?" Quinn mouthed with wide eyes, pointing with no attempt at discretion at the back of Peter's head.

Lena smiled and bit her lip, embarrassed. She wondered if they'd recognized his black hair.

BEVERLY

1936

. . .

The kitchen table was painted with rings of spilled coffee. Two cold mugs were all that remained of a rushed breakfast, cut short by the arrival of the moving truck.

"Hey Beverly! Where do we keep the towels?" Rachel's voice carried down the hallway.

It was a strange word, "we." She'd lived alone for so long. Beverly blushed. "Hall closet, top shelf!" she shouted over her shoulder while her hands, suddenly shaky, knocked the coffee mugs together on the shelf. It sounded like bells. Beverly was sitting up on the counter, her feet folded underneath her, reorganizing all the cabinets. They were going to need to use that space on the top shelf that neither of them could reach.

Rachel owned all sorts of things Beverly would've never thought to buy. Framed photos of her family, ceramic plates with little flowers painted on them. None of it was expensive, but it was still pretty just for its own sake. She wondered how Rachel would feel about the muddy wading boots that piled up by the door in the summertime, about the gap in the screened porch that let the bugs in at night. Beverly cleaned her dishes right after she ate and knew how to scrub a bathroom so it sparkled — her mother had made sure of that. The house wasn't dirty, but it wasn't beautiful. Beverly had never cared when her mother had said things like that, because it wasn't her mother's house. But she wanted Rachel to feel at home here. She wanted to use these plates with the flowers. Beverly could already picture how they would make a grilled cheese sandwich look like a gourmet meal. She wondered why she'd never used plates like that before. Her mother had tried to buy her some as a going-away present. Beverly had turned them down.

The dishes were packed in crushed newspaper, and Beverly had been unwrapping them in the kitchen while Rachel hung her clothes in the narrow closet down the hall. The house didn't have two bedrooms. They'd put a bed in the smaller side room that didn't have its own closet and was barely big enough for the mattress, but it got great light in the mornings.

Rachel's humming floated down the hall. It was like the entire house was more alive now that she was here. "Bev!"

"Yeah?" Beverly didn't think anyone had given her a nickname before. Not one she could remember, anyway. Rachel Poole felt totally comfortable with anyone, it seemed. Or maybe not. Beverly hadn't seen her interact with that many other people. Maybe Rachel just liked her.

"Can you guess the song?" Rachel's humming got louder as she came back towards the kitchen. Her humming blurred into lyrics, "*Ooh, what a little moonlight can do/Wait a while 'til a little moonbeam comes peepin' through.*"

"*You'll get bored,*" Beverly joined in quietly, barely audible over the clinking of the dishes as she lifted them into the cupboard. "*You can't resist him, and all you'll say/When you have kissed him is —*"

Rachel appeared in the doorway, her arms still full of clothes hangers, socked feet on the kitchen floor. "*Ooh, what a little moonlight can do!* Aha! I saw you singing!"

Beverly felt awkward sitting up on the counter. She shifted her weight and nearly fell, and reached up to grab the cabinet to steady herself. "Oh, no, you're mistaken. I don't sing."

"Nope," Rachel adjusted the hangers in her hands, "I know what I saw. You have a nice voice." The compliment hung in the air. "You're a Billie Holiday fan?"

"Honestly, I'm not even sure I knew who sang that song. I just know what I hear on the radio. Whatever they play after the President speaks."

Rachel laughed like this was funny. "All I heard is that I can drag you to the church choir rehearsals with me."

"Absolutely not." Beverly liked to sing. At home. Some things were just for home. And if this was Rachel's home now, then she would see the things that Beverly did at home.

"Alright, then, what *do* you do for fun? When you're done cleaning the microscopes or whatever."

"I played chess with my brothers a lot growing up." Rachel did not look satisfied. She continued. "In college, I taught myself a new language each year." Beverly picked at her cuticles. "Norwegian was the fun one. I ride my bike, I try to make new recipes sometimes, I have so many books I need to read —"

"What was the last picture you saw?" She prodded Beverly with one of the hangers. "Let's go see a picture!"

"Oh, no, I'm still putting away your plates, I've got to move the soup tureen from down there to up there, because I never make soup much anyway, and then you'll be able to reach the plates, so that's—"

"Up!" Rachel's fingers curled around Beverly's bicep, and she gently tugged her off the counter. "We've unpacked enough. I can finish the rest of this later. You never answered my question. What was the last picture you saw?"

Rachel took a big step over the box on the floor and tossed

the hangers on the kitchen table. Beverly didn't have decorations on her plates or nice curtains on her windows, but everything was always clean and in its place. It was the only way to keep up with everything. "We can't just leave this all here," she kicked the cardboard box, empty now except for the crushed newsprint, to prove her point. "We've made such a mess."

"I'll clean it all up later, I promise!" Rachel beamed. "Now, what was the last movie you saw?"

"There's never been a cinema in Marsden." Beverly said flatly, looking behind her at the clutter in the kitchen and wondering if this was what every day would be like in their house now. Rachel led her down the hallway towards their rooms without looking back.

"You didn't see any pictures when you lived in Philadelphia?"

Beverly blushed. "I didn't have much time." She didn't want Rachel to think she wasn't fun. She didn't know why that mattered to her, but it suddenly mattered very much. "One or two, definitely. I think one of them was, uh. Oh! Charlie Chaplin. Yes."

Rachel tossed up her hands. "I know you've got a Ph.D. and I haven't, and that's why you're doing research and teaching students and I'm just shelving books, but I'll be damned, Beverly, if you just sit and play chess all day."

It wasn't that Beverly didn't want to go to a movie with Rachel. It sounded like fun, but Beverly suddenly didn't know quite what to wear and had never cared about that before and didn't want to have to ask Rachel what was appropriate to wear to the cinema. "Alright."

Rachel spun on her heel, satisfied, and closed her door. Her voice was muffled from the other side. "I'm getting my sweater and we're going out. Grab your knit cardigan, the blue one, and run a comb through your hair. We're leaving in ten minutes."

Beverly closed the door to her own bedroom and felt uncomfortable, suddenly, that she had the larger room. Their rooms should be the same size; they were splitting the rent. She wondered if Rachel had looked inside already, and what she'd thought of Beverly's duvet and the print on her pillow-cases.

The closest cinema was two towns over. They rode their bikes, even though it was just starting to get dark as they were leaving. Under the bruised sky, Beverly wrestled her front tire out from the bushes and glanced nervously at the purple clouds overhead. "Are you sure this is a good idea? We'll have to ride along the highway."

"We'll be careful." And they were, as careful as Rachel did anything, which was always just careful enough. They rode single file on the shoulder of the highway, blinding headlights flying at them. Rachel rode ahead and Beverly followed, watching as her red hair streaked out behind her in the wind like ribbons. As the light changed, so did her silhouette.

There was something rather exciting about going to the cinema. The trees parted and the theater came into view up the road. The marquee glittered in the blue night air and cast a yellow halo that bounced off of the shiny hoods of a row of parked cars. Rachel sucked in a breath of cold nighttime and shouted, "Race you!" Beverly pedaled so fast the chain on her old bike threatened to snap. They careened into the gravel parking lot like they were on the run from the cops, laughing and shouting at each other. The apathetic women smoking under the awning, bathed in gold light and clutching the arms of their dates for the evening, looked at the two panting single women with disgust — Beverly wasn't sure which part was more disgusting to them, the red exhaustion on their cheeks or the fact they were unaccompanied. They left their bikes by the side of the building and went inside.

Everything in the lobby was dark red and smelled like popcorn and hot oil. Pink-faced theatergoers chattered loudly in Beverly's ear. Rachel dragged her to the candy counter. They bought two sweating glass bottles of root beer and a tin of Raisinets. It was more money than Beverly had spent on a night out in a long time — maybe ever — but Rachel insisted that they'd worked up an appetite on the ride over and would need the sugar to get themselves back home. "It'll be colder on the way back," she reasoned, "and you burn more calories in the cold."

"Is that so?" Beverly said, amused at Rachel's confidence and grimacing as she put the few bills back in her wallet. When did root beer get so expensive?

"Yep. You should trust me." Rachel swept the bottles off the counter and clutched them to her chest, the condensation darkening her sweater. "I know a lot about *science,*" she said with a wink, and walked down the carpeted hallway to the theater. Her red mane shook with giggles at her own joke.

The theater was already dark inside. Rachel sat down on her left. She flopped into the chair like she'd been here before; Beverly was pretty sure she hadn't, but Rachel seemed like the kind of person who was at home wherever she went. Rachel rattled the tin of Raisinets in Beverly's direction. "Want one?" she whispered. The bright white reflection of the screen flashed in her eyes as they darted to Beverly's face.

Beverly nodded. Rachel leaned over the armrest so her green cardigan brushed against Beverly's. She shook the tin and a few chocolates fell out and bounced on Beverly's palm. "I've never had these before," she whispered. "Do you like them?"

"Oh, I practically *lived* on them in grade school," Rachel laughed, probably louder than she should have. The pair sitting behind them shushed her. "I think I'm the reason the corner store by my house stayed in business for so long."

The screen blurred into focus, a hazy halo of white bursting through the blackness. It looked like a microscope slide, before the knobs are adjusted. There's just an indistinguishable something in the midst of a lot of nothing.

They always showed the world news before the pictures. Some man with a mid-Atlantic accent narrated grainy footage from places she'd only ever read about. Beverly had forgotten they did that. It made her wonder where in the world Scooter was. She opened her root beer with a hiss, just to do something with her hands. Rachel looked up at the screen, rapt. White reflections danced across her face. Beverly opened Rachel's root beer, too.

The picture was one of those stories about a pouty woman with a lot of money who tricks a few men with a lot of money into giving her their money, or into marrying her, or something. It wasn't really Beverly's thing. They all had eyebrows that were too thin and made them look eternally surprised.

"You know, Bev," Rachel whispered without turning her head, "sometimes, when I was younger and I didn't have the money to buy the Raisinets, I would just slip them into my purse in the store."

Beverly turned to look at her. Rachel's eyes were still fixed on the picture, the curves of her long eyelashes pointed up at the white screen. Her whole face was reflecting light, like a full moon. The shadows flickered across her face as the figures on the screen moved and danced. "You stole candy?"

She had let Beverly in on a secret — one she would keep, not because it was important, but because it was one of those tokens exchanged in the embrace of darkness. Words spoken under your breath in the cinema or at church or any other place where you're supposed to face the same direction and not speak. Those are the words that are so funny your sides split. The words that no one else can hear, the words that were just for you.

"I guess I did!" Rachel turned to Beverly, an embarrassed smile playing on her lips. "Oh my goodness, I'm a thief!" Rachel dropped her hand to Beverly's arm as they fell forward in giggles.

"I'm not sure I can have a criminal living in my house," Beverly teased, as they both tried to stifle their laughter. She wondered if the blush had climbed to her face, and she was glad it was dark.

Beverly glanced at Rachel, who had fixed her gaze back on the screen while her lips shook, trying and failing to suppress her smile. Her cheeks glowed, even in the dark. Rachel, blushing. Beverly squeezed her sweaty hands in her lap.

So Rachel liked Raisinets. Chocolate candies. It was good to know what things Rachel liked. Beverly thought perhaps they should have a supply of them in their kitchen, in a big bowl that you could take a few out of every time you passed. And even though Beverly knew she could never afford to keep candy in the house all the time, it was nice to think about it for a moment. There was the raisin in the center, of course, which was a fruit, which provides some vitamins. The tin said right on the front, in gold letters, *"Tasty and Healthful."* It wasn't even that terrible of an idea.

Rachel's sudden laugh at the film sliced through the clouds in her mind and Beverly realized she hadn't been paying attention. On the screen, a woman with pin curls sidled up to a man with a mustache. She had milky skin and fleshy, bare arms and a dark dress that snaked around her in curves. She moved like water, every step and bend of her wrist was fluid. The camera zoomed in on the mustache man's face as his eyes lingered on her jaw, soaking her in, sizing her up, almost like he was afraid of her. She plucked the cigar from the mustache man's lips and took a long drag.

LENA

2016

. . .

There was a giant decal of a gummy bear on the wall. It was one of the yellow ones that Lena could never decide if it was pineapple or orange flavored, and she was distracted by the thought. White highlights on its transparent body traced its snout and eyes. The decal was behind Peter's head, and when he leaned back in his chair, the gummy bear ears peeked out of his hair.

"I cannot believe you've never had frozen yogurt before." Lena laughed and studied the walls of the shop so as to avoid his eyes. Alex and Quinn had discovered this place. One wall was painted hot pink, and another one was lime green, and the seam where they met seemed to vibrate. It hurt her eyes. She didn't know how decorating a store this way could possibly help business.

"My dad was lactose intolerant. We didn't eat much dairy as kids. Never really acquired a taste for it," Peter said, pink from laughter and from the cold sundae in his hands.

"So what's the verdict?"

"I don't know how it's legal to deprive children of this," he said as he reached across the table to steal another spoonful from her cup. He hadn't been able to decide between flavors, and when Lena had gone for the strawberry, he had proclaimed to the entire shop that he only had a girlfriend so that he could have twice the flavor options. The red on Lena's face still hadn't faded — mortification and a little pride.

"Is that coming from another documentary?" Lena teased. They'd watched four documentaries in the last two weeks, sitting side-by-side on the futon in Peter's dorm, a healthy inch of air between them. Only last night had Peter finally put his arm around her. Even though they were dating, he still didn't seem sure if he could touch her — a quality she quite liked.

"Actually, no, my oldest brother took a few child psychology classes in college and he'd tell me about it. Fro-yo is definitely going in the 'critical for childhood development' category," Peter said, laughing and watching the melted yogurt drip off his spoon. Lena had noticed that when he laughed at something she had said, his eyes crinkled in a way that they didn't for anyone else. It always made her happy and also nervous at the same time. Her foot started bouncing under the table. "Is that your way of saying you thought that documentary was boring?"

"No, I told you, I love stuff like that. Plus, you'd said it was one of your favorites, and that taught me a *lot* about you." She gently shoved his arm. "I was just teasing. I watched documentaries as a kid with my dad. Whenever I'd asked him a question he didn't know the answer to, he found a video that could explain it instead."

"I can totally picture a tiny little Lena, incessant questions," Peter said. Crinkly eyes. "Did your mom do stuff like that with you, too?"

Lena stirred her melted yogurt. "My dad always said she was smarter than him," she laughed, the hollow kind that sometimes feels necessary to make the other person more comfortable. "So when she was around, he would tell me to ask her. But when she got her fellowship and I guess he didn't want to move and so she left us, he started renting documentaries from the library. I was still so little and... I think he wanted to prove he didn't need her, you know." It was the only time Peter had asked about her mother outright, like he had been afraid to bring her up. "It's okay," she said, finally meeting his eyes. "It was a long time ago. My dad, he always made me feel like it was okay to ask questions. Any question. Even if he didn't know the answer, that didn't make it a stupid question, you know?"

Peter didn't say anything else after that. It didn't feel uncomfortable, either. They didn't need to fill every second. He hesitated and then grabbed her hand from across the table.

"So. I guess, it's, um. Happy anniversary," Lena said, suddenly shy. It had been three whole months, which felt like a lot for someone who had never cared about relationships before. *Anniversary*, she knew from her SAT flashcards, came from the Latin root *ann*, meaning "year," so she knew it wasn't really an anniversary at three months. To most people it wasn't really worth celebrating.

Peter brushed his black bangs from his eyes. "You too, champ." He punched her in the shoulder. Her cheeks felt hot, like they did that first day they spoke. He was close enough she could smell his toothpaste. Spearmint, not peppermint. Good choice.

Lena gripped her knee so tightly under the table that she could feel the half-moons she left in her knees through the denim. She couldn't get her leg to stop bouncing. It was like she'd had caffeine, a lot of caffeine. It was the way she felt before a big test. She wondered if you could fail a relationship.

Peter's eyes swept over her face for a moment. Professor Knowles had told her to go on the date with the boy when he asked. Maybe she hadn't meant *this* boy, but still, Lena was just doing her homework — and rationalizing it was the only way she could shrug off the guilt for the Friday nights spent watching movies instead of quizzing herself and reading ahead.

Peter leaned back in the plastic chair and stretched his legs out under the table so they brushed hers. The yellow gummy bear ears on the wall were centered over his head. This must have been a pineapple gummy bear, because if it was supposed to be orange-flavored, the gummy bear people would have made it orange. Peter looked at her with a slight smile. "What are you thinking about?"

"If the gummy bear was supposed to be orange-flavored, they would've made it orange, right?"

Peter was stunned for a moment, and followed her gaze to the decal on the wall behind him. "My god, Rivera, your mind." He laughed, hard. His eyes did the crinkly thing. "So then, what flavor is it?" He tried to pull himself together and treat this like a serious conversation.

"Pineapple."

"Obviously." He nodded like that made sense. Amusement twinkled in his eyes, but it didn't feel like he was laughing at her. He folded his arms behind his head and might have just as easily been on a beach or swinging in a hammock. His hair looked like it was mussed by wind, even though they were inside. Peter was comfortable in every room: in this fluores-cent frozen-yogurt shop, in the crowded cafeteria, in the football stadium, in the biology lecture hall. Every place that she was nervous and skittish, he was calm, confident. Except, of course, in a dark dorm room by the glow of a laptop playing a movie. The two-week lead-up to Peter finally resting his head on her shoulder had been an awkward dance. "You know I've never been in a relationship like this before?"

"What do you mean, 'like this'? Is 'this'... bad?"

Peter snapped back to the table and became very inter-ested in his melting yogurt. "No, I mean, I've actually never been in a relationship before. Like this, like you and me, three months. I'd never even been on a second date before you." It was strange to think there was anything Peter hadn't experienced. He'd had a head start, like if life was a race, everyone else was running, but he'd been given a jetpack. That was what it had always felt like.

"I'd been on a few first dates, my brothers—" he meant his fraternity brothers, she had learned, not blood relatives, "set me up a few times. But I never felt a connection. Like, I want to talk about more than just who's taking who to the formal and where we're all going for spring break." Peter turned the chocolate soup over with his spoon. A gummy bear slipped beneath the surface. "I didn't think I'd be with someone who would want to watch the Discovery channel with me and not get bored talking about microorganisms. Lena, you're — I just. I didn't think I'd get this lucky."

Two years flashed before Lena's eyes. She'd had a few good friends in high school, her best friend since middle school was a dorky guy who asked her out senior year and she turned him down. She liked Matt, really, but it wasn't about Matt. She didn't know how to date, how to take herself seriously. She had thought he was joking. He wasn't joking. They never are.

"Peter." Lena pictured spilling her melted yogurt all over herself. She had that kind of luck, really. Maybe Peter would fetch the napkins. Maybe this top — her favorite top — would be stained.

"Lena," he answered, mimicking her tone and mocking her playfully. Was it normal to feel this lucky and also, sometimes, wonder if she should just break up with him? Get the inevitable over with and return to reality?

Lena blew her bangs out of her eyes and sketched his face for a moment. She let her eyes wander around his jawline, the curve of his cheeks and the vein in his forehead. His lips parted, and she remembered he was still waiting for her to say something. The air in here was stale, the way an ice rink smells — cold and sweet, a dry feeling that sticks in your throat.

"Peter. I —" She wrung her hands under the table. "I —"

He looked up from the spoon he was playing with to keep his hands busy. His gray eyes found hers immediately. "I love you too." He didn't hesitate. There wasn't any hint that in his eyes he was wondering how it would feel to get up and run away. But she did, all the time.

He pressed a kiss to her cheek, which was exhilarating and mostly embarrassing because they were in public. Peter smiled like he meant it, the way little kids do when they don't even try to hide their joy because they haven't been taught to be ashamed of it yet, and that was wonderful and terrible. "Ready to go?" He threw their cups in the trash.

Lena nodded. She was just doing her homework.

. . .

Steam fogged up the professor's glasses as she poured from the boiling kettle on her hot plate. "Tea, Lena?"

"Sure. Uh, chai."

Professor Knowles placed the mug on the low table in front of Lena and sat back at her desk. They considered each other for a moment; Lena was still uncomfortable interacting with her professors, and Knowles always seemed very comfortable with silence. After a moment: "How are things going?"

"Okay. I'm starting to get the hang of my classes. It's... an adjustment. Like they said it would be. But I feel like I'm figuring out how to study. Stuff like that. It's hard, but it's good."

Knowles took a long sip and raked her eyes over Lena in the silence. Lena's gaze dropped to her hands, which were sweating, and she didn't feel like she could wipe them on her jeans like she would normally do because the professor was looking at her and she would notice and then she would realize that Lena was nervous and there wasn't anything to be nervous about — not really, right?

"What about all the other things? The not-class things, Lena? We had discussed —"

"I auditioned for an improv troupe."

Knowles seemed surprised. She had raised the mug to her lips and didn't take a sip. "Good for you."

"They didn't want me, of course, but I know that's not the point."

She waited for a response and got none.

"And. I'm dating someone. So that's...new."

"Good for you." Knowles smirked. Her computer dinged an email, and she turned to dismiss the notification. Seconds felt like eternities; silence was agonizing. "I'm really happy you're trying to leave your comfort zone. I know it's not easy."

"I thought about it, and I guess you're right. I mean, that's all science is, right? You push forward, even if it's uncomfortable and you don't know what's going to happen?" Lena laughed hoarsely. "That's what everyone has to do at some point. That's how discoveries are made."

For just a moment, her mother's face flickered before her, hazy and warm-toned, the way faces crackle in old home movies. *She* hadn't been that kind of scientist. *She* hadn't tried to pursue the postdoc and the family, the career and the love. "Right," Knowles interrupted, and the image faded. "You push forward."

Lena nodded. That's how discoveries are made.

BEVERLY

1938

. . .

Beverly Conner could not feel her left eye.

She had been wholly enraptured and lost track of time. Her samples were just a row of glass tubes filled with an opaque sludge. The wind chime sounds of empty glass clinking together were dulled by the sample at the bottom, transforming into a heavy thud that smelled like salt and sounded like earth. This algae could grow on anything. No sunlight, no heat to speak of. No encouragement. Still, it grows.

Her eye had been squeezed shut for twenty minutes as she peered through the microscope. But she couldn't tear herself away, even as muscles in her face she didn't know existed were aching in protest. Some people see the body as one with the mind; others see it as a vessel. Beverly had long since mastered her body. Its job was to keep up with her racing mind. The eye stayed shut.

On the slide below, backlit and glowing around its edges like the moon in an eclipse, was pressed the most beautiful emerald-colored specimen. It sprawled in intricate tendrils like a fine lace, something rare that people would pay a lot of money for. It turned reddish-brown at the edges, like an apple oxidizing. Beverly could understand why someone would spend their time looking at a plant like this, but not a lace tablecloth. The lace in her mother's house was artificial, repeating itself in predictable floral patterns that swirled the same each time. But algae? You couldn't predict it. It was like it had been painted right there in the water by a shaking, brilliant hand. One emerald brushstroke in a painting that only she was looking at.

It had already been a little over two years since her first meeting with Dean Peabody. He'd been in touch, visiting occasionally and more often sending her letters giving updates on his progress in his beautiful scrawl. She'd kept them all in a neat stack in her office, between the employee handbook, which she never looked at, and the Green Book, which she flipped through often. The Dean's most recent letter had mentioned that if she could get something else published, something big — something so big that they couldn't ignore her, because the *thing* would squeeze out all the air left in the room — he thought he could tip the scales. She'd be Professor Conner. Associate, at first, but still.

Every surface in this closet they called an office was covered. By the door, in a well-organized heap, sat all of her collection equipment, most of which she'd made herself from things she'd scavenged from around the house. Rachel was getting fed up with what she called "The Curse of the Disappearing Kitchen Appliances," but Beverly didn't have enough funds from the department to buy new equipment. Her muddy boots were in the hallway, drying on a sheet of newspaper she'd taken from the faculty lounge — she was assuming everyone was finished with that article about the new Kodachrome. And her microscope — her treasured microscope — claimed the precious real estate on the shelf she'd been left for a desk.

Her right hand flew, pencil on paper, as her left maneuvered knobs on the microscope and coaxed the slide across the viewer. The rock in her throat was growing. This thing, this feeling that was spreading across her chest. It was new. It was looking at something new. There was a word that bubbled up in her mouth, but she kept forcing it down.

She kept waiting for it to make sense, for what she was seeing in the microscope to suddenly crystallize into focus and look like one of the hundreds of other samples she'd preserved on matboard or illustrated for textbooks. Twenty minutes, thirty minutes, of her pulse beginning to race and doubt, certain doubt, forcing it back down. But that jagged edge that dappled like lace and seemed to melt into the water on the slide, like it was so fragile it might just disappear — something was not adding up.

Algae produces between 30 and 50 percent of all the oxygen usable by humans. Beverly took a deep breath. The crude oil in a gurgling engine, the natural gas in her stove — all the remains of ancient algae. It was the currency of the world. The sample pressed here, paralyzed between sheets of glass, it was of the same heritage. Whether it was new or not, it was a part of that same beautiful harmony.

Beverly's hands twisted the knobs on her microscope. Too excited, she threw the image out of focus. The viewfinder blurred to a solid green shape.

If there was a totally unique kind of algae living in the lake at Marsden, that mattered. Maybe it was found elsewhere, too. Maybe it had come from somewhere else and evolved. Algae, the pond scum that could grow where nothing else could and silently, thanklessly, offered up the most precious gift in the animal kingdom: oxygen. It needed to be protected, studied, and the only way Beverly knew to do that was to understand it. Fully.

Beverly leaned back in her chair, her vision flashing cyan and magenta as her eye adjusted to being open once again. She always rather enjoyed the tricks that exhaustion played on her senses. Most people tried to convince her that the way that she experienced the world, the beauty she found in the shapes of cells, the organic geometries and brilliant colors, existed only to her. Where she saw two dozen different shades, like facets on a cut gem, the untrained eye simply saw green. So the hallucinogenic spots that present themselves, like ghosts, when you've been staring at a sample too long — those made sense to her, too. Beverly understood that she had always been seeing things that others swore weren't there.

But this slide, glowing in her microscope. It was no hallucination.

The word was back on her tongue. Her mouth tasted like metal and her vision dotted with magenta and cyan. Discovery. Beverly could hear her pulse in her ears. Her pencil flew. This new species that Beverly Conner might have just discovered.

Fucus evanescens. The Latin always sounded nicer than the English: *Fucus,* meaning algae. *Evanescens,* vanishing, fading. Disappearing.

LENA

2016

. . .

"Are you trying to get high off highlighter ink?"

"Excuse me?"

"Lena, your face is so close to the textbook — just — give — me — that," Peter's hand wrapped around hers and wrestled for the highlighter. It was hardly a fair fight. When he got this close, Lena could smell chili peppers on his breath and his deodorant, which she thought smelled like the ocean. She let go.

"You're overworking yourself." He tipped the lid of the textbook shut, which collapsed its pages, dangerously nearing a thousand, onto the table with a loud thud that punctuated his sentence. They listened to it reverberate off of the cinder block walls.

"I am not," Lena finally mumbled.

"How many cups of coffee did you drink today?"

"Beside the point. I like things that are, you know, iced and caramel. The coffee just... *happened* to be there. More of a reason to have whipped cream, really."

Outside, there was snow. Soft January midnight in the window bounced bright from the sheets of white on the grass and the trees. Lena hadn't seen a lot of snow in Virginia, and she'd never seen it glowing a sort of ultramarine under the dark sky, or reflecting green stop lights, red taillights, orange streetlights. The dorm room smelled like sickly-sweet instant hot chocolate powder, even though their mugs had been cold for hours, and the vague notion of peanuts from their Pad Thai.

"Lena." He ran his fingers through his hair, which probably meant he was frustrated with her. Small veins leapt from his wrists, and his dark eyes were fixed on her face. "Lena. Look at me. Come on. What are you trying to prove?"

"I'm not trying to *prove* anything. I can do this. I can be better, I am better. I got a B on the first quiz of the term, and the next one's coming up, and if I don't wow this professor, then how am I going to get a letter of recommendation to get a summer internship to make me a connection that will get me into grad school?"

"Lena." He reached for the highlighter again.

"Peter, if I don't get an A on the next quiz, I'm not going to grad school."

He started to laugh. "That's it! Get up!"

"What?" He was already sliding his hands around her neck and knees, lifting her from the chair and gently tossing her onto the bed, which was jacked up high enough to fit the mini fridge under. "Put me down! Peter!"

"You're losing it. One quiz is not going to make or break your future."

"No. One quiz is not going to make or break *your* future. It might for me. You know, opportunities don't come as easy to everyone."

"What's that supposed to mean?" His laugh faltered only for a moment.

"I'm not joking, and this isn't funny." She tried to sit up on the bed, but he was right about the exhaustion, and decided she could be angry while lying down.

"Lena, come on."

"Your parents are both chemists with Ph.D.'s. You had braces so all your teeth are where they're supposed to be. You know the right words to say in an interview and how to write the thank-you note afterwards. For God's sake, you were family friends with the chair of the Biology department before you had even applied to Marsden!" She looked down at her hands. "I wasn't sure I was even going to get into a place like this."

Most people, Lena thought, would be offended. Perhaps Peter should have been, but he didn't react at all, not in any way that was visible. "This is just leftover freshman nerves, Lena. You'll hit your stride. You'll see." He studied her face. "You're lucky I'm not the TA of this class, too, or I'd just fold and give you the answers."

Lena didn't laugh. "You're not listening to me. I need to keep working. I can't slip up. I don't have the same cushion if I fail."

He looked at her, at her eyes and at her hands, like he was trying to paint her. His eyes moved frantically around her face, her eyes, which she was sure were ringed in smudged mascara, her lips which were chapped and red from her biting on them while she studied. Peter had never been a very good artist.

She wished he would speak. "Peter."

He reached for her hand and held it, considered it. Her small hands made his look awkward, angular, with fingers that were too long and thumbs that were square. Her fingers trembled, probably from the caffeine, blue chipped polish making a jagged shape in the center of each nail. The inside of her left pinky had ballpoint pen ink, blue that dries with a purple sheen, coating each fine crack in her skin. Her favorite pen had exploded last week. Her right hand still carried her high school class ring, on the middle finger, because her father had bought a size too big, and that was the only finger it fit on. She had been proud of it at first. Now it felt more like a reminder of the desire to get into college, to get out, graduate, champing at the bit to get started in life. Prove yourself, prove yourself, prove yourself. And if you ever slow down, you can look down at your shaking hands and see a gleaming reminder that you didn't work that hard to not work this hard.

"Peter."

He dropped her hand.

Peter reached forward and took the textbook into his hands. He almost dropped it. "I swear it was lighter when I took this class," he mumbled as he caught it. "Jesus, did they add a chapter?" Whatever was rising in Lena's throat was threatening to burst.

"Alright, Lena. Explain chapter four."

"Peter?"

"Too easy for the champ?"

Lena stared up at the ceiling and traced the cracks and water stains.

"Chapter four's next week."

"It's highlighted already."

"I read ahead."

He leaned forward so quickly she didn't have time to flinch. He softly kissed her forehead. "I know you did."

She turned away from him so he couldn't see the tears that sprang into her eyes. Men, she'd found, didn't understand the range of very logical reasons to cry. Her dad always started to panic when she'd cried happy tears because their cat was extremely cute and sometimes that was overwhelming. She didn't want to have to explain to Peter why her eyes had welled. She wasn't sure herself. Her hands were still shaking.

"Thank you, Peter."

"I'm still waiting for an explanation of chapter four." She

didn't turn around, but she could hear the smile color his voice. He nudged her with his foot, and she turned. He was looking out the window. Lena followed his gaze and saw that it had started to snow.

BEVERLY

1941

. . .

The Second World War hit Marsden about as hard as anywhere else. If you asked the people there, they would have told
you it had hit a little harder, since the town had an unusually
high percentage of young, able-bodied men. And it's always
hardest right wherever you are, isn't it? The struggles of
others can slip into background noise. Whatever was happening in a train station in London was just ink on a newspaper.
It's loudest right here.

Franklin Delano Roosevelt's gravelly voice entered the
whitewashed house through the radio, the uninvited but
nevertheless welcome third roommate. Someone had to look
after two single women. He was a smooth-talker, punctured
by crackling radio waves. She'd never heard anyone speak
who could really change the way she looked at a problem
before, but Beverly was comforted by him. Rachel, in those
days it seemed, wasn't comforted by anything.

*"The Japanese have treacherously violated the longstand-
ing peace between us. Many American soldiers and sailors have
been killed by enemy action."*

"We've got to do something, Bev." The nervous chatter

was a part of the tradition now. Rachel would pace around the screened porch at night while they listened to the fireside chats. Beverly would sit in her wicker rocker and draw illustrations for science textbooks to earn some extra money. They needed it, since their salaries from Marsden barely covered their rent. And like Rachel, all this talk of war made her jittery. They both needed to do something with their hands.

Tonight, though, "We've got to do something" sounded like a question, not a statement.

"Oh yeah?" She barely looked up from the tracing paper in her lap. The sharp pencil tip followed the wavy silhouette of a plankton. "What do they need us to do, mend the soldiers' uniforms? I haven't done a clean whipstitch since I was a girl."

"We are now in this war. We are all in it — all the way. Every single man, woman, and child is a partner in the most tremendous undertaking of our American history."

"I wish you wouldn't talk like that."

"Like what, how everyone else talks? How we're supposed to talk?"

"There's a lot we can offer."

"I know that. You think I don't know that?"

"All the men are shipping off. They're going to need bodies, Beverly. Hands." That much, at least, Beverly couldn't argue with. They'd seen their vibrant Marsden — gossipy and old-fashioned, perhaps, but vibrant all the same — evaporate into a ghost town seemingly overnight. The grocery store bagger, gone. His father, the grocer, working overtime, since he was too old to join the boys in uniform. The mail was only coming sporadically these days. The postman, gone.

Beverly set down her pencil. "Where?" The graphite rolled across the page, slicing a jagged line in the plankton's antennae. Then the pencil clattered onto the floor.

"Everywhere," she paused, looking past the screened porch towards town, where the sun was setting in brilliant oranges and purples over the mountains. "I'm joining the fire department."

"*Every citizen, in every walk of life, shares this same responsibility. The lives of our soldiers and sailors — the whole future of this nation — depend upon the manner in which each and every one of us fulfills his obligation to our country.*"

Beverly opened and closed her mouth. There was so much that Beverly felt like she should do and say to soak up all the fear from Rachel's brow and wring it out into a bucket. It might not have been that hard for someone else, who had been taught how to do these things. But the people who taught her were her brothers, who showed their care by giving you a swift shove down the grassy hill out back and laughed as your feet went over your head. She should have looked at Rachel with the kind of look that says, "Everything will be alright," even though it might not. There had never been a war like this before. She should have reminded her that they were capable and were scraping by and that was more than anyone had expected of them. That they had a loaf of bread in their breadbox and it wasn't likely that the Japanese were going to attack again, and if they did, it wouldn't be here in New Hampshire. That should be enough.

Beverly didn't say any of those things. She just grabbed Rachel's hand and watched the sun set with her. They had both decided that their screened porch had the best view in town.

"*It is our obligation to our dead — it is our sacred obligation to their children and to our children — that we must never forget what we have learned.*"

Rachel Poole was five years Beverly's junior. Marsden hadn't yet beaten her into silence, which seemed to happen to all of the other women Beverly had met, the faculty wives and the women who ran the museum. And time hadn't yet sapped her strength or her ambition. Rachel Poole was joining the fire department, so Beverly Conner would go with her.

"Have the firemen asked for women to volunteer?"

"No." Rachel turned her head towards the periwinkle mountains and her hair covered her face. "But they will."

Beverly nodded.

"There is no such thing as impregnable defense against powerful aggressors who sneak up in the dark and strike without warning."

The sun surrendered to the treeline. As twilight washed over the town, blanketing bricks and roof shingles in a heavy blue, Beverly wondered when night in Marsden had stopped feeling safe. Anything could be out there. She wondered if it was quiet enough in New Hampshire to hear a plane if it was flying overhead.

"We're going to be awfully tired, Rachel." Rachel turned and tucked her hair behind her ear. "You know, a full day of work and then a shift at the firehouse."

Rachel said nothing but started to smile as she closed her eyes. "Thank you." She let her head fall onto Beverly's shoulder, her hair fanning across Beverly's chest.

"We will know that the vast majority of the members of the human race are on our side. Many of them are fighting with us. All of them are praying for us. But, in representing our cause, we represent theirs as well — our hope and their hope for liberty under God."

Beverly looked down at the top of Rachel's head, bobbing as her own chest rose and fell. The rhythm was peaceful, which was strange, listening to the President speak of fighting and liberty, while Rachel's breathing slowed. Then Rachel's hand twitched, as though the contact had been a mistake, and her thumb folded over Beverly's hand in her lap. Beverly froze, in case it had been an accident, and any movement would wake Rachel up and shift her away. The crickets were performing a symphony in the grass.

Perhaps Rachel fell asleep. She stopped moving either way. The President's broadcast ended and the radio cut to a shaky static. Beverly sat, listening to the crackle of the radio and Rachel's even breathing, as she scanned the night sky. What she was looking for, she wasn't sure, but she knew she wanted to see it before it saw her.

LENA

2016

. . .

It was unseasonably warm for New Hampshire in April. Lena knew it had been known to snow as late as the end of March, sometimes even early April, since those were the kind of statistics she knew about every college she'd even considered applying to. 10.7 inches of snow in the month of March. It had said so in her college admissions binder. But today it was unseasonably warm, and Lena had nervously left behind her puffy winter jacket and had left her room with bare shins showing. That glorious First Warm Day.

Alex rolled over in the grass so the sunlight could warm her face. Oblong shapes of yellow and shadow dappled her nose, cut by the tree branches and the leaves above, young green things that had appeared overnight. "Can someone read the chapter to me? I'm sick of reading." The heavy textbook was open and lying across her stomach. "Lena?"

"Mmm," Lena responded, crunching one of the pretzels that had scattered across their picnic blanket. "Sorry. Finishing my lab report." It was hard to see her laptop screen in the bright sunshine, but after the long winter, she refused to work inside, even if the squinting was giving her a headache. It still felt good.

Lena had been content working alone under her oak tree, but Alex and Quinn had spotted her when they were leaving Carlisle. They'd invited her to join their picnic study session, and it was unclear if they'd really meant it or if they'd felt like they had to invite her because they were passing by. Lena hadn't known how to say no.

She hammered away at her lab report, pausing only to watch the shapes of the shadows from the tree canopy dance across her knuckles. A bug she didn't recognize landed on her wrist and she let it walk along her vein, a tiny mountain range, until her typing forced it to flutter off.

Lena didn't notice as Alex and Quinn argued about the answer to one of the practice test questions. She wasn't that nervous about their upcoming midterm — the absence of the emotion left her feeling empty. Something was missing, the tensing of her stomach and the clawing at her throat. But she was doing really well so far. She had her system for studying, it was working, and at Peter's pleading, it involved a lot fewer flashcards than she'd relied on in high school. She was on track to finish her lab report today, and it was due next week, after the quiz. Alex and Quinn hadn't started theirs.

There was a breeze. It mussed her hair like an older sibling might. Lena didn't reach up to smooth it.

"I'm sure Len knows which of us is right," Alex said, as she dramatically clapped her textbook shut. That caught Lena's attention. "Y'know, because her *boyfriend* gave her all the answers."

Lena had at least two issues with what Alex had just said. First, she was doing well in her classes this term, which was a marked shift from the struggles of the previous one, and it was no thanks to Peter. He wanted her to prove to herself that she didn't need any help — so he'd never offered any. Second, she did not know Alex well enough to have earned a nickname.

"Len" was something that Peter called her; no one else had earned that right.

She kept typing, pretending not to hear the teasing. Quinn closed her textbook, too, and tossed one of the pretzels at Lena's keyboard. "Earth to Lena. Can you help us?"

Lena didn't look up, but took the pretzel from her spacebar and chewed it slowly. "Peter didn't even take this class. Neurobiology isn't his specialty. This is an elective course." The words came out slowly. Quietly.

Alex and Quinn exchanged the glance one musters when silence is overbearing. It was easier to pretend that Lena was overreacting to a joke than acknowledge that they all knew there was a truth buried somewhere. "C'mon, Lena, I was kidding. I just mean, y'know, that you should help us. You're not even studying for the quiz."

Lena closed her computer and watched for another moment as the leaf-shaped shadows fell across the peaks and valleys of her hands. She sucked in a deep breath that smelled like springtime and tasted like new humidity. "I know you thought I was sleeping with the TA to get help on the tests or something. If you think I'm cheating, then I can't be of any help to you anyway, because clearly, I don't actually know the material."

Quinn reached down to adjust something on her shoe. Alex stared at Lena and only glanced away when Lena noticed.

"I mean, it seemed like you guys only wanted to hang out when we were working together." A grasshopper sprang from a blade of grass and landed on a sunny patch on Lena's knee. She considered it, the geometric, pale green face cut into facets like a diamond. Somehow proud, despite its size. "Am I your friend? Or just the answer key?"

Alex opened and closed her mouth. The grasshopper leapt to the safety of the shade, where the sunlight didn't blind or scrutinize.

Lena stuffed her laptop into her backpack. "I forgot. I have, um, a meeting. So. I gotta run."

She stood and brushed the pine needles from her legs. Bare calves, the sharp line down her shin gleaming in the sun like a sword. The First Warm Day brought something out in her. She didn't recognize herself. "Oh, and Alex was right. The answer's B. It's on page 265."

Lena didn't walk back to her dorm right away. She wandered around campus until the sun set and the darkness rolled in and reminded her what April in New Hampshire really feels like. Springtime in Virginia was warm. It didn't trick you like New England did, offering enticing patches of sunshine and a chill that sneaks up on you. For a moment, she thought of the bed of flowers outside of her house and wondered if the daffodils had bloomed yet, if anyone had remembered to water them without Lena there to drag out the old garden hose and hold her thumb over the spot with the hole in it so the water didn't spray everywhere. Just thinking about it, she could picture the squelch of water in the grass.

Professor Knowles had told her she could have it all — the social life, the good grades, the career, the hobbies and club sports teams — if she wanted. And she'd told Lena that she would be a better scientist, more recharged and focused, if she had a support system. Lena was sure she was right. But she was pacing around campus, alone. Not sure where to find those things, even if she wanted them.

There were no daffodils blooming yet in New Hampshire. There hadn't been enough sunshine. Lena typed out a text to Alex and Quinn apologizing. Then she deleted it, unsure exactly what she would be apologizing for. She saw a missed call from Peter. She didn't call him back. She felt something like anger, though it couldn't be anger, because there was nothing to be mad at him for.

I found this practice test that's pretty helpful, she texted

Alex and Quinn and sent them the link.

Lena looked at the goosebumps rising on her legs and wrapped her arms around herself.

New Message from Alex: OMG! You're the best!

The grass turned dark blue, and the streetlights glowed orange and it was hard to remember that the sun had just been shining. It gets cold quick.

. . .

It wasn't a disciplinary hearing. Not really. But the chair of the department had called her in for a meeting to discuss "a situation" that he had recently become aware of. Peter. And her.

"Ms. Rivera, please, have a seat." The Chair, Professor Ng, gestured to the seat in front of him. It was a nice office. Bigger than Professor Knowles', in a part of Carlisle she hadn't spent much time. "You look alarmed," he said with a comforting smile. "You're not in trouble, Lena. We just wanted to figure out what was going on. Make sure no one has broken our *Honor Code.*"

She was sure Alex and Quinn had filed a complaint of some kind. She couldn't prove it, but it felt like retaliation for what had happened on the quad last week.

"The department has become aware you're..." Professor Ng looked uncomfortable; he looked at spots on his corkboard, or the tile floor, or out his window. Anywhere but her face. "Romantically associated. With another student in the department, who was your TA in the fall. You didn't disclose this relationship, and we take these...offenses. Seriously." Professor Ng had squat, rectangular fingers that he studied in his lap. A pink face, though maybe he was just embarrassed. Black hair that was turning gray.

Lena thought she might throw up. She opened and closed her mouth, weighing her words, because she knew as soon as she started speaking the words would just tumble out.

"Peter and I barely ever even spoke about the class. We weren't dating for the first few exams of the term, so there was no way he could have helped me more than any of the other students." Lena's leg was bouncing violently. She had never been accused of cheating. She had never really been accused of anything. She'd contemplated shoplifting once, just to see what it would feel like, and the guilt she had from even acknowledging the thought had haunted her for weeks. "I can...have my friends write a character reference. I'm sure there's camera footage from the library, on those, security... cameras. You can see I sat by myself every day for hours and studied. I can show you all my practice tests. I got so many answers wrong I wouldn't have bombed all the practice tests if I was getting answers from my boyfriend."

Lena's entire body was hot and getting hotter. Her leg was jerking against the tile floor. She felt like her stepmother's tea kettle, which filled with pressure in a way that sounded uncomfortable until finally, in an ugly protest, it started to whistle. She had to keep the lid on.

Professor Ng sucked in a few deep breaths. "I appreciate your willingness to prove yourself." He scratched at a small stain on his khakis like it might come out. His breathing was loud, there was a ringing in Lena's ears. "But even the optics of the situation —"

"Why didn't you bring in Peter for questioning?" Lena could not believe she was interrupting a professor, but the words kept spilling out of her mouth. "I mean, please, sorry, Professor." He glanced at her and back to the wall. "But Peter's the one in the position of authority, he's the —"

"A separate investigation will be conducted —" Ng shook his head.

"But you think it's more likely that the freshman girl is promiscuous and wants an easy way to the top, than that the sophomore frat brother might ever use his position to prey on younger women?" Professor Ng was pressed back into his seat like he'd been slapped. "N-not" — Lena caught herself — "that either of those things is true. I mean, Peter didn't *prey on me.* Jesus. No." She was making everything worse. Her stepmother's kettle let out a jet of steam when it was finally boiling. As a kid, she'd made the mistake of reaching for it and had burned herself. "I'm sorry. Professor. This is just very upsetting; I hope you understand. Peter has been incredibly supportive of me as I've gotten adjusted to college classes, to the department, and neither of us has ever dreamed of cheating."

Ng finally fixed his eyes on her face, like he wanted to believe her. She swallowed hard, since her throat was closing the way it always did when she was about to cry, and if she cried in the Chair's office when he was accusing her of sleeping with her TA to get ahead, well, that wouldn't much help her case.

"I worked very hard to get to Marsden. I wouldn't throw it away for a *boy.*" She couldn't believe she'd had to say that, and she really hoped that she meant it.

They stared at each other for a long moment.

Alex and Quinn were probably eating dinner together somewhere. Lena wished that in that moment she had another thought in her head besides the fact that maybe she didn't have any friends here at Marsden. And maybe Knowles was right; maybe that did matter.

"Just." Professor Ng raked his fingers through his hair and didn't look up from his desk. "In the future, Ms. Rivera, you should consider how your actions present yourself to the world. As a...woman. In the field. It's not fair — I get that. But it's still there all the same." Lena was certain he did not get it.

"Thank you, Professor." She thanked him for confirming that all the moments she had wanted to hide Peter from the world, embarrassed of him and what it might say about her —

she had been right. Lena liked to be right. And it would have been lovely to be wrong.

"Lena, you seem to have a bright future." Ng looked out the window. "I don't want this misunderstanding to get in the way of that. But please do be careful."

"Always, Professor." She wondered for a moment if she could ask how the department had heard, who had told them. But he was going to let her go — after she'd interrupted him, said things she couldn't imagine ever saying to a professor, about things she couldn't imagine ever speaking to a professor about. It wasn't worth knowing if Alex and Quinn had been behind it. It didn't matter. "Will Peter get in trouble?"

Professor Ng sighed. "You can go, Lena."

"Got it. Yes. T-thanks." The door was heavy, and she closed it slowly behind her.

BEVERLY

1941

. . .

Rachel was right. The fire department had not wanted any women, but the question came down, as most do, to the "yet." Beverly and Rachel rode by the fire station on their bikes before work on Wednesday and asked the fire chief if they needed more volunteers. He was sitting in a folding chair on the driveway, looking out onto the road. He took his cigarette out of his mouth and blew smoke in Rachel's direction. He took them in, and Beverly could picture how they must have looked: two skinny, pale academics and their cardigans buttoned up to their throats. Then he started to laugh. But five days later, when they rode by again, the department had lost all of their strongest men to the war. Their lockers inside the garage were cleared out. Ghosts, everywhere.

The fire chief's name was Walt. He dropped the cigarette to the ground and crushed it under his shoe. "Let's see what you've got." And then he got up from his chair, folded it and tucked it under his arm, and went inside the garage. Beverly and Rachel looked at each other and silently decided that was as much of an invitation as they would get around here.

The garage housed two fire trucks, engines 12 and 13, and

was punctured with niches that served as lockers stuffed with wooden ladders and metal helmets. It was cool inside, the way rooms with concrete floors always are. Two other new volunteers — gangly Marsden students who hadn't shipped off to war yet — were sipping coffee in the corner with the three remaining firemen in town, recognizable by their uniforms. Their stiff laughter bounced around the room. The emptiness was a little suffocating. Beverly wondered what it had sounded like when all the firemen had stood in the garage, whether they could hear each other over the din of laughter and conversations about their wives' pot roasts. "Boys," Walt said, appearing behind her and snapping her from her trance. He clapped one of the men roughly on the shoulder. "We've got two new *recruits*."

The men looked around for who Walt could be referring to.

"Hi," Rachel said.

"Absolutely not," one of the men in uniform said to Walt. "You want me to put out a fire *and* rescue her when she trips on the hose?"

Walt smirked. "All I said was we got volunteers. Next we're training." He turned to Rachel and then to Beverly, who was reminding herself over and over again that this was Rachel's idea. "Can you run in that dress?" He looked pointedly at Rachel's skirt. Beverly was wearing pants.

"Faster than you." Rachel looked pointedly at his soft stomach that spilled over his belt. One of the boys in uniform choked on his coffee. Walt turned red.

"If you're gonna be a fireman, you're gonna respect your fire chief. Got it?" Walt barked. Beverly kicked Rachel. Walt waved around him and added, "Grab some uniforms, all of you. Quick, like there's a fire. No time for lolly-gaggin' in this business. Meet us around back and we'll see what you've got."

Beverly ran to grab one of the folded uniforms from the

cleared-out lockers. She slipped the jacket on, a double-breasted coat, dark blue. The sleeves were so long they covered her hands. She looked up in time to see Walt shove a metal helmet into Rachel's chest. Rachel put it on with a defiant laugh, and it rolled down her scalp so the molded lip covered her eyes. Beverly reached for the pants and panicked. There was no place to change. This locker was in view of the open garage door and the street beyond. She slipped them on over her pants, wool scratching wool. They were too big, and she cinched up a belt around her waist, hoping it would hold. She had to bow her knees to walk normally. "Rach, hurry up!"

The men had gone out the back door. Rachel was still getting dressed, fumbling with the buttons. The male volunteers had already dressed and left in a matter of seconds. *Everything is quick when you aren't worried about scandalizing the neighborhood with your bare skin.* "Go on, Bev. Better that he likes one of us." Frustration shook Rachel's voice.

Beverly grabbed a pair of pants from the nearest locker and pushed Rachel behind the engine. "You're going to have to take your dress off. I'll cover you."

"Bev, I can't —"

"Hush," Beverly snapped. Rachel looked up at her, a crease deepening between her brows. Beverly tried to soften her face, but wasn't sure she knew how. "You wanted to do something. We're doing it." It was the way her brothers would have treated her. *You wanted respect? Respect is earned. There's no room for softness.*

Rachel nodded. She pulled her dress over her head and threw it on the floor, not looking at Beverly, as though she was embarrassed maybe for the first time. Her stomach and arms were white and fleshy. Beverly tried not to stare. It made sense, though: shelving books didn't give you much muscle. Beverly held the pants out and helped her into them, awkwardly bending her wrists so her palms didn't brush Rachel's thighs. "You can do this."

"I don't know if I can." Rachel's eyes were wet. "I'm not used to this, Bev. I'm not the only woman in the room, not ever."

Beverly buttoned up Rachel's coat and dusted off the collar. "You don't want them to talk to you that way? Show them that." She picked up Rachel's dress, folded it, and set it in an empty locker. "Let's go."

Outside, the men were squinting in the sun. Walt had equipment strewn in the grass, a ladder and a bundle of hose and a few crowbars and pickaxes. The uniformed men stood behind him, eyes glinting with amusement, arms crossed. "Took you long enough. We were starting to get worried," he scoffed as the women joined the group. "The vetting process involves a written test, which you'll take tomorrow. And a physical exam." Rachel caught Beverly's eye nervously. Neither of them wanted to be *examined* by the swollen, pink-faced fire chief or his uniformed squad, but Beverly wasn't as concerned as it seemed like Rachel was. Maybe it was that she'd been examined by the men at the office every day. Or maybe it was that she'd been expecting this. It made enough sense to Beverly — if you can't carry the hose, or bash a window open to let someone out of a house, or the other things she imagined firemen had to do, then you probably couldn't be a fireman. Firewoman. Simple enough.

Rachel steeled herself. Beverly found herself more focused on watching Rachel and suppressing her desire to protect her from these men and their eyes. The first drill was just carrying the rolled hose while running. It was heavier than it looked, but all of them managed, even Rachel. The other recruits seemed surprised to see the women close behind them. It just felt good to be running through the grass again.

The drills got progressively harder. Beverly suspected that some of them were improvised by Walt on the spot. Surely the state-authorized physical exam did not include tests of flexibility, which he said were necessary "in case you need to fit in tight spaces." Rachel could do a perfect split, which Beverly did not know.

The day dragged on and the sun climbed higher in the sky, hidden as it was behind opaque clouds. Walt told them there was one last exercise. "Does that mean we've almost passed?" Beverly asked. Walt did not answer. Rachel squeezed her arm.

"Put these on." Walt gave them each a helmet and a belt with a fire ax and a crow bar looped through it. The ax was heavy and the oiled handle bounced off of her thigh when Beverly walked. He led them to a fence. The uniformed men crowded behind them to watch the action. "You're each going to carry all that, and you're going to slide under this fence, run down that way, climb that tree," he pointed one sausage finger towards an oak in the distance, "and retrieve one of the helmets I left up there. Then you're gonna run back, shimmy under this fence again, and give Scott here the helmet."

"Sounds easy enough," Beverly said.

Walt grinned. "Then you get to go first." Rachel looked over at her, face pink with exhaustion and excitement.

Beverly nodded and stepped forward. "So do I just start running?"

"Wait." Walt grabbed a bucket of water. The volunteers watched as he poured it at the base of the fence, turning the soil beneath the lowest slat to mud. He stirred it with the toe of his boot, so the group heard the squelch.

Walt turned back to the onlooking volunteers, suppressing a smile that crept into his eyes, anyway. "Go ahead."

Beverly took off running, the ax and crowbar slapping her legs and the helmet bouncing against her forehead. She sucked in a deep breath of January air and tossed herself onto the ground, sliding through the cold mud and under the fence. The helmet clanged against the lowest slat like a bell ringing in her ears. Wet earth streaked the front of this, someone else's uniform, and was already starting to freeze. The fabric stuck to her stomach.

She streaked through the field. With the firemen behind her, she could almost trick herself into thinking it wasn't demeaning, but freeing. Just grass and trees spread out before her, under the white winter sky. The wind whirled around her face.

At the base of the tree, she realized she'd been tricked. Walt had put the helmets on a branch totally separate from the rest of the climbable sections. He must have used a ladder. The branch was thin and crawled out away from the thickest part of the tree. The boys were far behind her now, but she could almost hear them laughing. She was still panting from the running and her hands, pink in the cold, slid off the tree as she tried to get a good grip. Her hands weren't as callused as they should have been, and the bark scraped the pads of her fingers. Even if she could have climbed up the trunk, she couldn't reach the helmets from there. And the branch was too thin to support her weight.

Beverly looked back over her shoulder. Rachel was the size of her palm in the distance, but she could almost make out the hope on her face. Her red hair blew around her and she shivered in the uniform that was too big for her. Beverly chewed her lip, quelling the rising panic in her chest. She had to do this. She had to figure something out. The mud on her chest and the metal tools were turning cold against her. Then Beverly reached down and took the ax from her belt, lifted it over her head, and threw it at the tree. The ax stuck in the thin branch for a moment, and then the ax crashed down to the ground, the heavy metal head tumbling first. The bough and all three helmets came with it.

She put the ax back in her belt, clasped the helmets to her chest, and ran. Rachel's cheers wafted through the wind as it picked up speed. Frozen earth sounds hollow when it's pounded by heels. Beverly slid back through the mud and stood, dripping with sweat and dirt, and tossed the stack of helmets at Walt.

He caught them with bewildered eyes.

"I'll be damned."

Beverly tried to wipe the mud from her face and spread it around further. Rachel laughed and looked over at the boys. They just stared at the creature covered in earth. Her chest rose and fell. "So, are we on the squad? Chief?"

Walt shoved the helmets into Scott's chest and stalked off.

LENA

2016

· · ·

"This one's yours, 3B," the man, whose workman's jacket said "Hank," whether or not that was his actual name, jiggled the key in the deadbolt and kicked the door as he opened it for good measure. "Hank" was the property manager for the building, a squat cluster of low-ceilinged apartments above a liquor store in Roxbury. It was the best place Lena could find on short notice.

The wood floors in the hallway sank in the middle, and the whole building was haunted by the humid, cloying smell of the liquor store downstairs. But on the whole, it was livable. "Hank" left her keys on the counter in the kitchenette and vanished down the hall. Lena dragged her suitcase inside and set about acquainting herself with the locks on the door. There were three, but only two keys, and even when all the way shut, the door wiggled in its frame. She locked it after a few tries with both keys and pushed her suitcase against the door as if that would add some extra security.

It was a studio apartment. She surveyed the entire space from her vantage point by the door. One window that let in gasps of noise from the street below, the occasional tire squeal or siren. A sunken futon with mysterious stains Lena would force herself not to think about as she slept, a kitchenette with a mini fridge, microwave, and hot plate resting on sage green linoleum counters. A single lightbulb above the microwave and one above the futon.

It would be fine. Lena wiped the sweat off of her forehead. Carrying all of her belongings up three flights of narrow stairs in June, afternoon heat had sapped her. There was no time to lose, though. She'd arrived in Boston Friday night. Work started Monday morning.

Professor Knowles had pulled a few strings to get Lena this internship. She had heard about Lena's meeting with Professor Ng, but she assured Lena that she had found the whole thing an overreaction and she wouldn't retract her recommendation for Lena to work in this lab. It would have been nice to spend the summer with her family, but Knowles made the lab sound like it was a big opportunity. Lena wasn't yet sure what that meant.

Her first apartment, all her own.

Peter called as she started unloading her clothes into the shoebox of a closet. She put him on speakerphone and shouted at him as she tried to beat the wrinkles out of the only two work-appropriate outfits she owned. "How's the place?" She could hear the smile in his voice.

"It's...great. It's the right size, you know. Just for me. My first apartment!"

"Is it safe?"

"Yeah, of course."

"Is there any security in the building?"

"Yeah," she lied, thinking of the grate "Hank" had unlocked at the street entrance. "Super safe. How's home?"

"It's so nice to be back, Len. My sister says hi!" he started to shout over the other voices in his room.

"Aw, tell her hi back. And your parents? They're good?"

"Yeah. My dad took me suit shopping today to get ready for work on Monday." Peter was starting his internship at a lab at the University of Chicago. Lena hadn't heard much about what he'd be working on, but she had already heard of the lab, which was more than she could say for her own job.

"Do you really think you'll wear a suit to the lab?"

"No, he was just trying to be supportive. We had a good time."

"Did you go with pinstripes? I think you could pull it off," Lena said, shutting the door to the closet and watching it spring open again. It looked like the hinge was broken.

"I don't think people wear those anymore, Lena," he laughed.

Lena carried the phone with her as she ventured into the bathroom. "Sure, you know, in movies," she said. Tiles everywhere that had once been white, gridded in blackened grout. A small shower, a cracked medicine cabinet she was scared to open. Lena studied her sweaty reflection. She could almost trick herself into thinking she was old enough to be doing this.

"Like mob bosses?"

"First impressions matter, Peter. It's important they know who they're dealing with." She smiled as she set her toothbrush on the rim of the sink. All moved in.

"You're probably right," Peter said. "You know, I'm really looking forward to this job. I'm, like, actually excited to go into work. I'm officially old."

"Not old. Just doing what you're supposed to be doing."

Peter paused. "Yeah. That's nice."

"It is." She absentmindedly picked at a hangnail on her thumb, then stopped. She wondered how bad it would be if she got cleaning chemicals in the cut on her finger.

"You're ready for Monday?"

"Getting there. I need to get some food for my... fridge. Tomorrow. I just ate granola bars on the train."

"Get some takeout tonight!"

"Yeah." Her stomach growled at the thought of some Pad Thai, but she knew she was too exhausted to venture back out into the city. And getting it delivered was not an option; she was unwilling to pay extra for the luxury. "Maybe."

"Len, I gotta go. Talk to me tomorrow after you've got some food in your house!" Peter said quickly, like someone was rushing him off the phone.

"Bye!"

"Love you." He managed to squeeze it in before the line went dead. Lena let the last sounds of Peter's voice wash over her. She always felt calmer after she talked to him, just hearing the hum of his laughter relaxed the tension in her shoulders. It was going to be okay. And now it was time to get to work.

There was a bottle of bleach in the bathroom. It might have been older than Lena; the label was peeling off, and it was scarred with a large square patch of dust in the shape of the sticker that had once marked price. It would have to do. Lena stripped down to a tank top and shorts from high school gym class, piled her hair on top of her head, and set about wiping down every surface in the apartment. The sink in the bathroom, the toilet seat and handles of the faucet. The doorknob, the locks, the counter tops.

She crawled around the kitchenette, the peeling sheets of lacquer on the floorboards flaking off and biting into her bare knees. Flecks of things, the accumulation that comes when one decides to deep clean, covered her legs. Kitchen. From the Latin *coquere,* "to cook," which became the German *kūche.* Everything was an SAT flashcard.

She discovered an ancient mousetrap in the corner and hoped its age meant there were no mice left to kill.

Lena flinched at the sound of every footstep in the hallway, stopped to check twice that the curtains really were closed and her door really was locked, but after about two hours, she was finished. She collapsed onto the futon and tried not to think about how comfortable Peter's bed must have been at home. Monday was coming. It was really happening. She was here, and she was doing it all by herself.

The bleach-soaked towels reeked in the corner. She'd have to find a place to do her laundry in the morning.

BEVERLY

1941

· · ·

Black grease coated Beverly's hands. There was a smudge on her elbow and her temple and her chin. She was straddling the fire truck, like it was a pony and not a machine that choked on its own exhaust and wailed under its own siren. She blew her hair out of her face as her slick hands finished rolling up the hose and tucking it back into place.

"Hey Bev!" Scott, one of the few boys left in town, called from the coffeemaker. He was pouring himself a cup and had already poured one for her, without asking. It was steaming on the counter next to him. "Come and get it."

"Scott, you know she's not coming down until every bit of equipment's put away up there," Rachel teased as she rounded the corner. Her hair was piled up on top of her head, tied up with that red kerchief, and the short pieces around her face had stuck to her forehead. Beverly thought she looked best that way — when she had a whole day's work behind her and usefulness and pride in her hands shone out of her eyes and her blushing cheeks. "You know my Bev. Most at home on the engine."

It was true, but Beverly laughed and dismissed them. She

stumbled over her words as that "my" bloomed on her cheeks. My Bev. "I'm almost done."

"Coffee's getting cold."

She liked it up there, picking her way across the ladders and hoses and things that were stored on top of the truck. She was like a cat, who defied gravity with an arched back and precise, weightless feet. She had a purpose. She could do something. And — unlike in her office in Carlisle Hall, where all of those things were also true — after she'd proven she could do it, all the men backed off. Engine 12 was basically hers now, no questions asked.

The lockers weren't as empty as they had been when Beverly and Rachel first volunteered. Some plucky high school seniors had arrived at the fire house a few days after Beverly and Rachel had, and the garage always had at least a few men and the radio on. One by one, the uniforms were getting tailored to their new wearer's proportions, and Beverly and Rachel no longer had the worst-fitting jackets in the station. As soon as her own sleeves had been hemmed, Rachel started teasing the seventeen-year-olds who looked like they were wearing their fathers' coats.

John, Scott's little brother and the only one left in the station who still tried, fruitlessly, to flirt with Beverly, lumbered in through the open garage door. He walked that way, like he just liked to hear the heavy sound his boots made. "Beverly Conner, you've been working up there for four hours. Would you come on down here and have something to drink?"

Rachel touched his arm with fingers that looked delicate even when she had grease under her nails. She whispered something in his ear that made him chuckle his husky laugh despite himself.

Beverly didn't like how much better Rachel was with people. It came naturally to her. Every eye in the room flew to her when she walked in. Beverly swung her legs around so they dangled off the side of the truck, and the metal lip bit into the undersides of her sticky thighs. These weren't feminine, toned legs like Rachel's. These were white as milk so you could see the smattering of hair on her knees, thick and strong and peppered with bruises. But she had quickly become the station's most diligent worker. And that was true no matter if they hung on her every word.

Rachel led the men out of the garage. Rather, Rachel walked out of the garage and the men followed her. Beverly climbed down from Engine 12 and took a swig of cooling coffee Scott had left her. He knew exactly how much sugar, which was swirling in crystals on the bottom of the mug. She stretched and looked around as she gulped the coffee down. It was good to use her muscles. On the bulletin board, pinned above pictures of David's kids and a thank-you card from the Women's Club of Marsden, were two of Beverly's favorite items in the world. A newspaper clipping of an article from last month. In the grainy picture, Rachel and Beverly, with sweat dripping down their wide, exhausted smiles, stood atop Engine 12 with their arms slung around each other. "Local Girls Make Good Firewomen," the headline, simple and not nearly as complimentary as the article went on to be, but still — seeing it in ink stamped on the page made something melt in her chest. And next to it was the award they'd given her last night, a certificate of honorary membership of the station and full voting privileges. Even Rachel didn't have that yet, making Beverly Conner Marsden's first volunteer firewoman.

She touched her hand to her face and spread the grease further from her cheekbone to her neck. Outside, Rachel stood as the sun glared horizontal rays just before dipping over the tree line. She laughed at something Scott said from his shy post at the other end of the driveway. They were too far away for Beverly to hear what they were saying, but Rachel's red hair was on fire in the sunset and Beverly had worked all day long and she was happy to lean against the siding and watch this effortlessly graceful woman start to dance to the radio. She could almost forget that tomorrow was Monday, and that the professors at Carlisle would ignore her again. For now, she existed. She could feel her blood racing and the sun that made her eyes squint. She was sure that only people in love can feel so lucky to be alive.

Beverly stepped out onto the driveway into the setting sun and felt the warmth hit her face. "There you are!" Rachel's voice sounded like bells as she grabbed Beverly's stained wrists and gave her a twirl. Beverly awkwardly stumbled but laughed; if anyone else had tried to make her dance on the street, she would've insisted she had no rhythm and was a better onlooker. But she didn't want Rachel to drift farther away. "Come on, bend your knees!" she playfully kicked Beverly's shin, and they spun down the driveway. No one found it strange, these two women with callouses dancing with each other. It wouldn't have mattered much if they had. The world blurred from shapes into colors. Rachel's hands slipped from her wrists and she twirled away, her hair fanning out around her and then swirling to a rest on her shoulder.

All eyes were on Rachel. But when she stopped spinning, laughing at herself, and turned back to the group, her eyes were on Beverly. She shivered, even though it was warm. Everything was frozen. The radio crackled with static, and then the song changed.

LENA

2016

. . .

The apartment looked its best in the early morning light. Pale blue came in through the windows and washed everything. Lena lifted the blinds as soon as she woke up and watched the bands of light stretch across the floor as she got ready.

"I'm so excited for you," Peter's smooth voice crackled over the phone. "First day, first real research lab. Are you excited? I'm excited."

"I'm excited," Lena agreed, tossing an apple in her purse for her commute. It was the only thing in the fridge. She'd eaten everything else she'd bought on her nervous trip to the bodega on Saturday morning. Once she got paid, she could go grocery shopping for real.

"You sound distracted. Len, take a minute. Soak it all in today, okay? You've worked so hard for this."

"So have you." Lena pictured Peter's parents packing his lunch, peeled orange slices and sandwiches cut in triangles. Probably a nice home-cooked meal when he got home at night. She smiled at the thought. It was to be a summer of instant ramen and white bread. "I'm proud of you, Peter."

She hadn't told him about the bleach and the mousetraps.

Peter still thought there was a doorman to her building, since it wasn't worth correcting him. She tried to focus on her day, on the job, on making a good first impression. Everyone might be a letter of recommendation for grad school. But still, just hearing his voice was enough to make Lena wish she was in Chicago instead, even if it meant giving up an internship she'd been twisting Professor Knowles' arm to get. Lena didn't want to be the kind of girl who would give up a summer internship to be near her boyfriend. She wasn't sure what "that kind of girl" meant, but she knew that she wasn't it and didn't want to be it and she wasn't sure but she could almost, almost smell the musk of his body wash through the phone. And that shouldn't be possible.

"Have a good day at work," she shouted into the phone as she reached to hang up. She looked down at her wrinkled button-down shirt she'd bought at a thrift store back in high school and wondered if she was going to look out of place at the lab. Like a child.

"I love you." He sounded like he meant it.

"I love you too." Something clawed at her throat that tasted like metal. She did love him. Apple, bag, computer. Lock the door. Lock the door again. She loved him, and that was the problem. There wasn't room for him and everything else, and if she got more attached, she might just pick him instead. Keys, purse. Phone? Phone. Downstairs. Bus stop. Work.

The phone call was on her mind all morning. The bus, which, to Lena's dismay, smelled like gasoline even when you were inside of it, was full. She stood in the aisle and tried to steady herself on the bar overhead. "You've worked so hard for this," and "I love you," rattled around in her head like the bus windows rattled in their frames. The bus hit a pothole.

They gave Lena a nametag in the lobby. A real one, the kind that goes in a lanyard with a plastic sleeve on it. It had her photo and her name and which lab she was assigned to, all printed right on the plastic, permanent and official. She put the lanyard over her neck, which she soon realized absolutely no one did, and headed inside. It was a hallway full of frosted glass doors and logos of small biomedical startups and university labs. Her new boss showed her the lab, explained their research. It was a team of mostly women, which was exciting and surprising, since the lead biochemist on the project was a woman named Jordan, and for some reason, she had assumed Jordan was a man. Jordan wore running shoes and a sweatshirt from the Gap under her white coat. Lena was actually overdressed in her thrifted slacks and button-down, which was a relief, because she didn't have a week's worth of those. The whole lab was casual. Comfortable. These were people who looked like Lena and who remembered being her, beaming back from behind clunky safety glasses. They were doing really innovative things, partnering with the university's hospital to trial a new drug-delivery system that targeted viruses on the cellular level. The drug could permeate the cell wall, be accepted inside. It was amazing, the kind of stuff Lena would have read about in a textbook and felt goosebumps rise on her skin. All the boring flashcard stuff was finally usable, needed. And helping people.

But Lena couldn't focus. And she hated that she couldn't focus. It was Peter's fault.

There was no way out. Distancing herself from him wouldn't suddenly sharpen her world into view. She was in too deep to be able to cut him out and have everything snap back to normal. The pangs of jealousy, the ease with which he seemed to skate through life, they haunted her. More than anything, though, she missed him. And that was much worse.

The women got her set up in the corner, pipetting an agent into this plastic tray. They'd need to run hundreds of tests, so they'd need hundreds of agents prepped. It wasn't the flashiest part of the lab; she wasn't lighting things on fire and nothing was changing colors. But it was what Lena had come here to do. Was Peter pipetting? Perhaps he was doing something more important. Perhaps they'd taken one look at him, smiling like he was in a toothpaste commercial, and they'd promoted him to their full-time staff. In the moments of clarity she could find when her inner monologue paused, she was hit with a giddy wave of pride. In the other moments, she was glad the task at hand was so monotonous that she could think and think and think and still get the work done. Not a drop spilled, not too shabby for a first day. Her fingers ached. How was Peter's first day?

The trays piled up and the hours passed. Her supervisor examined the refrigerator full of prepped agents, their plastic wrap coverings labeling them in Lena's shaky handwriting. They would chill overnight in there alone, as Lena suspected she would in her dark apartment, and be ready for work tomorrow. The perky supervisor feigned more enthusiasm than Lena thought was appropriate. "This looks great! Good job — you're a fast learner. I had trouble with those little guys on my first day!" And perhaps on any other day, Lena would've warmed at the words. Encouragement didn't come often enough, and it wasn't like her to dismiss it. Her childhood bedroom was still tattooed with the gold stars she'd peeled off of elementary school spelling tests.

Lena got home that night, exhausted. She'd need new shoes; the beat-up tennis shoes she'd brought weren't going to cut it. She'd be on her feet all summer. The ramen was already in the microwave when Peter called. Her finger hovered over the "accept" button. And then she declined the call.

He wouldn't be offended. He didn't know exactly what time she got home from work. He wouldn't know that she was blowing him off. And she wasn't *blowing him off*, exactly, she just needed time to collect her thoughts. She used to be able to do that on her own, without using Peter as a sounding board.

Lena hadn't turned on any of the other lights in the apartment when she'd come in. There wasn't much to see, anyway, so she sat on the floor of the kitchenette, her face in the microwave's glow. This place really wasn't clean enough to be sitting on the floor, even after the bleaching. She reminded herself once again that this was the best she could afford. Her phone started vibrating on the floor next to her. He was calling back.

She still saw pipettes when she closed her eyes, and her blood was ringing in her ears. Forty-five seconds left on the ramen. How was she going to make it through the summer? Her work was amazing and thankless, and her apartment was so tiny that the hum of the microwave seemed to reverberate off the walls. Maybe she wouldn't call Peter tonight. She typed out a few texts, something about having a headache or being stuck in a long commute on the way home or treating herself to takeout and it being too loud in the restaurant to call. But she didn't lie to Peter — she didn't really lie at all, but there was something especially sacred about him that she couldn't violate, even when she wanted to run away from him.

And it wasn't him she was running from — it was the fact that she didn't want to run away from him at all, and she didn't recognize that in herself, and she needed to push him away, just to prove to herself that she could.

Her phone vibrated again. *New Message from Peter: Made it home from work just now. The guys took me out for a drink. Call me whenever! Can't wait to hear about your day!* And suddenly she was gripped by the desperate need to hear his voice. He answered the call immediately.

"How was it?" Peter couldn't contain the excitement in his voice. He was really that thrilled to hear about her first day. What had she been so afraid of?

"Peter. It was." She opened the door to the microwave and

pinched the phone between her shoulder and her ear. How to describe her first day. The faces of the women in the lab stared back at her. "Peter, it was amazing. Jordan is a woman, apparently, not even that much older than me. Or she looked young, you know, anyway. And they were so excited to have me! I thought it would be scary, like, men in tweed jackets talking about molecules or something. But my boss, she's so cool. I want to be just like her when I grow up." Peter started to laugh, but she didn't let him cut in. "Peter! Their work! They're targeting the virus *on the cellular level.* I think they mentioned something about it in Bio 101, but it didn't hit me until I was standing there in the lab that the stuff they're do-ing —"

"The stuff you're doing," he corrected.

She smiled. "Whatever. The stuff we're doing, it's not just flashcard stuff. You know? It's going to help someone, maybe, someday."

Lena hadn't allowed herself to feel the weight of the day until she narrated it back to Peter. Perhaps the rest of it could be forgiven, the guilt and the feeling of lack when he wasn't around. Because she would've just kicked off her shoes and stayed buried under the grayness of exhaustion. But when he called her, she was reminded why she had wanted to work in a lab in the first place. And it wasn't just having *someone* to talk to at the end of her day, it was having Peter, who under-stood this work, who genuinely wanted to see her do it, whose smile she could hear in his voice when he spoke to her.

"Lena! That's amazing."

She fell onto the futon and heard one of the springs finally give up on living. Lena slurped ramen as Peter started telling her about his day. The lab sounded more important, the people sounded more important. But maybe it was just that she always felt like Peter was more important. She tried to push the thought away, but she kept thinking of the new suit his father had bought him. Maybe he really had worn a suit on his first day. Maybe it was the kind of place where you had to wear a suit on your first day. It was the kind of place, apparently, where the new intern gets taken out for a drink with "the guys."

Peter rambled through a detailed description of the exact shape of an ethanol molecule while Lena listened to the car horns and wailing sirens of the city. For a moment, they drowned him out.

BEVERLY

1943

. . .

The stairs were faster when you took them two at a time. Beverly fisted her skirt in her left hand, hiked up to her hip, and clutched the fat folder to her chest with her right. The stack was uneven; a few translucent onionskin sheets stuck out from the folder and fluttered as she climbed. Sometimes the light would catch through the tracing papers and silhouette just her graphite markings, fibrous and oily like some sort of membrane. Her footsteps and panting breath echoed in the stairwell and slowed as she reached the last step.

She was out of breath. It had been a while since she'd run up this stairwell. It had been a while since she'd visited the supply closet and its sweet smell and warm embrace. She'd been spending more and more time in her office, as the research gathered momentum with a fervor, like she was chasing it down a hill.

But these illustrations needed to be sent back to her publisher today, otherwise she wouldn't get her check before the rent was due. And the only envelopes big enough to fit a stack like this were all the way upstairs.

Beverly's head was down, checking that everything was in

order in her folder. That's why she didn't see him until it was too late.

Beverly and her folder bounced off Bell's chest and his crisp white shirt. The illustrations fluttered through the air and landed in a wide halo around her on the floor. It was safe to say they weren't in order anymore. Beverly hit the floor, her chin biting into the ground hard enough to tell there was concrete under the carpet. She'd have a neat purple mark there on her face for a week and a half.

"Miss Conner, keep your running to the gymnasium," Bell said, eclipsing the lone lightbulb in the ceiling. His silhouette loomed over her, fists at his sides. He did not move to help her.

"*Dr.* Conner," she muttered as she pushed herself to her elbows. The carpet had thin stripes on it. She had never noticed that before.

"What is the meaning of all this?" Bell moved in a small circle, sweeping his eyes across the hundreds of translucent sheets. One dark pencil line on each page, looping around the perimeter of some plankton or algae. She could see that he understood that this was the sort of work done under the flicker of one lamp, the work done after everyone else has gone to bed. It was clear, in the precision. You don't get those kinds of lines when someone is looking over your shoulder and talking. It's quiet work, and it was work he never had the patience to do. When Bell swung back around, any flash of wonder in his eyes had already been replaced with disgust.

"They're illustrations, sir." Beverly stood and brushed off her knees and elbows. "For textbooks."

"I don't recall that being in your job description." His voice deepened. Beverly was certain he couldn't recall her job description at all.

"Sir. I draw illustrations in the evenings. Not on work time. It all gets done, sir, and I do my job well. Dr. Bell." She turned her back to him and started collecting the sheets from the floor, gingerly placing each one back in order in the folder like she knew them all as individuals. "I trust there have been no complaints with the work that's in my *job description.*"

Bell's patent leather shoe crashed to the floor, inches from her fingers. The toe pinned a drawing to the carpet, and she winced at the sound of the sheet crumpling. Beverly considered herself in the reflection of the shiny black loafer. Red face, hair stuck to her forehead. She looked small, distorted.

"Beverly. You cannot have another job if it interferes with your first one. It's embarrassing for a Marsden...*employee* to be working odd jobs in the evenings. I will not have it." He lifted his foot.

"Dr. Bell," Beverly reached for the last sheet, "I don't believe there have been any complaints about my work." She shut the folder and pressed it against her chest. "So I don't believe anyone could say drawing a few pictures is *interfering.*"

"It's college policy. You wouldn't want to be an exception to a rule, Miss Conner?"

"Sir. I cannot pay my rent on the salary Marsden pays me. I trust it would be far more embarrassing for the College for me to be homeless?" Bell lowered his eyes.

"It's not proper to discuss money —"

"Then let's not. If you'll excuse me, I just came up here for an envelope." Beverly pushed past him, confirming that his bicep was as stiff and cold as the rest of him. She skittered down the rest of the hallway to the supply closet and didn't look back to see if he had moved.

When Beverly got back from the post office — she'd decided not to wait until after work and mail the illustrations right then, in case Bell returned later to seize them — a thick envelope was waiting for her, squeezed under the door to her office.

She ripped it open, right there in the hallway.

It was the letter she'd been waiting for. From the president of the American Phycological Association.

Dear Dr. Conner,

Thank you for your lovely note. I've cross-referenced my own notes about the New England region as well as the field drawings of our late great Dr. Stefanik and I can find no such species that matches your description of this fucus evanescens. It's not entirely unheard of for ponds and lakes, isolated from other bodies of water, to evolve their own unique strain of vegetation, though of course you know that.

I'll cut to the chase — submit your paper for peer review. I believe the community will agree that you've discovered something totally new here.

I've included carbons of the notes I referenced, in case that's of any help to you. Do reach out if you have any more questions. Between you and me, I did my post-doc with a few of the boys at Marsden and I'm very glad to have someone looking for newness there. I've gotten the impression they're quite fond of the old ways of doing things.

Best of luck.

Beverly dropped the letter onto her desk. She wasn't the type of woman to faint at good news — or bad news, for that matter — but she clutched at the cinder block walls just in case. They say there's a first time for everything.

Dr. Bell could report her for all she cared. Beverly Conner had just discovered a new species, and in a few short months, everyone would know.

Maybe then she wouldn't need another job. Maybe Rachel could buy cheese again.

LENA

2016

. . .

Sophomore year could have been off to a better start.

It simply wasn't possible, this number. Lena Rivera was no failure. Freshman year had gone better than all those voices in her head had told her it would go. Lena had never failed a test in her life, though she'd had a very realistic series of recurring nightmares about the subject in the past. But this paper she was wrinkling in her sticky, shaking fingers was real. So was the grade in the top corner — a fifty-five.

Lena started to get dizzy. All the students in the two-hundred-student lecture had filed to the front of the lecture hall to retrieve their graded exams from one of three tables, divided alphabetically by last name. She'd immediately unfolded it to read the grade, as had everyone. Most, though, quickly folded it again, good or bad, and made their way back up the aisle to get their bags and leave. Disappointment looked the same as joy, everyone taking long strides to take the sloping aisle stairs two at a time and get out of the lecture hall as quickly as possible. To celebrate or to consider dropping the class.

Lena hadn't started back up the aisle yet. She started to

sway, something hot and quickly expanding rose in her throat. One hand grabbed the folding desk on the armrest of the seats in the front row, but it hadn't snapped into place yet. When Lena leaned her body weight on it, the desk folded closed.

She was so lucky that Peter was not the TA for this class. No one was to ever know. She folded the test in half, the crease sure to stick from the sweat on her hands. Slowly, Lena made her way up to her seat. The murmurs of conversations grew unbearably quiet as everyone else trickled out of the lecture hall. The mess of papers went firmly into the backpack, into the darkness. She was hot and could not catch her breath. Lena jerked her jacket off of her shoulders and shoved it in the backpack too. She zipped the bag shut.

She'd need to shake this off before tomorrow. Professor Knowles had arranged for Lena to present about her work at the lab last summer at a virtual panel. The Biology professors had invited their colleagues from other universities and from private biotech companies to come hear the student panel. It would be Lena's best shot at a better summer internship for next year, if she gave a good presentation and played her cards right. Lena had been thrilled the day before when Professor Knowles managed to squeeze her onto the panel at the last minute. But who would want her now, Lena the Failure? She wasn't sure, having never applied to any jobs before, but she imagined that one of the qualifications besides a bachelor's degree in an associated field was, of course, not being a complete failure of a person who couldn't even pass a midterm.

Things were better when she got outside of the lecture hall. When you see just how far the Earth stretches in every direction around you, something like twenty pages stapled together feels a little more insignificant. If you put a ruler up to any straight edge, you could see it head steadily toward the vanishing point on the horizon. Everything was angles and math. Lena forced a deep breath as she found the tree line, bouncing up and down as she walked like she was mad at the Earth. Without even thinking, she had gravitated back to the oak tree and leaned against the bark. Sitting on the ground was good. The red that flashed in her vision was all but dissipated with fresh air that smelled like flowers, which smelled like new life, which reminded you that there always would be, you know, something new. Whether she failed a test or not, the trees would still stand and the sun would still shine.

She had studied for that test. Hard. This feeling that clenched and unclenched her fists wasn't just anger at herself for not being perfect, it was also anger at a field that didn't reward her for the things she'd given up. She had been invited to dinner in town at a dive bar with a couple girls from class. One of them, Nisha, had just turned 21 and was going to have too many margaritas, and maybe, if they were lucky, muster her nerve to do some karaoke. Lena really liked Nisha, maybe the first friend she'd made at Marsden that she actually really liked. But she had said no and spent her weekend studying for this test in her room, then the library, then her room again. Her classmates texted her photos of themselves straightening each other's hair as they all got ready for their night out in one tiny dorm room. But Lena had been told that sacrifices pay off, and she'd downed the rest of her iced latte at 8 p.m. and traced diagrams on her whiteboard until she saw molecular structures when she closed her eyes. And it hadn't mattered.

A few leaves shook themselves free from the branches above her head. She watched as they zigzagged back and forth in front of her face, suspended in the air. Did she really want to spend her life devoted to something that didn't care about her? Was it worth caring about something so much it hurts if that thing never seems to care about you?

Lena pulled the test back out of her bag and folded it flat. She flipped through it. Of course number six was wrong. She'd misread the question in her haste. She knew that, too. The back page, same thing. Words she knew, concepts she could explain backwards and forwards. She'd mixed them up in her panic. Perhaps the issue wasn't that she couldn't understand the material. She just wasn't enjoying it anymore.

In high school, science classes had been *fun*. Teachers had lit things on fire and frozen a bouquet of flowers with dry ice until it shattered. Textbooks had explained the world and barely even felt like studying to read about. This weekend, poring over her practice tests, hadn't been filled with the secrets of the universe that only she had understood. It had been dulled by caffeine-induced panic attacks. Did she enjoy this anymore? Did she even want to be a scientist?

She laid on her back in the grass, feet up on the trunk of the tree. That was supposed to keep the blood flow in your chest and brain. That was supposed to help with a panic attack, if that was what this was, which it probably wasn't.

With her hands folded behind her head and her eyes squinting in the sunlight, she had a view of clouds like marshmallows and leaves that lit up, golden, transparent. They fell around her, and she picked up one that landed on her chest. In this light, down here, by her face, it was a dull green. Opaque, closing itself and hiding its mysteries away. She eclipsed the sun with it, her arm outstretched, and it burst open, revealing a skeleton, a network of fine lines and geometric cells.

Lena dropped the leaf back to her chest and closed her eyes, seeing the sun through her eyelids, everything awash in red and warmth. She'd loved doing that as a kid, seeing, but not seeing anything in particular. Just color. Just light.

It seemed that eternal questions weren't how everyone defined science, not for a Ph.D. and certainly not for grant funding. Suddenly everyone cared about all these things she wasn't good at, like writing grant applications and publishing research papers as soon as possible and faster than everyone around you. Everything had been easier when she was a kid. And everything had seemed hard then, too.

In the middle of a beautiful sunny day, it started to rain. One fat drop splashed in the corner of her eye, hard, snapping her from her daydreaming. Some people say sun showers are lucky, but Lena never cared about luck. She cared about how something so spectacular was possible, and sun showers were just another thing Lena didn't understand. A lot of water was rolling down her face. Lena sat up on her elbows and saw her backpack darkening with rain. On another day she might have been mad. Today, she laid back down in the grass and listened to it squelch around her. For a brief moment, she had a vivid memory of the daffodils in her backyard, the ones only she would water. She liked them best because they grew first. The rain slapped her face and her arms, and as the smell of earthworms and humidity swirled around her, she could picture her childhood home. The old pair of sandals she kept in the garage that she'd slip on just to tend to the bed of flowers. The garage, which smelled like the ancient lawnmower that belched gasoline and cut grass. A raindrop rolled down her nose, and her fingers started to prune.

The mulch around the tree was saturated with water. Lena picked up a piece and bent it with her fingers. It splintered when it was dry. It's funny how rain hits you hard but makes everything soft.

She stayed outside until she was soaked through and then walked home as the sidewalk began to dry. Her wet hair stuck to her head in dark, dripping clumps. Lena's phone. *New Message from Nisha: I might have bought too much vodka, since I can do that now. Come to my room! We're going out tonight!*

New Message from Nisha: and don't say you have to study, I know when that test was!

The last party Lena had been to was her freshman year.

The night she met Peter, actually. It was long enough ago that the memories of sweaty Basketball Jersey Guy falling face-first in his own vomit were just beginning to be a funny story. Maybe it was the fact that she failed her first test, and people who fail things are supposed to be reckless. Maybe it was the fact that she was sad and, for the first time maybe ever, had someone who understood that to talk to about it. Her teeth chattered. She typed a response. *Screw it, why not? I'll be there in 5. You have to help me fix my hair. Will explain later.*

Nisha's dorm was nearby. It was starting to get darker as the sun slanted further in the sky, and since it was a Friday afternoon, that meant music was already pulsing from the brick building. Lena swiped herself into the building and knocked on Nisha's door. A loud pop song about a breakup was blaring inside already.

"Lena!" Nisha threw her arms around Lena's neck and pulled her into the room. She smelled like strawberry vodka and hairspray. "Why's your hair all wet?"

"Oh," Lena laughed as she dropped her backpack onto Nisha's rug, "it started raining. Got caught in it, or, um, I didn't bother getting up."

Nisha's room was the coziest dorm Lena had been in. She had photos of herself and her friends and family taped up on two of her walls, hiding the fact that they were cinder blocks. She burned scented candles, even though candles and hot-plates were strictly forbidden, so it always smelled like caramel, plus the added rush of having broken a ridiculous rule. The windowsill was lined with succulents, which, apparently, all had names. The aloe plant in the corner was named George.

Lena debated whether or not to tell Nisha about the test as Nisha set about drying and straightening Lena's hair. She also determined that Lena's shirt was not party-appropriate and offered a few of her own. "I'm so glad you came over. I needed a girls' night, you know. I mean, a night without Steven." Lena nodded. "You seem a little, I dunno, down?"

"I failed the midterm," Lena said quickly as she tried on the first top.

"No! Really? But you studied so hard for it!" Nisha didn't mention her birthday dinner that Lena had skipped. Lena wondered if karaoke would have been a better use of her time.

"Turns out it wasn't enough." Lena blinked back tears and tried to laugh at herself. "Maybe I'll switch majors! Who knows?"

Nisha was also a biology major. She got it. "Listen. If I was talking to Jolie, or really any of our other friends," Nisha started, which felt odd to Lena since the only friends she had were these new acquaintances she made through Nisha, "I would probably turn off this music and turn on a sad movie and order a pizza and talk about it. But girl, I've never seen you show any emotions, and here you are about to cry over one bad midterm." Nisha reached for the bottle of vodka. "You need to put this whole thing behind you. Come on! It was one test. You can't change it now, and you're *not* switching your major. We'll get back to work tomorrow."

Lena considered the bottle on the desk. It did smell like strawberries.

"Okay."

. . .

Sunlight streaked into the room. Lena's face was pressed into her arm, spread out on the hard floor. Nisha was in her bed at an angle that suggested she might have been thrown into bed. One arm hung off the edge of the mattress. Lena's eyes were sticky. She blinked a few times and finally noticed Nisha's alarm clock. "Shit."

Nisha moved slightly, her tangled mess of hair covering her eyes. "What?"

"Nish, it's noon."

"Yeah? You been hungover before, kiddo?"

"I missed the panel."

"The what?"

Her head was pounding. The panel had ended an hour ago, and so had Lena's chances at a better internship for next summer. Lena fished her phone out of her backpack, which was still slumped where she'd left it yesterday. There were only two notifications. *New Message from Peter: How did the panel go? Let's get coffee at 2 and you can tell me all about it?* And an email from Professor Knowles, sent right after the panel adjourned. Lena didn't have the courage to open it. The screen hurt her eyes. Nisha rolled over, facing the cinderblock wall. She was still wearing her sequined tank top and only one of her beer-stained sneakers. Lena had also slept in her jeans and the top of Nisha's that she'd borrowed for the night. The print of the carpet squares gridded her arms, as though in the night she'd tried to melt into the floor. That sounded like a nice option right now. Her eyes felt like they might fall out of her face.

Lena didn't feel the urge to cry. She didn't feel a rising panic in her chest, a heat that spread across her face and neck and arms. Everything was numb. She leaned back against the wall, which was colder than she'd expected. It was dark and bright at the same time, the grayness inside from the overhead light still turned off, and the glimmers of an orange daylight through the window. It was disorienting. The empty bottle of vodka laid on its side on the college-issued desk that Nisha appeared to be using mostly as a vanity. A tray of makeup and a hairdryer were scattered next to the bottle, as well as Nisha's diligently-colored-coded calendar. Nisha probably wouldn't have slept through her own meeting.

Lena's phone vibrated again. It was probably Peter. It could've been her father, she realized, slowly, who she had also told about the panel. She wasn't sure if it would be harder to face Professor Knowles or her dad.

Nisha's wooden bed frame was covered in graffiti. Permanent marker initials of couples who had probably broken up, grooves etched into the wood by a ballpoint pen. The letters of a fraternity, a lazy cube traced through with lines in a different color, maybe by a different hand. Many people had slept here. Perhaps some of them had woken up here, too, and wondered how things had broken so quickly. So easily.

BEVERLY

1946

. . .

Beverly sat in Dean Peabody's office alone. He'd been called out of their meeting by the President's secretary — a mousy redhead in a sweater that was too big for her — and after apologizing profusely, he'd left her in his office, promising to return soon. It had been about ten minutes, listening to her heartbeat in her ears the way it always did when she was in one of these stuffy leather-covered rooms. Her eyes ran along the desk. A smoldering cigar died in the ashtray. Manila folders were heaped on top of each other. The top one was labeled "Physics Department," the one beneath it "Arctic Studies Programme." He spelled it the British way. She found it insufferably pretentious. The one beneath it. "Beverly Conner Memos."

For a moment, she considered what to do. She was not the kind of woman who snooped around in other people's offices, but anyone would agree that this was not snooping: It had her name on it. That was the kind of thing she was entitled to read.

She tugged it from the middle of the stack. Onionskin carbon copies from the Dean's secretary's typewriter fluttered out of the folder. Letters — dozens, perhaps. Peabody had been collecting them for months, corresponding with the department chair, with botanists and zoologists and more than a few frustrated to be disturbed while on sabbatical, to weigh in on what he dubbed the "Beverly Conner Issue." The confidential folder ranged from honest to brutally honest. "It is my belief that Beverly Conner," one anonymous source drawled in spiderweb cursive, "had the misfortune, one, of being a woman. And two, of looking for work in the Great Depression. Should she be paid more? Perhaps. But the department does not possess ample funds, even for our men."

She shifted her weight in the chair, one of those leather things puckered with buttons which presents luxury but is much harder than it looks. *Beverly Conner had the misfortune of being a woman.* The words rattled in her head like the jingle of an ad on the radio. The Dean had mindlessly underlined them over and over, so hard he'd almost torn a hole in the paper, as if that would illuminate some truth, some solution. She did not consider herself misfortunate.

"Dr. Conner." The Dean appeared in the doorway. Beverly dropped the folder onto the desk.

"I'm sorry. I —"

"I should have told you."

Beverly wrung her hands in her lap and listened to his heavy footsteps as he came over and took his chair, the larger one with the wingback, behind the desk. Leslie picked up the cigar from the ashtray and cursed under his breath to find it cold.

"What are they?" she asked quietly, after a moment.

"I'm building a case," he said simply. "We're going to get you promoted. It takes time."

"Because I have the misfortune of being a woman," she said bitterly.

Leslie sighed. She could tell he was studying her face, but she refused to look up at him. Beverly Conner was not often angry. It was a waste of energy. But she did not enjoy being written about. Perhaps this emotion wasn't anger at all — she felt she might throw up, which would certainly ruin the leather chair and the Persian rug.

"I've lost sleep." Leslie said, his voice gravelly. Almost a whisper. "I take these long walks around the country club at sunset. My wife is getting concerned, I'm —" he sighed, then laughed sadly. "She probably thinks I'm having an affair; she just hears me on the phone late at night, the only time I can get the bastards on sabbatical to take my calls." Beverly did not move. Something twitched in his cheek. "I'll handle this. I made you a promise." She understood it wasn't that she was a woman — Leslie Peabody was no gentleman. He was a scientist, in pursuit of facts that helped make sense of the world. There were several facts she knew they both could not ignore.

Fact. Beverly Conner was one of the most competent scientists at Marsden. She had already published ten papers, which outpaced the men in her department with few exceptions. One of the memos mentioned something about discovering a new species, which should, Peabody thought, make her the most valued member of their department.

Fact. Beverly Conner received correspondence from all over the world, answering questions of scientists on nearly every continent. The letters were coming in frantic flurries every week now, after her latest publication had received so much attention. She had taught herself four languages, including Latin, to keep up with the letters and to read publications from outside of the states. None of the Marsden language classes, which were open to faculty hoping to expand their minds, were open to women. Fortunately, Beverly was a great teacher.

Fact. Beverly Conner was not getting paid enough. She made ends meet by illustrating textbooks with her steady hand and hawk eyes, a fact she had sheepishly forked over after much needling from the Dean, who insisted that she couldn't be paying rent on her salary alone. "I've seen the salaries of the entire department," he said nervously. His voice dropped, and he moved closer to her, slate-gray eyes fixed on her face. "You're making —" She looked up, defiant, and he swallowed his words. "It doesn't matter. I'm going to get you a promotion. And a goddamn raise."

She dulled herself with time, by intention, so that perhaps if she didn't stick in anyone's mind too long they would forget she was there and let her, quietly, carry on with her work. Beverly knew he didn't know quite how she did it, as it was a skill he'd never had to learn. But every time her face appeared, it shone the light back to him, something he'd thought only the moon could do.

"Shall we resume our meeting, Dr. Peabody? We did have some business to attend to, before this," she swept her hand over the desk, "digression."

He nodded. Beverly smoothed her pants. She was suddenly aware of what she was wearing, something she didn't think of often. Her pants were dark blue, and her cream-colored blouse was tucked into the wide waistband. Leslie had told her once that his wife never wore pants. She said they were mannish. "I'm bringing good news," she said, distracted by the papers she was shuffling in her lap. She sensed his eyes skating over her clothes and did not look up to acknowledge it. "I'm getting another paper published. It will be the first mention of a species called *fucus evanescens*." The color on her cheeks spread up to her temples and down across her nose. Then, rather suddenly, she held out the papers to him. "I thought you might want to read it."

He didn't reach for the papers immediately. He didn't move at all. The papers slid on the slippery satin of her pants. "I'm sure you're too busy."

Leslie Peabody shook himself. "No, no, of course not.

Never too busy for you. What's this about?" He took them from her hands. For a moment, they both saw how much larger his hands were than hers.

"A new species."

"Well, I'll be damned." He thumbed through the pages of tiny black type and laid them flat on his desk. He looked up at her bright face. The sunlight coming in through the window behind her caught half of her face in silhouette. The edges of her hair glowed orange, highlighting the individual stray hairs that floated around her head like a cloud.

She watched as he read the paper with rapt attention, the embarrassment of moments ago totally forgotten. His mouth formed the words as his eyes darted back and forth across the page. Beverly wondered if it would be enough. She wondered whose handwriting it had been, that she had been so pityingly misfortunate. She wondered if Dean Peabody had agreed with that shaking hand.

He looked up from the papers and smiled. She forced one back.

LENA

2016

. . .

Lena liked the sound her boots made on the floors in the biology building. The echo was incredibly satisfying because the hallways were narrow and the ceilings were low, the way that old buildings always are. Lena wondered if people had just been smaller in 1930.

The first and second floors of Carlisle Hall were where the classrooms and labs were. They'd redone the lecture halls in 2000 and in 2010 had raised a few million dollars to revamp all of the labs. There were two clean rooms and an electron microscope. Down there, everything smelled like rubbing alcohol and all the doors were glass. The third and fourth floors, though, were Lena's favorite. The professors' offices were in the older part of the building, where the sweet smells of small rooms still hung in the air. It was like going back in time. Mahogany door frames had brass room numbers above them, and they were all slightly different sizes, or the wood had warped over the years. Some were too big for the doors, others always got jammed.

It was what a collegiate hallway should look like. Between each door frame were cork boards that were layered with job postings and grad programs like fossils. If you went back far enough to actually unearth the cork again, you might find an advertisement for an internship program from the '80s, maybe, on brittle, yellowed cardstock.

The door on the left was Professor Knowles'. Lena hadn't seen her since The Incident, only exchanged a few sheepish emails. In her last note, she'd said she would stop by during Knowles' office hours. The handle was one of those ancient brass ones with the button to press with your thumb. It always got stuck.

Lena finally jerked the door open, a little harder than she meant to because of the handle situation. Professor Knowles was sitting at her desk, facing a student, who was crying into a tissue. An assignment of some kind, a test maybe, was spread across the coffee table. Knowles looked up at Lena. The student did not.

"Lena. I'm with a student. A moment, please." The amused smile was gone, the murmur of empathy in her voice, gone. The Professor's face was pale and taut with shadows around her eyes. She looked exhausted.

"Of course," Lena said immediately, ripping her eyes from the room and shutting the door behind her. She should have knocked. Why hadn't she knocked?

Lena sat on the bench outside the door. It was one of those leather ones that looks like it will be much more forgiving than it is. The leather was hard and cold and was beginning to peel off in jagged pieces. She placed her palm down, realizing that it was shaking, and when she lifted it, flakes of stained maroon leather stuck to the sweaty pads of her fingers.

First, she'd slept through an important meeting that Professor Knowles had set up for her. Now she'd barreled into Professor Knowles' office unannounced. Like she'd expected the professor to sit there, waiting for her, all day.

The door was still slightly open. She was already mortified

and fiddling with the door handle now in the silence would be too awkward. Through the crack, Lena could hear the murmurs of the conversation. The tearful student shuffling through the papers to ask another question. And then to ask the same question again, since she hadn't understood it on the test and she hadn't understood it just now. Professor Knowles' voice sounded raspier than usual, Lena noticed. She picked at a hangnail on her finger mindlessly. It was a habit she had tried to kick in high school, after her anxious picking had led her to bleed all over the scantron sheet for her PSAT. She'd needed wound-free fingers when handling chemicals, for safety reasons, and she'd wanted neat, clean fingers for interviews. The student in the office started crying again and Lena pulled at the flap of skin next to her thumbnail until her flesh turned scarlet.

Professor Knowles' phone kept vibrating. Low, dull hums traveled farther than the words they were saying. Knowles must have been silencing it when it started to ring; it only got to the third ring or so each time. But someone kept calling.

The echoes of other footsteps down the hallway were starting to irritate Lena. Her boots had sounded so adult, so confident, when she walked in. They had those wooden heels that make everything you're doing sound so assured. But these kitten heels of the department administrator sounded timid and heavy at the same time, and she kept walking around. The sound, along with the pounding of her own heartbeat, was making her anxious. Lena was not good at waiting.

She decided it might be a while, and she tried to take her backpack off as quietly as possible. Other professors' doors were open, some were on phone calls and some were talking to each other. Lena always thought you should be quiet when you were the only person with nothing to do in a hallway full of busy people. That, and she didn't want Knowles and her student to hear a heavy backpack crash to the floor.

Despite all that, the bag slipped on her arm and hit the tiles with a smash. Lena's various keychains — trinkets she'd preserved from high school and refused to part with, like the photo of her and her father on a roller coaster that they'd gotten printed at the giftshop in a glittery acrylic frame, which had felt like a big purchase at the time — jangled together like wind chimes. Lena cringed.

Inside, the conversation did not pause. Maybe they hadn't heard. The student's voice was growing more hysterical, but Lena still couldn't tell exactly what she was saying. Maybe she'd failed the same test Lena had. Her throat was starting to feel dry. Professor Knowles' phone was vibrating again. The administrator's heels were clicking. Lena wanted to scream.

The tiles on the floor were a black-and-white checkered pattern. Nobody puts tiles like that in their buildings anymore. Lena wondered if there had been black-and-white tiles on the first and second floors, too, before the renovation.

Her thumb was bleeding. A small dot of blood had soaked into her jeans.

BEVERLY

1955

. . .

Beverly Conner's mother was right about just about every-thing. If you asked her, anyway. She picked a new obsession once every few months, learned everything there was to know on the subject, so that she could swiftly explain to you the moral superiority of That Thing and why She Was Right and, unfortunately, You Were Wrong. Today, she wanted to be just like Jackie Kennedy. Well, she wanted her haircut, perhaps, and some nice pearls. Beverly's mother had decided that she was the height of class and fashion and any sensible woman, as she believed herself to be, would want to be just like her. She'd always had a mind for things like that. But Beverly's mother had had five boys, and her little girl was the youngest. Beverly Conner had never liked being buttoned into dresses.

"Do you still take your coffee black, Mother?" Beverly asked from the stove. She was always uncomfortable with her mother in her house, this place that was all her own.

"Yes," was the distracted reply. Her mother was fidgeting with her knock-off pearls she'd bought at the drugstore and liked to imagine nobody could tell the difference. Beverly wouldn't have noticed, not having the eye for that sort of thing, except that she knew her mother couldn't afford any-thing genuine. Her mother's hair had been gray for years, the kind of gray that keeps its chin up and shines silver in the sunlight. But in the past few months, she'd begun dyeing it and insisting that it had always been that way. She'd cut it shorter, just below her chin, so it swung when she turned her head.

Beverly set the mismatched mugs down on the linoleum table haunted with yesterday's coffee rings. "Any word from Scooter?"

"Not in a few weeks. Last I heard, he was doing alright."

"Well. That's Scooter."

"Do you still send him money?" The question surprised Beverly. She had never discussed such things with her mother — she had never told her she had helped Scooter cover his bills every now and then.

"Scooter can take care of himself."

"That's not what I asked."

Beverly's mother had always said there was something wrong with Scooter. Beverly had always said he was special and needed a little extra time. And even if there was something wrong with him, Beverly understood that as well.

The air was still in this room. Normally, Beverly kept the windows open so in the spring and fall, the kitchen smelled like sweet earth and damp air. She liked to watch her lace curtains whisper in the wind, she liked to open the house up to sunshine and life. Her research was outside, *life* was outside. A house, as she saw it, was just a place to keep your briefcase when you got home from work and a place to keep you from getting rained on in your sleep. It wasn't a point of retreat or a way to impress your guests. But Beverly's mother didn't see things that way.

"You know I've always had a soft spot for Scooter. He's figuring out his way in the world. If I can make that any easier,

I will." Someone had to. She knew what it was like. "And how are the rest of the boys?" Beverly wiped her hands on her skirt. All of her other brothers still lived in town with her mother. Except Scooter, of course, but everyone had always known he was going to leave.

"They're the same. We all had a meatloaf the other night."

"That's nice."

"What is there to do in this town? Is there a cinema?"

Beverly laughed and remembered a blustery bike ride in the dark that she had forgotten about. It felt like a lifetime ago. "I...wouldn't really know, Ma. I don't have time for much beyond my work."

"I didn't see a cinema on my drive in."

"If you didn't see it, we don't have it. I think you've seen all our roads." She didn't look in her direction but could tell, could feel, that her mother was staring at her. "Come to think of it, there's a cinema next town over. If you're looking to see a picture."

"I wasn't looking."

"I hear there's a new one with Cary Grant."

"Beverly, I didn't say I wanted —"

"And Grace Kelly, too, I think."

Her mother dropped the pearls. They clattered against her collarbone with a dull thump that sounded like it might have hurt. "I do like Grace Kelly." Beverly looked over, finally. Her mother kept talking. "She's got everything a person should want, you know. They just announced her engagement to the Prince of Monaco. I'm sure her mother's so proud."

Beverly took a hard sip of her coffee. "I think the picture's called *To Catch a Thief*."

Her mother raked her fingers through her hair, flattening her lips into a line. Beverly wondered if the dye ever came off on her fingers. She'd never dyed her hair before, but she thought perhaps if it was cheap dye, that might happen.

"I don't think I could live in a town like this, Beverly."

"Well, you don't. I do. And I like it here."

"But it's such a sleepy little town."

"It's where my work is, Ma. Not everybody's willing to hire me. I can't choose where I work based on the proximity to the nearest cinema. Besides, this is my home now."

"Beverly, you study biology. I may not have gone to *college*, but I do know that's about life. Don't you want to be a part of it?"

"I am living my life. It's a good one. I'm sorry it doesn't look like Donna Reed's, but that's my choice to make."

"There's more to life than your work. You don't want children of your own? You'd rather teach a bunch of rowdy prep-school boys?"

"I can live fully without a husband. Or a child."

"You're missing out on the best parts of life. I mean, *love,* Beverly."

Beverly paused. It was a low blow. "Love takes many forms. Mother."

"You're not proving a point, you know. Come on, Beverly. You've been paying your own bills for decades. You've got your fancy education and your science career. Those things can't be enough to make anyone happy."

Perhaps Beverly had more in common with her mother than she had different from her. Both were deeply passionate women. But someone had actually given Beverly a microscope and a Ph.D. That is, someone had given Beverly an outlet for her passions. Even if it wasn't her mother who had encouraged them, someone had. And Beverly's mother had had five boys and a girl who didn't much care for dresses.

"Are you even listening to me?" her mother's voice expanded like hot air. If she kept going like this, the whole house might just lift off of its foundation. Beverly continued looking out the kitchen window. The lace curtains bent in the breeze, the curtains being the only thing in the house that Beverly's mother approved of.

"Of course, Ma. I listen to every word you say."

Beverly looked a lot like her mother. She had the same sharp features, the same full lips and long eyelashes. They were women whose faces almost demanded to be painted. But Beverly had different eyes than her mother; they saw the world in a different way.

"I need a cup of tea. Can I get you anything, Mother?"

"A cup of tea. I'll be damned. We just had coffee."

Beverly heard Rachel at the back door. "Bev! Home from work!"

"Come on in!" Beverly placed the tea kettle on the stove and started boiling some water. This house needed some more steam. She glanced at her mother, who was sitting at the kitchen table with her arms folded like a pouting child. "You're going to be nice to her," Beverly scolded quietly, feeling quite maternal. "Rachel," she hollered again, "come on in here and meet my mother."

Her mother's red, drugstore-lipsticked lips mouthed Rachel's name to herself silently. Considering it. *Rachel.*

LENA

2017

. . .

Lena was sitting on the pool table, her hands behind her on the green felt. The textbook was in her lap, and she read aloud to the other girls in her study group, who were dancing as they answered questions with pool cues serving as microphones and props. The whole billiards hall was empty, and they'd finally finished their term project — a massive, glossy poster with what had felt like a hundred graphs and size 10 font. It had taken two of them to carry it from the specialty printer in the library to Carlisle Hall to hang it. All that stood between them and Christmas break was this one last final. They'd searched the student center for a suitable place to work, and Nisha, the loudest of their group, had suggested the empty billiards hall would be "way more fun than the library." Lena had never considered whether or not the library was fun.

"Can you please focus?" The third member of their group, Jolie, shouted at Nisha over the music she was playing. "Lena, I didn't hear the question. Can you repeat it?"

Nisha tossed a handful of popcorn at Jolie, only one of which she caught in her mouth, and chorused with a laugh, "I heard the question, and the answer is phospholipid!"

Lena rolled to her stomach on the felt and shouted out questions about the peripheral sheet of the smooth endoplasmic reticulum to Nisha and Jolie, and she had to admit that this was a better way to spend a Friday night.

The study session dragged on until around midnight, when Jolie took the textbook from Lena's hands and threw it onto the ground, insisting that they'd studied enough. "Give it back!" Lena had wrestled for the book with a laugh but didn't fight that hard. The three girls ended up in a pile on the floor, Nisha passing them handfuls of snacks. Lena suddenly found herself with Jolie's head on her shoulder, braiding Nisha's hair.

"It just sucks, you know, because my parents want me to take over the family business." Nisha said with her back to them as Lena sectioned off her hair for the French braid. It was easier for her to talk now that she didn't have to see their eyes staring back at her, and the words kept tumbling out. "And I love them, you know, but they never went to college. They don't get it. I want to support them, like, that's the only thing I care about. But I can support them much better if I'm a dermatologist than if I am balancing the books at their hair salon."

Jolie sat upright and stifled her yawn. "Dude, that's insane. Like, yeah, I get that that's their life's work, but you came to Marsden to get a better shot at your dream, right?"

Nisha was quiet for a moment. A blush spread to the tips of her ears. "Well, they don't know that I'm a biology major."

Lena didn't say much. It was easier to listen. She liked these girls, and she didn't want to ruin it by giving them advice she wasn't qualified to give.

"What do they think you're doing? Accounting?" Jolie said as she licked the icing out of an Oreo. Lena didn't understand how she could hear someone saying things that were hard to choke out and just answer so casually. The braid was snaking down Nisha's back and she focused on her hands. Nisha had beautiful hair.

"Well, I mean, economics, yeah."

"When are you going to tell them?" Jolie pressed. "I mean, they're gonna see the diploma, right?"

"I'm going to! I am. It's just. When I'm here, I'm who I'm supposed to be, you know. I'm taking these classes that I love, and I have my friends and my roommate and everything makes sense. Even when everything isn't perfect, it's still mine. And I only have to deal with that when I go home and they ask me questions and —" Nisha sighed. "This is what I'd dreamed of. Being at a place like this? Coming from my high school? Statistics tell you I shouldn't even be here. I just want to be *here* when I'm here, you know?"

Jolie nodded, and added, "But it's like you can't forget that this place isn't built for you. It's like they want to remind you of it, every minute, all the time."

"Yeah." Lena was surprised to hear her own voice cut in. "I've had, what, two female professors? Three? I wasn't expecting it to feel like you're going to someone else's school. I mean, it's not 1950." She hadn't ever thought about it like that before, at least, she hadn't thought that she had. It's strange to hear yourself say things to others you'd never said to yourself. "I never thought about all those things in high school. I mean, I don't think about it much now. It's just a gut feeling. I don't know what I expected, I guess. Not to feel it?"

"Or at least for it not to be so constant! Or for people to talk about it!" Jolie said bitterly, drowning her sorrows in more popcorn.

"They make you fight so hard to be here that you feel like you have to be a certain kind of successful, like, justify why you're here. Why you put yourself through it." Lena peeled a hangnail away from her index finger. "Like maybe I don't want to be world-renowned, and I wouldn't even know it because you get brainwashed —"

"Yes! Oh my god yes, I know I'm going to apply to a dual M.D./Ph.D. program just because it will make all the other honor society kids absolutely *die,*" Jolie whispered with a sick laugh.

"I haven't even stopped to think about what I want. I don't think," Lena said. Hadn't she?

Nisha tossed a piece of popcorn at Lena's face. "Don't do it! Introspection is a trap!"

The girls laughed, and then they stopped laughing, and everyone was afraid to speak.

"I had never thought about who pays for things." Lena stared intently at her fingers, weaving back and forth through Nisha's long black hair. "It looks like so much of this field is going to be scrambling to get tenure, or a secure job at an independent lab. Like you're not spending the majority of the time actually researching, you're trying to get people to like you enough they'll fund your research. And then you're going to conferences to present on your research, and hope that someone there will give you a job or a grant or —"

"And they do all that to keep us out of the lab," Jolie said. "I'll say it. I mean, I might sound bitter, but, like, I am. Nobody taught me how to schmooze at a conference, so I'm behind."

Lena almost dropped the braid in her hands. "Yeah, exactly."

"I've had so many arguments about this with Steven. Like, guys, I think I have to break up with him," Nisha's tone slid into levity, picking at the chipping nail polish on her thumb. "I keep telling him you're doing better in this class than me, yeah, but you're not *smarter* than me. Your daddy bought you a tutor, y'know? Like, you're family friends with the professor. You have adjacent lake houses or something." The girls laughed, even Nisha. "Guys, I'm serious! He doesn't get that things are easier for him. Yeah, he's smart. He's brilliant. I love him. But he's a guy. He's in science, he's from like forty minutes away in some swanky Boston suburb." She dropped her voice. "Guys, I think his mom still does his laundry."

The girls squealed, thankful that Nisha lightened the tension. It was good to talk about these things — Lena had never heard them said out loud — but she was afraid of how heavy the words were. She hadn't considered these things before. Or maybe she had. She didn't know anymore.

"Do you guys have dreams about presenting at conferences, too?" Lena asked.

"Oh my god, yes, and then all my teeth fall out when I stand up to speak," Jolie laughed.

"I had a dream once where I was accepting the Nobel Prize in Medicine and Brad Pitt was there for some reason and he was like, 'She doesn't deserve that!'" Nisha shouted.

"Oh my god. Why would Brad care?" They fell into a heap of laughter.

"Hey." Jolie popped up as Lena finished tying off Nisha's braid. "Who wants mozzarella sticks? I think the café's still open."

"How can you still be hungry?" Nisha shouted after her, but they gathered their books and dashed up the stairs, relieved to have something new to talk about.

Lena's phone vibrated. *New Message from Peter: hi len. Good night w/ J + N?* Lena couldn't shake the conversation from her shoulders. She wanted to talk to Peter about it — she talked to Peter about everything, of course she should talk to Peter about this — but she doubted she'd ever find the words. It felt strange not to talk to him, like she was keeping a secret. *Yeah,* she typed back. *Just studying.* There shouldn't be guilt about feeling like you don't belong; like a space was designed for someone, just not you.

"Lena, hurry up!" Nisha's voice carried from the top of the stairs. Lena ran the rest of the way.

BEVERLY

1956

. . .

"This looks great, Bev." Leslie Peabody had been reading the grant application in silence for ten minutes, his heavy-lidded eyes shifting between the creamy pages in his hand and Beverly's expectant face. She needed more money, and the department wasn't going to give it to her. She'd be a compelling grant applicant, though. The whole thing had been the Dean's idea, and he'd offered to help her write it.

"You really think so?" The air in her swelled chest let itself out on its own, like a pressure valve had been released. She needed this money. It was all she'd talked about for weeks.

"I told you it would make a great application." She blushed and her eyes darted all over the page, trying to see over his shoulder which sections had received the most red marks from his pencil. "Bring your chair over here. Let's go through it."

Beverly had never been on this side of the Dean's desk before. It was a wide mahogany table littered with important-looking documents: a heavy paperweight that commemorated 20 years of service to some organization or another. A stand to hold his fountain pen and its corresponding glass jar of ink.

This was an *office*. She was still working out of a closet. It smelled like leather and cedar and tobacco, and the sun sliced through the blinds in golden ribbons. It was exactly the sort of room that things like grant applications get written in. Suddenly, Beverly felt out of place, even though she was the one who'd written it. She hesitantly dragged her chair towards the corner of the desk and leaned over to read the page, so the sharp corner bit into her stomach. It was uncomfortable, and she did not say anything.

"Tell me what you were thinking here." Leslie gestured to the third paragraph, next to which he'd written only an exclamation point in his fine, shaky scratch.

Beverly hesitated. "I wanted to convey not just why I'm the right person to do this research, but how much this research *needs* to be done." Her eyes searched his face, but he only tipped his head in a slight nod. "I mean, if we can properly understand the range of living conditions that a few, or even one, of these species can survive in, we could really change how we look at ocean life, too. It's not just about rivers or lakes." She could see all the things that she was describing, like if she reached out and dragged her fingers below her she might make ripples. She might feel the cold water rush around her, warmed in random, oblong patches from the sun. "My research, of course, has been about the lakes and ponds in New Hampshire and Massachusetts," she said through the cloudy pond water that swirled around her. The microscopic organisms danced beside her, translucent green corkscrews and geometric, angular things. Fleshy stalks, feathery tendrils. A rainbow of colors. "Small-scale organisms, not even microscopic ones. But in the ocean, sea kelps can be hundreds of feet long."

They could smell the salt. Thin sheets of leathery fiber bent in the water, soft. Totally transparent greens and yellows that become dark and opaque when they clump together. They never stay still in the current. "So this could have implications for oceanography, too. For what we think can live in the twilight zone, or even lower, where there's almost no light at all." They dove deeper, where the water turned purple, and the sun was just a pinprick above them. Where the water got colder. And then the water went black. It was like she was far away from him, speaking her words into bubbles of oxygen that had to travel to the surface to be heard. But it was also like she had taken his hand and plunged him under and showed him that he could breathe where he thought he couldn't.

Beverly glanced at Leslie as she spoke, as though she could see him coming up for air, mesmerized. It must have been from the algae, the journey she was taking them both on. It could not have been anything else; she was not mesmerizing. His eyes were fixed on her face, but that was because she was talking. His eyes were tracing her jaw and the corners of her eyes and the cloud of stray hairs that must have been framing her face the way they always seemed to when she got excited — but that didn't make sense. There was nothing special about her. What was special was the algae, a whole earthy rainbow of colors that glow, the way everything underwater seems to when it's struck by light.

"Could you even imagine how much more could be out there?" She sighed as she floated back into the room. "I want to be the person to do it. So, anyway. That's why I put that paragraph above the one you've circled."

She lifted her eyes to his and found him still staring at her.

In an impossibly long instant, as though he hadn't yet thought about what he was doing and before she could tell him to stop, Leslie Peabody reached forward and ran his thumb softly from her temple to her chin. As if he was touching something breakable, as if he had to check to make sure she was real. His other fingers curled, dragged along her cheek.

His hands were softer than she'd thought that they would be.

Beverly was too shocked to move for a moment. The side of his hand rested there, caressing her cheek, until she had the wherewithal to pull away from him. "Sir —"

"You're exquisite." It was so quiet, neither of them was sure he'd said it. His hand slid down, slowly, until his fingers were tangled in her hair. "Exquisite." An eternity passed. Beverly froze. She had never been afraid of Leslie before, and she wasn't afraid of him now. She was afraid of what he might do, which was an entirely different thing.

Leslie's face was clouded, his lips parted. And then she watched him realize where he was and what he'd done, all at once, like he'd been drunk on his own thoughts and then suddenly sobered. Beverly had never been that kind of drunk.

"My...apologies. Beverly." She didn't meet his eyes, but was already shaking her head politely to dismiss his apology. "*Dr. Conner.* I just. I do believe it's quite a shame you've got no one to love you. When you talk about these things, it's like the world makes sense. Like you're seeing things nobody else does."

She only lifted her eyes when she heard him sink back into his seat. Beverly understood she was looking at a man who thought he had fallen in love with a shooting star — that is, he should have known better, really. No one has ever caught a shooting star; when it comes down to earth, you realize it only glittered when it was in the sky. Down here, in your realm, it's a skid mark of burned grass and a steaming moon rock.

She steeled herself. Her hands could shake later, the lump in her throat, the quiver in her voice. There would be time for all of it. She took a breath of stuffy, mahogany office air and tried to fix her eyes to make them kind. She didn't know how other people could do that at will.

Beverly leaned in close enough that only he could hear her. Not the walls, which heard everything, or the paperweight on the desk or the sun, slanting low and orange in the sky through the window. "I really value your friendship, Leslie." She let her eyes graze the brassy wedding band that squeezed his swollen finger like a sausage casing. She lingered there long enough for him to trace her gaze and look down and see it, too. It had fit him years ago. He had grown since then.

She was sure it was the first time she had called him Leslie. She decided it would also be the last.

"I should head home." She gathered her cardigan from the back of her chair and stood quick enough that she hoped he wouldn't notice her hands shaking.

"I'm. I'm so sorry, Beverly." His voice squeaked out, barely audible. Leslie twisted the wedding band on his finger, so the shiny side rubbed gold from the pads of his fingers faced out, where he could see his reflection. His image was barely recognizable in the twisted shapes; he only got flashes as the image wrapped around the ring.

Beverly squeezed his hand quickly, and then she was in the doorway. "See you next week, Dean." Dean. Not Leslie.

"Oh," he looked up, but not far enough to meet her eyes. "You will?"

"Tuesday. I need help with another grant application."

"Yes."

"You're sure you have time?"

"Yes."

They were bound in their mutual dependence, their need for discretion. The married man. The woman who didn't belong.

"Great." She forced steadiness into her voice. "See you then."

Beverly walked out and listened to the sound of her own footsteps on the checkered tiles. She sucked in a few deep breaths; she felt her heels strike the Earth. Rachel was waiting for her in the lobby, perched on the edge of a bench, her cardigan hanging from her willowy frame. She leapt up and launched into the saga of her day and the drama at the library. Beverly could barely hear her over her roaring thoughts.

These were unrecognizable feelings. Dean Peabody had been the reason, the only reason she'd gotten a modest raise. She knew he cared about her — if he didn't, she and Rachel would barely make ends meet. She hadn't meant to make him think she cared about him, make him look at her with the eyes that he did just then. She was confused. Honestly, Beverly wouldn't have known how to make someone think that if she tried.

It hadn't been the first time that men in her workplace had touched her in ways they never touched other men. The first had been at Penn. There had been Sam at Woods Hole, three years older than her and assigned to teach her how to rig the boats up when she'd first started working there. He'd been friendly enough until they got out onto the water and nobody was around. There had even been other men at Marsden. But this was the first time that one of them seemed to be interested not just because she was a woman, but because she was *Beverly* — because of the sound of her voice and the way her hair glowed in the sunlight. It was being seen in a way that wasn't just nakedness, because she knew her own naked body. It was that he saw things she'd never seen in herself, and he had been transfixed by those things that he thought only she had, the quirk in her voice when she smiled while speaking and the scent of cedarwood and orange when she tossed her hair over her shoulder. That wasn't nakedness. That was something else entirely.

Beverly took a deep breath and felt something in her throat tighten.

It was too much. It had been upsetting and humiliating when the reason why men touched her was because they didn't think of her as a person. It was somehow much worse for the reason to be that he saw her as a person, championed her, admired her, and still noticed how her hair looked in the sun.

"Bev. Are you listening to me?"

"What? Oh. Yes."

"Are you alright?"

"Why wouldn't I be?"

"Okay."

Beverly decided that Leslie Peabody was a decent man. A married man, who loved his life and had enjoyed Beverly's friendship and was bored and confused and not seeing straight, probably. It was just a misunderstanding.

Most men, Beverly thought, were decent men. It was an easier way of looking at the world.

If she was uncomfortable the next time she saw him, she would swallow it. She needed his help, and he was a decent man. And eventually, the way her stomach clenched when his eyes grazed over hers would lessen, until she forgot about it entirely. She didn't see many other options. Everyone can do impossible things when they seem necessary.

"So I couldn't believe she spoke to me like that, when it's my turn to host book club, and she knows that." Rachel said, punctuating her words with passionate footfalls on the tile. "I just thought about what you would do."

"And what's that?" Beverly heard the quiver in her own voice and hoped Rachel hadn't noticed.

"I bit my tongue, and I smiled. And then I told her, nice and calm, that she was wrong." Rachel flipped her hair over her shoulder as she reached for the door. They were hit with a wall of warm air that smelled like honeysuckle. "I get why you like it. It's very satisfying."

Beverly shivered, even though it was hot. Rachel held the door for Beverly and studied her face for a moment, like she was searching for something she knew was there.

LENA

2017

. . .

Summer in Virginia was hot, hotter than she'd remembered, even. Lena's bangs were sticking to her forehead and her thighs were chafing right where her shorts ended. Carefully, she balanced the tray of gelatin on one hand and pressed the door open with the other. She had hoped to do the activity with the kids outside, so the disruptive ones could do a lap on the burning blacktop instead of interrupting her, but the forecast was calling for rain. A single purple cloud hung in the sky like a threat, and Lena had been told to bring it all back inside the classroom. She liked it inside, anyway. There was air conditioning, at least, and all those laminated posters on the walls with inspirational quotes.

Working at her former middle school hadn't been her big dream. Two weeks before her internship in Chicago was supposed to start — she would've lived with Peter's family in their *guest house* — Lena's father had gotten laid off at the grocery store. Her stepmother was back in school, trying to get her master's so she could finally get promoted at work. They needed help caring for her little sister, and any money, too. So Lena had canceled her flight to O'Hare and started writing lesson plans for summer school for seventh graders.

The twelve-year-olds looked up when Lena came back inside the classroom. They liked her, or at least they liked her more than the former librarian brought out of retirement who was teaching their science class. Mrs. Kimball. Lena was technically a "Teacher's Aide," and getting paid like it, but she'd written all the lessons herself. The kids had been eyeing the tray of supplies all morning, likely wondering what lime gelatin and gummy bears had to do with their otherwise painfully boring day of classes.

"Only one more hour until lunch," Kira, the girl in the front row, mumbled to her friend. At twelve, it seemed, the kids were too cool to show any interest in their classes, especially these kids, who would be held back a grade if they didn't pass their summer courses. The girl's friend didn't hear her, or at least made no indication that she had. She scrolled on her phone silently. Lena hadn't had a phone in the seventh grade.

Mrs. Kimball was playing solitaire on the desktop at the front of the room and loudly eating a Caesar salad with anchovies out of an ancient Tupperware stained with the orange memory of marinara sauce. Two weeks into this job, and the two of them had settled into a symbiotic relationship. Kimball was there for legal purposes; she'd call the ambulance if one of the kids, as she put it, "cracked their head open." Lena would teach.

"Kira, what do you know about cells?"

Kira looked up from the hangnail she'd been busying herself with, surprised she'd been singled out.

Lena had been nervous to teach at first. But they were just kids. And it was in this classroom that Lena had fallen in love with science. If a middle-aged man and some student-grade Bunsen burners had been able to do it, she could do it. Or so she told herself.

"Uh, I dunno. They're small."

"Right! Really, really small. But are they the smallest part of your body?" Lena ripped open the lime gelatin and started mixing it into water. The students giggled at the mention of the word "body." And maybe, also, "small." Maybe the two, considered together like that.

"Probably not, otherwise you wouldn't have asked it that way," offered Liam from the back row. His feet were up on the desk, showing off the pristine, never-been-creased basketball shoes that he was quite proud of. Lena looked up at him from the gelatin and he held her gaze for a moment. She nodded her head at his shoes, and he slowly put them down.

"Well, Liam is right. Inside of each cell, there're smaller structures called *organelles*. They each have a different purpose. And to help you remember them all, we're going to make a model of an animal cell, all of us."

The students looked at her hesitantly. Behind them, on the back wall, there was a poster of a school of fish, all swimming in one direction. One, a goldfish, smaller than the rest, swam the opposite way. "Dare to be different," it said. Lena couldn't remember if the poster was new or not. The room smelled like lemon furniture polish, and it always gave her a headache by the end of the day.

"Doesn't that sound like fun?" Lena asked again, hoping they couldn't hear the falter in her voice.

"I mean, we're not *kids*," Kira mumbled. Her friend giggled.

"Well, that may be, but I'm twenty and still remember the candy animal cell I made in middle school when I take my tests in my college classes. I guess we can just draw it on the board, if you want, and I can take all these gummy worms home for myself."

"No, I mean, we're not *kids*, but we can still do this thing, I mean, even if it is dumb," Kira said helpfully. "If it helps you."

Lena sighed. That might be as good as it was going to get. "Alright then. Everyone up, come on! Come up here. We need all hands on deck!"

Still unenthused, the students slowly got up. After the din of shuffling sneakers and desk legs squeaking on tiles, ten begrudging students gathered around Lena's tray. "This bowl is going to be our cell membrane. It's what keeps everything that belongs inside the cell in, and what keeps everything else out. There's a few ways that materials can pass through the cell walls, and those materials are the way that cells talk to each other — so it's important that we have our cell membrane first, because it's what tells the cell that this stuff is different from the cell next door." The kids leaned on the edge of the table, salivating over the candy or staring at the wall behind her. One snuck a glance at Kimball, but none of them seemed to be paying attention to Lena.

"The first thing we need is a nucleus." Lena took a jawbreaker and placed it in the middle of the bowl. It rolled around until it came to a stop against one of the grooves in the bottom. For a moment, the only sound in the room was the candy rolling against the plastic and Ms. Kimball crunching on her lettuce. "The nucleus holds all the cell's DNA, which is basically the instruction manual for the cell. We'll put it in the middle, so it's protected and so all the other organelles can get the information they need from it."

There were gummy bears for the vacuoles, jellybeans for the mitochondria. "Does anyone know what the endoplasmic reticulum is?"

"The textbook called it the 'highway of the cell.'" Kira picked at her fingers and answered the question without looking up. She had been steadily chipping all of the blue nail polish off her fingers all morning. Lena had done that when she was anxious before tests in middle school. She wondered if it bothered Kira that she'd been held back.

"Okay, Kira, that's a great start. Does anyone remember why we call it that?"

Silence.

"I mean, it's probably how stuff gets around," Kira said flatly.

"Right! We're going to use this licorice," Lena handed the candy twists to Kira, "because they're hollow in the middle, which is where the proteins might pass through to get to other parts of the cell."

Lena kept teaching but watched as Kira carefully folded the licorice back and forth on itself to make a bunched, oblong organelle. It looked just like the diagram in the textbook. Kira placed it next to the jawbreaker nucleus gingerly.

Liam snuck one of the chocolate chip lysosomes when he thought Lena wasn't looking, but he actually answered her question correctly, so she pretended she didn't see. At some point during the lesson, it did start to rain outside, smattering against the windows, but none of them noticed. Kimball finished her salad and won her game of solitaire, and fell asleep in the desk chair.

"Last thing," Lena picked up the bowl of lime gelatin, a shocking shade of green. "The cell needs something to keep all these organelles in place. Does anyone remember what that substance is called?"

"I do," Liam said a little too quickly, then looked down at his shoes to feign disinterest. "Isn't it cytoplasm? Sounds like ectoplasm, which is *sick*." No one laughed, so he added, "like *Ghostbusters*. You know?"

"Liam's right! We've got our cytoplasm right here," Lena poured the gelatin over all the candy organelles, "which holds everything in place and allows proteins to move around within the cell. It's way more important than it seems."

"Lena! Tommy's eating one of the vacuoles!" Kira pointed.

Lena laughed and looked over at Kimball, who was

snoring. Lena didn't know how she could sleep in here with the oppressive fluorescent lights and the whining of the kids. "You know what? Tommy's onto something. Vacuoles for everyone!" The kids fought over the best colors of the gummy bears, which were immediately determined to be the pink ones, and Lena washed the gelatin off of her hands in the classroom sink.

"I'm going to let our animal cell chill while you all eat lunch, and we'll all have some this afternoon while we prepare for tomorrow's quiz. Sound good?"

The kids nodded and bounded into the hallway for their lunch break. Lena sat down in the front row and pulled a granola bar out of her pocket. This was the desk she'd sat in when she was in the seventh grade. It probably wasn't the exact same desk, but it was her spot in the room, under the water-stained ceiling tile. She'd made a gelatin animal cell all those years ago, and still thought of the endoplasmic reticulum as the knock-off brand of sour gummy worms from the drug store, even taking exams in her classes at Marsden. Maybe Kira would be a scientist one day. It was a strange thought.

Kimball snored so loud she woke herself up. "Oh. Lena. The children?"

"Lunch," Lena offered.

"Wonderful." She spun around in the swivel chair and opened up Minesweeper.

Lena's phone buzzed. *New Message from Peter: Kids working you too hard today, Ms. Rivera?*

She smiled. *No. We made an animal cell. They seemed to like it!*

New Message from Peter: Gummy worms?

She'd told him that story before. *Of course.*

Lena ran down the list of things she'd have to do when she got off work. Her parents had asked her to pick up some stuff at the grocery store. They'd been shopping at the one across town, ever since her father got laid off, so she needed to get gas in her car to make it all the way there. Then she'd pick up her younger sister from the day camp they'd put her in at the rec center. She could get dinner started and then help her stepmother with the laundry and —

New Message from Peter: My mom was asking if ur still coming @ end of summer?

Peter's parents had invited her to come to Chicago after summer school ended, so she could still get at least a little time with Peter before they had to go back to Marsden. She hadn't mentioned it to her parents, since she had no idea how she'd pay for a plane ticket now. There was no point. *Probably. Not sure yet. Family stuff.*

The desktop computer jingled. Kimball had beaten the game. It must've been a new record.

New Message from Peter: I know I know. Mom's just excited.

Lena clicked her phone off and studied the classroom. The rain was hammering harder in the windows. Another poster at the front of the classroom said, "Character is who you are when no one's looking."

BEVERLY

1960

. . .

Beverly was drowning. She recognized the sloop that splintered in the waves as the one she and Mary and Louise had saved up for. But the curved wooden sides of the boat only came in flashes, lit up by white lightning and tossed around on the thrashing waves. Black water swallowed her. She kicked, frantically. She was wearing a wool sweater and could feel the cable-knit collar, saturated with water, start to pull her under like a weight around her neck. Her head was pulled under the surface for a moment, and her nose and ears were filled with frigid water. She coughed and sputtered.

Lightning flashed again. "Beverly!" It was Louise's voice. Her drenched curls appeared beside her in the water. She could feel Louise's shriveled hands clawing at her arm underwater. "Where's Mary?"

Beverly couldn't answer her. It was like something was stuffed in her throat. She kept reaching for Louise. And she was always just a few inches farther.

. . .

Buying the boat had been Mary and Louise's idea. Beverly had agreed, because if they were to be scientists, they would need a sloop of their own for samples. They bought it on August 7th, 1925, in the late afternoon when they were done teaching. The weather was perfect, and they took her for a maiden sail at sunset.

There hadn't been one cloud in the sky when they'd left, and they watched the sun paint the sky orange on totally still waters. A storm appeared out of nowhere before they'd reached shore, filled the sloop with water, cracked it, and sank it. The girls were thrown into the black water, which was cold and violent under the hammering of the thunderstorm. They made it to a sandbar, only a few hundred feet away, after what felt like an hour of treading water and swimming against the current. It was the only time Beverly had been afraid of the water.

They stood on the sandbar, rain slapping their pink faces, for hours until the Coast Guard rescued them. They screamed the camp songs they had been teaching their students all summer, and it was probably the only reason the patrol noticed they were out there. Their laughter had carried on the wind, the captain said when he helped them onto the Coast Guard's boat. It had been the nervous kind that makes you afraid to stop, because silence is always worse. They wrung their sweaters out over the side of the boat as it sped back to shore and were quiet then. No one wanted to say how afraid they had been.

The girls dried off all the next day, wringing out their clothes and hair and huddling under blankets, teeth chattering. Mary took interviews with the newspapers all day long, basking in the fleeting fame. Louise was a wreck, cursing the savings they'd all lost on the boat. Beverly had merely written two letters, one to her mother and one to Scooter, explaining what had happened, and wasn't that a wild time, and she was fine, and the boat was gone but that was okay, and no, she wouldn't do anything like that again.

From her bunk, Beverly had listened to the waves outside her window all day long. They wouldn't stop their crashing; it was getting impossibly louder still. She caught herself shaking, every now and then, under the blankets. Jerking like she was back under water. The feeling of the spray smattering her face and then swallowing her was haunting.

That night, after everyone was asleep, Beverly took out one of the little white-washed paddle boats. The cluster of buildings that made up Woods Hole Marine Laboratory were just flecks of light in the grass just past the rocky shoreline behind her. One window, still lit up orange, that was all. It was just Beverly and the black water that swirled around her oars. Just her and the stars and sometimes a fish that would crest the surface. One bubble, then it was gone. Like it was just checking that the horizon was still there.

She could paddle away from Woods Hole and never look back. She could flip the boat over and drown. She could stay out all night collecting samples, she could lean back and scream at the top of her lungs. Either way, no one would know. She was afraid that if she didn't get back out on the water now, she would be too afraid to go back ever.

She stopped paddling and let the oars rest on the floor of the boat. Beverly filled her nose and open mouth and lungs full of air that smelled like salt and sweet grass, just starting to rot at the end of the summer. She wouldn't let the boat drift too far from shore, at times close enough she could've reached out and seized a fistful of bramble. She let her eyes linger on each tree as the boat drifted past, each tree that clung to the last dregs of chlorophyll before it would give up on living and turn orange another year. Quite dramatic things, the trees, she'd always thought. Like people, in their emotions, but much more predictable.

"Beverly." Louise's milk-white face was glowing pale blue in the moonlight. She drew her cardigan around her shoulders and stepped one bare foot onto the dock. Beverly hadn't realized she'd almost drifted all the way back to the docks, back to camp. "Bev. Come on, what are you doing out there?"

"It's a beautiful night," Beverly said with a laugh. "I'm enjoying the trees."

"You don't have to —" Louise stopped.

"I know."

"Just —" she took another step forward and the wind mussed her curls.

"I'm not trying to prove anything." Beverly said, and she meant it. The water had learned its place. They had patched their friendship.

Louise sat down on the edge of the dock in her nightgown, her calves submerged in midnight-cold water. The boat floated up to the dock and Louise reached for the lip of it to hold it in place so Beverly could get out. Her face seemed full of something — not fear, because there wasn't any danger she could see, but perhaps it was the fact that she couldn't see anything that was concerning. Heavy purple clouds were rolling in; soon they wouldn't be able to see anything at all.

They tied up the boat in silence and sat on the edge of the dock. The black water crept up the hem of Louise's nightgown and it fluttered in the water around her fleshy knees, pale at the tops of her thighs but bright pink where the cold water was lapping at her skin. They should've been shivering. For a few moments, she was content to listen to the creak of the wood, the push and pull of the waves. And then Louise spoke. "Do you think we're gonna make it, Bev? I mean, like really make it. I've been thinking all day about it. We risked our lives for a few samples last night." She placed her hands flat on the dock behind her and pushed her chest up towards the sky, letting her head fall back. She closed her eyes. "I don't just want to do this for a hobby and then meet a nice boy and work on my tuna casserole. I want to be here. I want to support myself. I want —"

"Yes." Beverly said, tipping her head back to look at the stars. If she squinted, it was like she could see the constellations push themselves forward from the black sheet.

Beverly wondered for a moment if she could dive into the water and keep swimming forever. If she'd drown before she found something on the horizon, or if there would be something out there waiting for her.

Louise turned to face her. "What do you mean?"

"Yes." She ran her fingers through the water, wondering if the black wedges that fanned behind them were the presence or the absence of something. "Yes, we can have that. We will, we don't have to — dammit, Louise. We don't have to stop, ever. You hear me? You get back out on that boat tomorrow and you be the best damn scientist they've got."

"I hope that'll be enough, Bev."

"I hope so too."

. . .

Beverly was drowning. Ice cold water enveloped her. She opened her eyes under the surface and saw Louise suspended in the water, bluish and kicking. Louise locked her eyes on Beverly and reached for her. Bubbles poured from her mouth.

. . .

Beverly woke up in Marsden, space and time stitched back together. There were no waves outside her window, but there were still stars to look at, still trees that were about to ache and sigh and throw brilliant red temper-tantrums. Another year was starting.

Perhaps it wasn't Woods Hole she'd been trying to get back to in her dreams, perhaps it was the hurricane — it was as though she was itching to feel in danger again.

"Are you okay?" Rachel's muffled voice asked, scratchy, the way voices sound in the middle of the night when they shouldn't be talking.

"Yeah. Go back to sleep." Beverly couldn't shake the image of Woods Hole from her mind, it had been so vivid. Things had seemed brighter back then, with their whole future tumbling before them, glittering. "Rachel, actually."

"Yeah?" Rachel rolled over, her hair falling across her face. Still groggy, her eyes fluttered closed. Her hands found Beverly's arm and curled around it. They listened to their breath in the still night.

Beverly reminded herself that she wasn't drowning, and that Rachel was real. Sometimes she still had to check. Gentle pink fingernails that found her in the night.

"Let's make tuna casserole tonight. Dig out my mom's recipe cards?"

Rachel sat up on her elbows and snorted. "Why?"

"I want to feel like a housewife. See what my life would have been like."

Rachel rubbed her eyes in the darkness and shook her head. "Beverly Conner, you're —"

"I think it'll make me glad I have what I have now."

Louise might have been working somewhere, publishing essays in a journal or teaching classes. Maybe she'd had kids. Maybe she'd died.

Beverly slept for four more fitful hours, dreaming of her mother's tuna casserole. Silver fish scales and silver tin cans and things that shined.

LENA

2017

. . .

Lena's childhood home had a big, wraparound porch that stretched from the front door no one ever used to the backdoor that opened straight into the kitchen. Three years ago, the planks in the middle gave out — termites, according to a very overpriced inspector, but no one could take the time to go stay in a hotel while the place got tented. Lena was the only one brave enough to sit out there. She was still afraid of anything with more than four legs, but the porch had fond memories and she wasn't willing to surrender it to the bugs. She'd learned through trial and error which boards could still bear weight and picked her way across them. One of her parents had left a lone folding chair out there for her. She scanned it for spiders before she sat down. The fabric was stiff from baking in the sun.

Her little sister and stepmother were dancing to the radio in the kitchen as they made oxtail stew for dinner, an old family recipe preserved only on a yellowed index card. Melodies and occasional peals of laughter floated out from the back door. Lena leaned back and rested her head against the vinyl siding of the house, which had been white once. End-of-summer left a fine film of sweet-smelling dust on everything, dirt that mixed with rain and hardened like ceramics in the sunshine. Lena's eyes wandered across the yard. Jagged sidewalk chalk drawings crisscrossed the driveway. Lena's sister had used the potholes as the centers of her lopsided flowers. The tub of chalk was left, overturned, in the middle of the pavement. Lena wondered if someone should pick it up before her dad got home and crushed it with the car. That someone would probably be her, but she didn't get up.

A mosquito landed on Lena's arm and she didn't swat it away. She looked at its feet, which didn't seem much thicker than a hair, and wondered how it balanced there.

Lena's phone vibrated in her back pocket and made a loud enough noise against the chair that the mosquito flew off. *New Message from Peter: Long day at work. I miss u.*

Lena clicked the phone off and tried to put it in the cupholder on the arm of the chair. The mesh pocket had ripped, apparently, and her phone fell onto the floor. One of the surviving floorboards.

It vibrated again. *New Message from Peter: Can we watch a movie tonight over FaceTime or something?*

She reached for the phone. *Of course.*

New Message from Peter: Can't wait. I'll call you at 8 your time?

Sounds good.

Lena put her phone down and studied the yard. The neighbors had just started mowing the lawn and the dull drum of the motor carried over the fence. The smell of gasoline coated Lena's tongue. She didn't mind it. It reminded her of her dad mowing the lawn in the summers. She'd stretched a beach towel out on the porch before it caved in, and got ahead on her summer reading to the sound of the lawn mower. In high school, she'd brought her SAT prep books out. It was like he was keeping her company, even though if she'd said anything, he wouldn't have heard her over the roar of the motor. When he was done, they'd go inside and split a lemonade.

The garden hose was still out in the middle of the yard from where they'd left it last night. It had been especially hot and after Lena's sister whined all through dinner, her father took them all outside and they all ran through the spray from the hose.

The house seemed smaller this summer. From here, with Lena's head against the siding of the house, she could see the entire yard without turning her head, from the driveway on the left and the mailbox she'd painted with dinosaur stamps during a particularly fervent paleontology phase in the fourth grade to the half-fence on the right they shared with their neighbors. She remembered running for what seemed like miles out here when she was a kid. The single tree had been a forest canopy, the house finches that flew from the branches to their roof and back again had been a migrating flock.

Headlights appeared at the end of their street and as the car crept forward, Lena saw her father waving from the front seat. On the passenger seat next to him was a bag of the just-expired dry goods the new grocery store he was working at let him take home sometimes. Lena jumped up to get the chalk from the middle of the driveway, but he parked the car in the street. "Artwork like that deserves to be seen," he waved at the lopsided flowers on the asphalt as he got out of the car. He handed Lena the bag of groceries. "Bring those inside to the kitchen and then I thought maybe we'd go for a walk? Since you are heading back tomorrow and everything?"

She was trying not to think about it. Not that Marsden wasn't exciting. But it had been so nice to be home.

Lena ran up the porch steps, which creaked in protest, and threw open the door. "Can I interest you in some just-past-expired cereal?" Her stepmother looked up from the pan where she was stirring the stew with a smile. Her glasses were fogged up.

"Anymore off-brand Oreos? We're out and I love them. I think they're better stale."

"He didn't say." Lena left the bag on the counter. "We're going for a walk."

"Dinner in an hour."

Lena let the door slam behind her. The doors in this house were very satisfying to shut. They all bounced in their frames and had heavy handles that felt good to turn. Lena thought this was what all houses should feel like.

"Where to?" Lena's father was standing on the driveway, hands in his pockets, gingerly stepping around the chalk daisies.

"Down by the creek, maybe?"

They followed the small footpath out of the neighborhood. It led steeply into a small forest, never more than five minutes from a major highway, but quiet enough that Lena had been allowed to explore freely when she was a child. It had been years since she'd been back here. She'd drawn a map of the footpaths, once, and had marked one tree as "The Best Tree" and another as a place where one "Might Find A Good Toad." She wondered if she still knew the way.

They walked in silence for a moment, listening to the sounds breathing humid air makes and the way footfalls on hot, damp mulch sound different from any other time of year.

"Are you excited to go back?"

"I guess. I mean, it's school. I'm excited to be back with my friends. Not really excited to get back to studying." She reached down and plucked a leaf from the ground. Must have been one of the first of the season to fall.

"Oh, come on, Lena. You? Not excited to study?"

"It's not like high school. It's not about whether it's fun. It... *matters,* now, I guess."

They heard the first trickling of the creek. It was more of a brook, really, sometimes only a few feet wide, but her father had always called it a creek, and so Lena had, too.

"Is that what you told your students all summer? That their summer school classes didn't matter?" he teased.

"Of course not. And it always mattered, some, I just mean that if I fail now, I really fail. Like change-my-life-plan fail." She skidded a few feet down the sloped bank towards the brook and dropped the leaf. It landed on the surface of the water, held there, orange and dry. They stopped and watched it get smaller and smaller until it disappeared around the bend. The water flashed white and bright on the tops of slick rocks. "Of course the kids mattered."

"You seemed to really enjoy that class, Lena." She could tell he was studying her face, so she didn't look up. She brushed the dirt off of her hands. "Maybe you should think about being a teacher."

She snapped her head up. "I have a plan already, Dad. I'm going to get my Ph.D. Be a researcher, you know, in a lab. That's always been the plan."

He held up his hands. "Okay. Of course. Forget I said anything."

A successful scientist could pay off the student loans, could send some money back home. Her family wouldn't have to eat the knock-off Oreos, not that they would take anything she sent. That wasn't the reason to be a scientist, but it was the reason to be successful. To do what her mother should have done.

There was a woodpecker, somewhere in the distance. Bashing its head against a tree.

Lena turned to the oak behind her. The grooves in the bark were deep and covered on one side by a pale green fungus that feathered out like flowers. It was really quite pretty. "No way."

Her father looked up.

"I think that's The Best Tree."

He laughed. "I forgot about that map. You were somethin' else."

They walked most of the way home in silence. He told her some stories about his day at work and she laughed and really tried to pretend like she was a little kid again. Lena was sweaty by the time they got home. It was just starting to get dark, and the beads of sweat at the back of her neck were about to turn to chills.

Dinner was oxtail stew, canned applesauce, and some of the off-brand, expired Oreos that were, in fact, in the bag her father had brought home. Everyone begged Lena to play one last game of Monopoly, since it was much better with four people and this was their last chance. She and her parents had conspired to let her younger sister win. Lena wondered if they had ever done that when she was little.

When Lena finally went to her room that night, she found three missed calls from Peter. *New Message from Peter: Are we not doing movie night? New Message from Peter: I don't know where you are but I'm around if you still want to talk. New Message from Peter: Shit, sorry I guess this is your last night at home.*

Lena quickly typed a response. Her fingers were shaking. She didn't know why. *Dammit sorry I got roped into family game night. I'll call you when I get back to Mars tmrw?*

Lena took a deep breath. The house smelled like the brand of detergent they'd always used, and the spices in their kitchen, and the gasoline from the garage. It was a sweet, earthy smell. No one else's house smelled like this. She turned her phone off and sat on the edge of her bed and watched as her view of the yard got darker and darker. She strained her eyes to see it all. Maybe she would make a map of it, and maybe if she could draw it all out she would remember everything and it would seem as clear as it had when she was a kid.

BEVERLY

1960

. . .

She had been Louise Potter when Beverly knew her. Now, it seemed, she was Louise Reiser. According to the secretary at Woods Hole, at least, after a few minutes of sighing into the phone and rifling through the filing cabinet. It had cost her ten cents a minute to listen to the silence, since she had called from the payphone in the library. She couldn't wait until she got home. She had to know. And now she did. Louise Reiser, living in New Rochelle.

When Rachel got home from work that day, she found Beverly sitting at the kitchen table with the lights off. It had gotten dark since she'd come home, and when she'd sat down, the sunlight coming in the windows had still been enough. Her cup of tea was cold, the teabag was still in it and had turned the water almost black. She'd brought the telephone over to the table, as far as the cord would stretch, and had it pinched between her shoulder and her ear. Her feet were propped up on the chair opposite her — which she wouldn't have done if she'd have thought about the fact that Rachel would come in and see her like that — and she had covered a napkin in chicken scratch with a ballpoint pen that was leaking ink.

"Operator. Louise Reiser. I've tried the Reisers on Acacia." She crossed a number out. "Okay. Aberfoyle Road. If you please."

Rachel swatted at her to get her attention. Beverly covered the phone with her hand. "I'm looking for Louise. She's not Potter anymore, and there's four Louise Reisers living in New Rochelle." Beverly uncovered the phone, and Rachel turned on her heel and went out to the porch to get the mail. The screen door slammed behind her.

"Hello?" The voice that crackled on the other line was Louise. It had to be.

"Louise. Hi. You might not remember me." Beverly straightened a tangle in the phone cord. "This is Beverly Conner. From Woods Hole."

"Beverly Conner? That's really you? Well, I'll be damned, you sound the same." A dog barked in the background. There was the hum of something. Maybe a fan, a radio.

"I don't really know why I called, I guess. I just started thinking about the night we sank that sloop the other day, and I just wondered whatever became of you." It sounded wrong. You don't tell someone you wondered what "became" of them. It sounds like you didn't think anything had. It sounds like you thought they had died and you had forgotten to notice. "I mean, of course, that I was sure you'd gone on and had some marvelous adventure, and I wondered what that was."

Louise laughed. "Oh, well, I can't say I've — actually, could you hang on one second, Bev? I got a casserole in the oven that's trying to burn." There was the sound of the phone being set on the counter, an oven door opening and steam hissing. "I'm back. Yes. What were you asking — Oh! My grand life. Ah, that's hot. Sandy! Sandy! Can you come downstairs please and set the table?" Louise shouted. "Sorry about that, too, Bev. My daughter's moved back home. Trying to get her to help out around here. Yes. So. My life? I mean. I married a chemist — do you remember Dick Reiser? — he's working at Columbia.

We've lived in New Rochelle for, oh, I guess thirty years now? I love our neighborhood. I have a dog." Louise laughed, like something was funny.

"That's very nice, Louise. I know you always wanted kids." Beverly looked out the window. Something jumped into the bushes against the house.

"I did. I did. I guess I must've told you girls that. So did you get what you wanted, then? A new boat, after we sank ours?"

Beverly wasn't sure how to answer. She looked around for Rachel, but she'd dropped the mail on the counter and gone into the bathroom. She heard the shower running. "I'm working at Marsden. Have been for a few decades."

"I'm sure you are. You were always the one who could, you know. *The Little Engine.* I read that book to my girls." Beverly squeezed her hands together. Her nails bit into the flesh of her palm. "Are you a lab tech, then?"

"I help out around the department. I teach some. I fill in for the professors when they're on sabbatical or something like that. I've been doing a lot of my own research. I've been publishing, some." She didn't have anything to prove to Louise, but it felt like she might burst if all the words didn't come right out at once.

"You're not a Professor, then, after all that?"

"Soon, I hope." The shower turned off.

"You amaze me, Beverly. I couldn't stick with it like you did. Not for all those years. I wouldn't have gotten anywhere, anyway." Rachel's wet footsteps squeaked through the hallway. The bedroom door shut.

Beverly kept thinking of Louise sitting on the dock, her legs pink in the freezing water. She'd wanted to make it — even when she knew how much she was up against, she'd wanted to be a scientist. But that woman had been a dream. Louise had never said those things.

Louise was still talking. "Woods Hole is like a fun daydream for me now. Like a summer camp or something. I loved collecting and looking at stuff under a microscope. Do you remember the three-legged race that one summer? We beat all the boys."

"We did."

"I wonder sometimes — ah, forget it. Oh, Bev, my daughter Sandy is setting the table for dinner. I better let you go. I'm so glad you called. Sandy, this is my old friend on the phone, from when I was about your age."

"It was good to catch up, Louise."

"Oh, you too, Bev. All my best to your mother, and to Scooter and all of them."

"Of course."

"Bye, Bev."

"Louise."

The line went dead. Beverly looked around and wondered when it had gotten so dark in the kitchen. It was like she'd just woken up. Her tea had gone cold. She didn't remember making it. She turned a light on and pulled her cardigan around herself. The stack of mail Rachel had fetched was sitting on the kitchen counter. Mostly catalogs and bills. One letter, in a blue cardstock envelope, clearly on nice stationery — addressed to Beverly. She ripped it open.

Dear Beverly,

You don't know me, but I'm quite familiar with you. My name is Dr. Henry Nightingale. I'm a professor at Oxford and I became rather obsessed with the paper you published about the fucus evanescens *some fifteen years ago. I've gotten a deal to write a textbook. I've got a publisher and I've got a deadline. I'd very much like for you to write it with me. For a person such as yourself to discover a species, I know, must mean you have the drive to get things done. I need that kind of disposition.*

I understand this is a rather hefty proposition from a

*virtual stranger. My colleagues who have made the trip
over the pond for phycological conferences tell me you've
earned your reputation as a teacher. The textbook is to be
a definitive volume for introductory courses. I don't know
if you've much experience with freshmen, but most of my
colleagues feel a project like this is beneath them. I see it
as an exciting challenge. Shaping a new generation of
minds! I get the sense you might share my philosophy.*

*Do write soon if you're interested. I'm happy to
answer any questions you might have, and I'm sure you'll
have many. My thought was to do this mostly by mail;
we can divide up chapters that way.*

Sincerely,

Dr. H. C. Nightingale

Beverly let the letter fall onto the counter. "Rachel."

She turned the lights off in the kitchen and walked slowly
down the hallway. "Rachel." She opened the bedroom door.
"Rachel. Rachel." Rachel was sitting in the moonlight, her wet
hair parted in two dark, dripping chunks on either side of her
head. She was working on a crossword puzzle in her nightgown. Beverly stopped, her hand on the doorknob. Rachel
looked up.

"What is it?"

"Someone wants me to write a book."

Rachel's mouth opened and closed. "Really?"

"A textbook. An Englishman, a man from Oxford, some-
body-or-other. He wrote me a letter. All the way from
England. And he wants me to write it with him. T-the book."

Rachel's face turned pink. She smiled with her whole face,
where her cheeks pushed up into her eyes. She turned and
rested her head on Beverly's shoulder and they sat, looking out
the window. "So she's to be an author, too."

A few birds crossed in front of the moon. It wasn't a full
moon, but it was waxing and white. Rachel's hair smelled like

lavender. Her head rolled on Beverly's shoulder slightly every time she took a deep breath. It was like the tide.

After a moment, Rachel sighed. "Who were you on the phone with?"

"Louise. From Woods Hole."

"The one from the boat?"

"Right."

Rachel reached up to move her wet hair off of her night-gown. It was one of Beverly's favorites, with tiny pink flowers all over. "How was she doing?" she seemed angry. Or not angry, not really. Sometimes it seemed she wasn't sure what to say to Beverly.

"She's different, now."

Rachel put her head back on Beverly's shoulder. "Different can be good."

Rachel didn't mean it, and Beverly knew that. They sat in silence, listening to the bed creak beneath them. Rachel had moved into this room, the big bedroom, with Beverly years ago. It had been brighter in here, warmer somehow. She didn't know if she would be able to sleep without Rachel now.

Beverly let her head fall onto Rachel's. Lavender enveloped her and she could have cried.

LENA

2017

. . .

"This just won't do." Lena was standing in front of her closet, holding up her phone so Peter could see the hangers over FaceTime. "I have nothing to wear."

"Lena, I really think you're overthinking this."

"It's an *interview,* Peter. I think you're *under-thinking* it." She decided not to dwell on whether or not under-thinking was a word — she thought it probably wasn't, but it was the only thing to describe Peter's nonchalance. He was never worried about anything, or he didn't show it, anyway. "Help me, then. What do you wear to an interview?"

She was nervous about the interview, but not like she would have been freshman year. A younger Lena would have doubted that she was qualified for the job, or even if she could do it. This new, jaded Lena was pretty sure she could do this or any other job she applied for — but it was now clear that wasn't the thing that got someone hired or not.

"A shirt, collar. Tie, if it seems like it's formal. Slacks, or khakis, if it seems like it's not." Peter, it seemed, had not understood that yet.

"Anything else you do?"

"Brush my teeth, probably?"

"No special cologne you spray on that hypnotizes your employer into hiring you?"

"I'm very capable of getting jobs without divine intervention or magic of any kind," he retorted with an amused laugh.

She sat down on the edge of her bed. "I know that. You know I know that."

The interview was tomorrow morning at nine. She'd moved into her dorm a few days early to be able to apply for a research job this fall. Peter was still at home in Chicago. Lena never did fly out to visit, even though his mom kept asking. They never talked about why she hadn't come. Peter called her two whole hours ago after receiving a barrage of panicked texts about the interview. "Lena. Just wear something casual that looks like you care."

"Peter! What does that mean? A sweater? A dress? Like. What. Does that. Mean." She fell backwards and clutched her phone to her chest so Peter had the same view of her ceiling tiles. The room she'd been assigned was nicer this year, or maybe she'd just grown used to —even comforted by — a dingy dorm room with cinderblock walls.

"What do you wear to class?" His voice was growing exasperated, too. He'd never had to help Lena get dressed before, or any woman for that matter. He didn't know what girls wore to interviews. He'd never thought about it.

"Peter, I cannot wear a *Nirvana* t-shirt and jeans to an interview for Professor Knowles' lab."

"You wear that to class?"

"Peter!"

"I've never seen you wear —"

"Jesus. Okay. Hang on." She put her phone down and ripped a white button-down off of its hanger. She pulled it over her head without stopping to undo the buttons. "How's this?"

"It's... decent."

"Decent."

"Honestly, Len, I love you. But you look a little like my second-grade cousin at her science fair."

"What do you recommend then, Sage of Interview Attire?"

"Calling Nisha, probably."

Maybe it was unfair of her to ask Peter, whose life practically came with a uniform, to navigate the nuances of a female wardrobe. But he was the person that she called when she had a problem, and this was a problem, and normally he was helping, but he couldn't help with this one. He just couldn't.

"Alright. Tell your mother I say hello, and to give you a crash course on the difference between a pencil skirt and an A-frame."

"Do you even know that? I'm pretty sure you mean A-line. A-frame is the house, I think. I've never seen you wear a —"

"Goodnight, Peter."

He laughed. "Night, Len."

Her finger hovered over the hang-up button. "It's going to be okay, you know that? No one has ever gotten a job or not gotten a job because of the shirt they were wearing." And then he hung up the call himself.

Peter was very sweet. He was also wrong. Lena was certain that some people had not gotten a job because they wore the wrong thing to an interview. And she was not surprised that Peter did not know that.

Lena picked at her fingers. The nails were worn down to stumps. She called Nisha. "Help me pick out something to wear tomorrow."

"Oh gosh, you still don't know what you're wearing?"

"Nisha —"

"Let me guess. You called Peter and he said, 'I dunno, uh, a button-down'?" Nisha exaggerated a man's voice that sounded nothing like Peter but a little like Fred Flintstone.

"How'd you guess?"

"I'll be there in ten."

She wanted this job. She was doing this because when she was ten years old and watching flies skate on the surface of the pond near her house — the one that froze over every Christmas and they went ice-skating — she asked her father how they could touch the surface and land and not fall in. He didn't know. She asked where the ripples in the water went, and what happened when they collided. And he didn't know that either. And she looked up in the sky and saw clouds suspended there, like they were hung by string just for her, and she asked how they stayed up there. He thought it was something about the density of the air and the water. She asked what density was.

Lena pulled a cardigan from her closet and laid it out on the bed. She knew now why flies could walk on water and where ripples went when they met and what kept clouds in the sky, and it wasn't string. She could figure out what to wear to an interview.

Kira and Liam's faces flashed before her, just for a moment. They'd all passed, the whole class, and would be moving on to the eighth grade.

Nisha knocked on the door.

BEVERLY

1968

. . .

Beverly had marched her class out to go collect field samples, and she wondered now if she'd picked the wrong day. The sun was directly overhead and beating down on them. The way to the pond had taken twenty minutes; they'd followed the old railroad ties, overgrown with sprays of yellow grasses, and emerged from the trees onto the rocky edge of the still black water. If the students hadn't complained the whole time, she would've been patting herself on the back for the journey. Instead, they all had sweat in their eyes and were counting up their mosquito bites.

"Miss Conner! Don't fall!" The boys liked to tease. They were freshmen, mostly, and unaccustomed to being taught by a woman. Beverly didn't mind so much. They respected her as a teacher, for the most part, just not as a woman, which they didn't need to. She picked her way over the rocks that were slick with water and shiny moss. This had been easier when she was younger, of course, but Beverly aged the way that stubborn people do: if you pretend it's not happening, then it isn't.

"Why don't you boys just focus on collecting a single

usable sample and I'll focus on not falling."

Field trips were good for the rambunctious freshmen, whose energy and entropy expanded in those little classrooms if left alone for too long. She knew how to handle them out here; it reminded her of days way back at Woods Hole, or even further back, of picking her way through the backyard with her brothers. She could always keep up with them — being the youngest, she'd had to, of course, or they wouldn't have brought her along. No one wants to be a babysitter. And neither did Beverly. "Hurry up, boys," she clapped one on the shoulder as she passed. It was good for them to see her with salt spray on her face, she'd decided. It was good for them to see that she could keep up.

The boys were dawdling. The tallest one, with broad shoulders, threatened to push one of the other boys into the water. Beverly had pretended not to hear. It was important to know which threats to take seriously, a skill she'd been sharpening.

They'd only had her in class for a few weeks. Those who wound up in a class about algae, which most of the focused students had written off as boring or impractical, assembled a diverse team, none of whom wanted to be there. There was a boy who should've been a sophomore but had "taken some time off" at the request of the College and the negotiation of his family — a practice which Beverly still could not understand and often correlated to a lack of respect for her. A true scientist knew that correlation did not equal causation, but nevertheless, boys like Wilson reminded Beverly of chorusing lecture halls and a shiny red apple. Her foot slipped and her shoe soaked up cloudy water.

She'd gotten further ahead, towards a particularly promising shallow pool that lurked with life. The boys hadn't accounted for the fact that Beverly grew up with brothers, and she knew how to play. As she bent down to get a better look, the acidic whisper of boys who should have known better traveled towards her. "Can't believe they really let that bitch teach us. Y'know how much we pay for this school?"

"Certainly enough to hire a man."

The voice was Wilson's. She'd never been a fan of wars, and these boys weren't even alive back then, but she couldn't help but think that if a couple of these boys had been drafted into the military after Pearl Harbor their attitude on what was fair might have been a bit different. Beverly's grip on the rock in front of her tightened. Now would be perhaps the worst moment to fall into the green pool. But she didn't say anything, didn't whirl around and give them a proper image of a bitch, if they wanted one so badly. She finished gathering her samples, because Beverly Conner was here to study, and that was what she did best. The water looked clearer as soon as you put it in a test tube, with the sunlight streaming through it. Her tongue was going to bleed if she kept biting it like this. She pushed a cork into the tube as the silt started to sink to the bottom.

"My father would be sad to see how much worse Marsden has become than in his day." Beverly labeled the test tube and nearly broke off the tip of her pencil.

"You should tell him!"

"Is it really that bad?"

Beverly's fingers were flying. Corks in every test tube, labels in barely legible writing. She hadn't even realized that she'd started working faster, much faster, because all that energy brewing in her brain had to go somewhere to keep it from coming out of her mouth.

"All I'm saying is, when my father went to Marsden, the only women around were the girls from Smith that would come in for the weekend."

"That's more like it. My pal Stevie's dating one of those chicks."

"She's a good teacher," one of the scrawnier ones piped up, which must have meant a lot, since the scrawny ones have so much more at stake. "Lay off her, will ya?"

"Matthew, shut up."

"You shut up!"

And the last label was finished. She stood, and turned, just in time to watch the boy she presumed to be Matthew splash into the stagnant water. He was lucky he hadn't hit his head on the rocks.

A mosquito hung in the air above him, surveying the scene. For a moment, they all stared at each other, silent, except for Matthew's heavy breathing and the sound of whizzing mosquito wings.

"Boys! What did you do?"

"He fell." Wilson looked over her head, refusing to meet her eyes.

"Are you sure about that?"

A sputtering Matthew coughed from the surface, a stripe of seaweed plastered to his forehead. "Ma'am, I was push —"

"Matthew?"

Sheepishly looking up at the rest of the boys, Matthew sighed and plucked the seaweed from his hair. "Just a bit of a klutz, ma'am. Slipped on this rock. I-I'll be more careful next time." The cloudy water rolled down his cheeks, red from the cold, and left a trail of silt.

"Oh, that's alright, Matthew. As a matter of fact, I've just got some samples from that bit over there. Why don't you use these in the lab — they look quite promising — so you can go dry off. I'm sure the rest of your friends here will need to stick around and get some samples, so they'll have something *half* as interesting as you to report on. Head on back to campus."

The boys begrudgingly hoisted Matthew from the water. He took the samples from Beverly nervously, glancing behind him at the other boys, and skittered across the rocks back to shore. The class was quite silent after that. "Lab reports will be due on Tuesday," she noted over the clinking of test tubes as they made the trek back towards campus. "I'm just so excited to see what you all learned."

She decided, as she biked home, that she would only tell Rachel about Matthew and leave out the rest of the class. She liked these quiet rides home, especially now that spring had arrived with a vengeance and the pathways were overrun with branches and vines that had grown eight inches since breakfast. Weeds burst from the cracks between the sidewalks. Her white-knuckle grip on the handlebars loosened as she rode.

Beverly had received word yesterday, in another beautiful note from Dean Peabody. She'd be promoted to Associate Professor at the end of the month. No one was sure if she was the first woman to do it; they didn't keep those kinds of records, and that wasn't the kind of question that Beverly was going to ask. The note was still folded up in her breast pocket, and it seemed to radiate light or heat or some other kind of energy. She liked to have it around. She liked the weight of it in her pocket. Professor Conner. Only 30 years or so after their first meeting.

When she rounded the corner onto Main Street, the sky was painted in yellows and the pale, almost-white blues of early evening. She got a nod from the coffee shop owner, who was closing up, as he usually was around the time Beverly headed home. They were just boys. And Matthew had a scraped knee and hopefully, a new interest in algae, so it was all a net neutral. Her wheels wove between a woman walking her dog and the mailbox outside of the post office. The boys, as they were nothing but boys, had faded into a verdant memory that rippled on the horizon the way hot air does in the summertime.

She turned onto their street and felt comfort wash over her at the sight of their screened porch and a tree full of green buds. Rachel had been waiting for her on the porch and threw open the screen door when she saw her. It slammed behind her, coming down the front walk in bare feet as Beverly tossed her bike in the bushes. "How was school today, Miss Conner?" she teased.

"Oh, you know. Another day in paradise."

LENA

2017

. . .

The white lab coat was a little big. The sleeves covered her hands, and the hem was already turning yellow from where her clammy hands tugged on it. But it was a real lab coat, not the kid-sized one she'd worn to the science fair, and that was good enough.

Lena looked up from the stainless-steel countertop and the lab around her came into focus a little slower than usual from behind the warped plastic of her safety goggles. She was still sneaking glances just to make sure it was all still there, all real. It was her first day working for Professor Knowles in her lab — she'd gotten the job, thanks to an outfit she'd borrowed from Nisha and new stationery for her thank-you notes she'd bought at the campus bookstore — her first day of junior year, doing research part time while taking classes. She'd updated her resume that morning over coffee with Jolie, who had practically swooned at the sight of the words. "Research Assistant." Lena had just nodded and taken a sip of her coffee, waiting for it all to feel important. She'd caught a glimmer when she slipped on the lab coat, but still, it wasn't anything earth-shattering. It was a job.

Professor Knowles wasn't in today; a grad student had quickly shown her the ropes. "Enter through this door," he'd said curtly, "and always exit through that one. Sign in here, first thing you've gotta do is put on your eye protection. Even if you're not working with chemicals, it's — legal, something." It wasn't anything she hadn't seen in Boston. "You'll be working here," a gesture towards the last clean corner of the counter, "That's my office," a quick gesture to one of three equally mysterious frosted glass doors in the corner, "so that's where I'll be if you need me. Try not to need me." It wasn't clear if that was a joke or not. And then, suddenly, Lena was on her own, measuring and weighing powders for the grad students. It was quiet in the lab with him gone. Lena still wasn't sure what the measured powders were going to be used for, other than that the experiment they were conducting had something vaguely to do with samples collected from the pond near campus. The one past the old railroad ties; Lena had been once before.

The scale was rather finicky, as the grad student had mentioned in passing. He'd had better things to do, and he was a bit distracted as he gave her the tour. But he needed exactly 9.7 grams measured so that *he could do his work.* Lena's spatula shook as she added what looked like barely anything, just a few grains of this fine powder. 9.64 jumped to 9.72.

Nisha had been complaining about how boring she found menial tasks in the lab. She was also working in the department, for a different professor, and over dinner had regaled the girls with tales of woe from her first week of research. Nisha didn't like being alone with her thoughts; she liked talking to people and being in a busy workspace. The murmuring of a centrifuge and the gasps of a hood vent weren't enough company for some people. Lena was not yet sure if she was one of them.

Lena yanked on the sleeves of the lab coat. No one had told

her if this was her coat, or if someone else would wear it when she wasn't in. It felt like the scale was judging her. She tried to steady her hands.

9.68.

Labs have a certain smell to them. The scent of rubbing alcohol sits on the surface, and the air feels thinner because it's been forced through more filters than usual. Sterilized equipment, tile floors, doors that say "authorized personnel only." Lena liked clear labels and expectations. She liked the sound that her sneakers made on the floor, the hum of the centrifuge, the machines that made some corners of the room hot and others quite cold. It felt busy and quiet at the same time. There was a rhythm to rooms like this; something almost like music.

The crystalline powder glittered in its dish like gemstones, beautiful, certainly, but also complicated. She wasn't even sure what these granules were. Maybe they were toxic. Looking at the spatula this closely, she could see that each fine grain was twisting in fantastically complicated shapes that no one would ever see. She liked that there were still some things that were complicated just because that was the way things were, not to impress anybody or make more money or anything. Just because the way it existed naturally, organically, whether you were looking or not, was the single most perfect shape it could be. She shook the dish, and the fluorescent lights bounced off the granules.

"Come on," she whispered under her breath as she steeled herself for one more scoop.

9.70.

It should have been a victorious moment. But the tray of empty dishes yet to be filled stared back at her, unimpressed.

"I'm heading out for lunch, not sure when I'll be back," the grad student, whose name Lena never learned, pushed through the doors and called to her over her shoulder without even looking. "Good luck with the scale."

When the door closed behind him, Lena let out a sigh she didn't know she'd been holding in. Her breath scattered the powder across the countertop. The scale changed to 9.1. She dropped the spatula and it clattered on the stainless steel. Nothing else in the room moved. The centrifuges did not notice. The scale did not help her clean up the mess. Lena thought of her long summer in a low-ceilinged classroom. She'd been melting in the Virginia August and woefully underpaid, but she'd given her students all the time they needed. Patience. And after she'd gotten to know them, that hadn't been a lot to ask. She'd wanted to help. She'd slowed things down when they didn't understand. She'd learned all their names.

The lab didn't know Lena's name. It continued its hum, its hot and its cold. Perhaps someone else would wear this coat tomorrow and nothing would notice. Perhaps the scale would behave.

Tomorrow was Kira and Liam's first day of eighth grade.

Lena tipped the spatula gently. 9.69. She cursed the powders under her breath.

. . .

There was only one diner in Marsden. Uncle Lucky's. On the weekends, the line wrapped around the block, but today was Tuesday, the first day of classes, and most of the town's patrons were either students or professors — that is to say, there was no line. Lena and Nisha were sitting at the bar, the kind with those vinyl swivel stools that give you a view of industrial coffee pots and a flat-top griddle making enough scrambled eggs for the entire football team, even though it was three in the afternoon.

"I can't believe we're *juniors,*" Nisha said, nervously

flicking the pink sugar packets in her fingers. "That sounds so *old*. Like, *juniors* have to have their lives figured out. Can we be freshmen again?"

Lena snorted. "Really? That was better?"

Lucky's was an institution in Marsden, but Lena had only been here once before. In a town this small, there was always the fear of being seen, which was just slightly worse than not being seen at all. Nisha had wanted to come, and the start of a year is a good time to get over fears. Reinvent yourself. The kind of thing Professor Knowles was always telling her.

"The lab's good?" Nisha asked absently, while she read the plastic menu.

"Yeah. You know, I think it's a learning curve. I didn't light anything on fire," Lena said, absent too. She kept thinking about Kira, and Liam, and all the kids. And she kept looking over her shoulder at the rest of the diner, though for what, she wasn't sure. "I'm sure it will be fine."

Lena rested her hands on the counter to discover everything was vaguely sticky from the memory of maple syrup. Two girls in Marsden Cheerleading sweatshirts were sitting on the other side of Nisha. They seemed unbothered by the stickiness, the noise in here, or the fact that everyone could see them.

The waitress set down two mugs of coffee.

The paper placemats had the diner's logo — a cartoon coffee cup, with tendrils of smoke that curled to spell "Lucky's" — and several black-and-white photos of mustachioed men standing outside of the same storefront. The logo read "EST. 1980," but these pictures were much older than that. Turn-of-the-century cars were parked outside. Must have been the '20s, maybe, or the '30s. Nothing else was the same then, except for the waffles. In tiny type: "Restoring a Marsden Institution." Lena took a swig from her mug and dripped coffee across the men in the photo. Maybe one of them was

Lucky. Maybe Lucky was just a character. The placemat was thin and it soaked up the coffee; Lucky's face grew dark.

"What can I get for you?" The waitress was still standing there.

"I'll have a waffle," Nisha said. Lena laughed. "What? It's the first day. Plus, you know they're good here."

Lena hadn't looked at the menu. "Make it two."

BEVERLY

1960

. . .

Beverly should have eaten lunch. All of the other faculty had eaten early, since the noon hour was when their faculty meetings were scheduled once a month. She'd lost track of time, fiddling with her microscope, and suddenly it was 11:55 and she was almost late to her very first faculty meeting. It should have been a momentous occasion, but she spent the entire time salivating over the apple she'd left on her desk in her office.

"So, if there's no other motions to discuss, we can adjourn the meeting," the Chair said, sounding quite bored. His hair was slicked back and so full of gel that it was almost blinding in that beam of sunlight. The ribbons of light that streaked through the room showed all the dust hanging in the air, swirling around. She shifted in her chair, her stockinged calves squeaking against the leather.

"I have one," Dr. Bell's voice cut through the room. Shiny shoes, pressed shirt. He stood.

It was exactly as she'd pictured it. Parliamentary proceedings, people talking about themselves in the third person and debating about important things. Beverly wondered if anyone could hear the protests of her stomach. Probably not — there was a ring of empty chairs around her, the only empty seats in the room. She must have unknowingly sat near a draft, one that everyone else was aware of except her. Surely, that was the reason.

After establishing herself in the department and getting past the year or so of introductions, Beverly had been able to wear pants and loose things that let her legs move the way a scientist's should. Years ago, when her mother was visiting, she took one look in Beverly's closet and had tried to order her everything in the Sears catalog that was pink or cashmere. But Beverly had gotten used to her routine; people, she found, didn't bother you much if you didn't bother them. She did her work in her closet, published her books, and could collect water samples with her pants hiked up to her knees. She did everything she needed to do, quietly.

"The Chair recognizes Dr. Bell."

But today, Beverly was wearing a dress. A high-necked, shift dress that was apparently in fashion now, for women younger than Beverly. Rachel had insisted she get some new clothes after the promotion, and she had practically zipped Beverly into this dress herself that morning. "Trust me," she'd said as she smoothed Beverly's hair. "You need to look the part." For the first faculty meeting. Rachel was also frying pork chops for dinner. A sharp pain stabbed at Beverly's stomach at the thought.

"We need someone to teach a freshman seminar in the fall. Dr. Croasdale retired."

Beverly smoothed the skirt across her legs. You couldn't kick in a dress. You had to sit with your legs crossed at the ankle in a room like this, like even the strips of mahogany wood paneling expected her to be a lady.

"Would anyone be willing to take this on?"

Beverly stood. "If it pleases the Chair, I would be happy to teach it."

The room was silent. She could nearly hear the sound of throats clenching in their neckties and collars someone else had pressed. Men were wearing higher-waisted pants, belts no longer had to match their shoes. White patent leather things, hair that was longer than it should be, and parted down the middle. Forty-year-old professors thinking they looked like John Travolta — it did not look good. Someone coughed.

"I said, if it pleases the Chair, I would be happy to teach it. Algae and desmids make for good trips to the lake. The boys would have a good time."

Weight shifted from foot to foot. She knew that every man in the room knew the title of her book and had read about its success, whether they had intended to or not. It had been featured in the American Phycological Association newsletter. Bestseller, they had said. "I-I've gotten good reviews of my teaching in the past." She wondered if she was speaking too quietly or maybe she was shouting. "And I'd be happy to take on the additional workload." She counted the four other courses she'd be teaching on her fingers at her side and then clenched them into a fist. "I'm sure I could manage it all."

Someone swallowed audibly. Dr. Bell's Adam's apple tugged against his tab collar. Beverly bent her knees slightly. She'd heard that if you locked your knees, you could pass out. Her fingernails bit half-moons into the heel of her hand.

"Unless anyone else wants to teach it?" Her own voice began to sound strange to her, like she was shouting into an aluminum can. Her brothers had made one of those telephones with soup cans and twine when they were just kids. She'd always thought they didn't work, and it was like you were talking and only you could hear you, distant and tinny. "It doesn't seem like anyone else wants to teach it."

"Dr. Bell," the Chair said, "since no... *experienced* faculty are available to teach the freshman seminar, inform the registrar that this department cannot offer one."

Dr. Bell glanced at Beverly like she was a dog whining for a treat — genuine pity, tinged with condescension. You can never explain to your dog why it can't have some of your dessert. Bell's eyes settled on his shoes. "Understood."

"If there's no other motions?"

The sunlight streaming in through that window was making this room thick and hot. It smelled of the breath of men who had smoked a cigarette for lunch. Perhaps that was why she couldn't breathe.

"Meeting adjourned."

Beverly gathered her skirts in her fists and wished she was wearing pants. It would have been nice to kick something.

LENA

2018

. . .

There must've been a fox nearby. Perhaps it was a wandering house cat, or an especially threatening raccoon. Whatever had been spotted, the birds in the tree were on red alert. It's difficult to have a conversation when anything, even a sparrow, is vocally fearing for its life. It begs the question — *why aren't you this afraid?*

It was a gray day, the kind of mid-spring grayness that seemed to suit the mass of frightened birds. The sun had been emerging from swollen clouds for a minute or two at a time and otherwise hid between the flat white sky. When the sun was out, the chill was still bearable. When the sun went away, the cold started to creep in. New Hampshire springs were predictable and, Lena thought, over-romanticized.

Lena was distracted by the screaming birds and the metal armrest of the bench that bit into her ribs. "Sorry," she brushed her hair from her face. "Peter. What were you saying?"

Peter sighed and raked his fingers through his bangs. The birds were fluttering around in the almost-bare tree. Danger was approaching, or it was already here. "Lena, damnit, I'm trying to tell you something."

"Good news?"

"Yeah. I — yeah."

"I've never seen anyone this eaten up about good news."

"I got into grad school."

"Peter! That's awesome!" Lena ignored the sharp twinge in her throat. She was excited for him. The shadow of his graduation had fallen over the whole year. They had tried to go back to the frozen yogurt shop the week before, after she had joked that he should get one last yogurt before he graduated and left forever. He had reminded her he had months left before graduation, and there was plenty of time for yogurt. They had arrived to find the yogurt shop closed, permanently.

The birds kept screaming. "Yeah, it is awesome." Color returned to his cheeks. He let his arm fall across the back of the bench, his fingers brushing her shoulder blade. "It's going to be really great. A nice change of pace."

Which did she love more? Him, or the way he made her feel? If it was him, then she should want him to go. Take on the next adventure, realize his future, light the world on fire. But if it was the way he made her feel, then the weight of his absence would be heavier than the pride in his next accomplishment. And it was a terrible thing to admit, even to herself, that perhaps it had never been about him.

"Yeah, Marsden's such a small town. Think of all the different kinds of food you'll eat in Boston, Peter!" Every school he had applied to was in Boston. They'd talked about this. "And when I come to visit, we can eat our way around the world. Hungarian for lunch, Korean for dinner." He smiled stiffly. It wasn't Peter's smile. "I'm not sure what Hungarian food is, really, but we can find out, that will be part of the fun." His eyes didn't crinkle like they should have. "I bet it'll be a lot of stews. And we can have something French for dessert." She kissed his cheek; he didn't move.

"I'm not going to Boston." The birds wailed. Maybe she'd heard him wrong.

"What did you say?"

"Lena. I'm not going to Boston." His arm twitched behind her back, and she wondered if he was trying to take it off of her shoulders. The sun moved behind a cloud.

"Wh-where else did you apply? Every school on your list was in Boston." It was less than two hours away. She could visit every other weekend; she'd lived there before. They both had friends there. This had been the plan.

A fox leapt from the brush. The birds scattered.

"California."

"Oh. When did you decide? — I mean, that's great. That's great."

He sighed. "I'm going to Stanford, Len. I didn't tell you I was applying because I didn't think I'd get in. I mean, of course I didn't."

When Lena met Peter, she hadn't known that the moment beneath the oak tree would be important. No one had told her to pay attention. But now, sitting here with him beside her, she knew as she was living it that this instant would be burned into her brain. She'd replay the moment in her head for months, and she knew she would, as it was happening. It was strange to know that you were living in a memory as it was happening to you, like you're watching a movie of your life in muted colors.

Lena leaned forward, studying the trees. One bird had stayed behind when the rest flew away. It cocked its head at her and fixed its one black, beady eye on her. Then it hopped to another tree, close by, before it flew off, too. The silence they had left behind was deafening. "Lena, say something."

He moved his arm off the back of the bench and clasped his hands together in his lap. She hadn't realized that he had been blocking the wind.

"What is there to say?"

He nodded. "I don't know." His lips made a flat line and sighed through his nose, the way adults do when they're not allowed to have a reaction. Lena didn't want him to be an adult that swallowed his feelings and moved to California. He should be a kid, with her, eating frozen yogurt forever. Because if Peter was an adult that meant Lena was, too.

Maybe she didn't love him. Maybe this wasn't what love was.

Peter was looking at her, she could tell. "Lena. We don't have to break up. I mean, we've made it work, you know, before. When I was in Chicago."

The bird was back. The one who hadn't left with the pack, the only one who was stupid enough to stay.

"Come on. This isn't a summer internship. This is your Ph.D. You're going to be there for years. You're going to want roots." Something started rising in her chest. It felt like when she was a kid blowing bubbles on her driveway with her dad and just before the bubble burst, it got really big and round and shiny. You could see a whole rainbow in the sheen, our own distorted reflection. "You're going to make a whole life for yourself there." She swallowed, trying to keep it down.

"But you only have a year left. I mean, you could come and join me, right? California?"

"I don't know if that's what I want." The shiny round thing was getting closer to her throat. She wondered if you could choke on whatever this was. "I- I don't know anything."

The bird darted off. Its oily wings made a slapping sound as it leapt into the air. Lena wondered if it hurt to fly.

BEVERLY

1972

. . .

Sometimes the mountains look blue in the distance, a bright blue or sometimes a teal. Beverly knew that it was because of atmospheric distortion, that the more sky there is between you and mountains, it looks more opaque. But she liked to think that maybe it was that the mountains were really the biggest waves you'd ever seen, and they poked up behind the tree line every now and then to say hello. If you were paying attention, you might see them, and they might get white and foamy at the top and one day they'd finally crash.

Tonight was one of those nights. Beverly and Rachel were eating dinner in their yard and watching the sunset, and the mountains were periwinkle behind the black trees. They sat cross-legged on a picnic blanket they both had forgotten about, buried in a trunk and smelling of mothballs and lavender sachets. It was all because Rachel had bought them a puppy.

They got Lucky just a few weeks ago. They'd named her after that old diner that had been in Marsden when Beverly moved in, Uncle Lucky's, which had been the source of Beverly's daydreams of waffles for at least a decade. Beverly had been against the idea of a dog at first, since she was afraid she wouldn't have time to help take care of another living thing and she was also afraid Rachel wasn't in a position to be taking care of something without her help. Beverly hadn't said any of that, though. She said she hadn't wanted something tracking mud in their house. Rachel had asked when she was planning on cleaning up the mud *she* had tracked in the house, and that had been the end of the discussion. Lucky had one icy blue eye and one chocolate brown and white fur that got matted in seconds, no matter how often Beverly brushed it. It had taken only a matter of minutes for Beverly to wonder why they'd waited so long to get her.

"Go fetch!" Beverly tossed a knobby stick with one hand and ate her turkey sandwich with the other. Lucky tore after the projectile, a flash of white fur stained with verdant skid marks. "So anyway," she turned to Rachel as Lucky whined through the stick in her teeth, "The last faculty meeting wasn't so bad. And I think they're going to have me teach two courses next term." Lucky dropped the stick on the ground and Beverly picked it up. It was slick and warm with saliva.

"That's good. Which two?"

The dog lunged back and forth in the grass, snapping at the stick in Beverly's hand. "Fetch!" Lucky and Beverly both traced the stick's arc across the orange sky. It landed, Lucky took off, and Beverly answered, "Introduction to Biology and my Algae and Desmids seminar."

"So you'll finally get all that stuff off our dining room table then?"

Beverly chuckled. "Yes, I thought you'd be thrilled. Lab equipment for twenty rambunctious boys, out of our house."

"I still don't know why the department couldn't buy that stuff for your class. You're telling me you really had to make it all out of, what, pantyhose and can openers?"

"Rachel —"

"I know, I know. Pick your battles."

Lucky was tired. She lumbered towards the blanket. Rachel scratched her ears as Lucky dove nose-first into Beverly's lap. Her eyes sank shut. Beverly kept talking and one hand absent-mindedly wandered to the dog's back, which she stroked while she babbled on about her courses.

It was starting to get chilly. "Do you want to head inside, Bev?"

"I don't think we should disturb Lucky, you know? She's actually sleeping. I think we should take our victories." Beverly rubbed between the puppy's ears. Her fur was still short and soft as she grew into the skin that rolled off of her muscles. "Plus, you know, we have to take her for her next round of shots tomorrow, and she's going to hate that, so let's let her rest now."

Lucky's breathing was heavy. Her flank rose and fell between them, pressed up against Rachel's bare calves. Her mud-coated paws hung over the edge of Beverly's crossed knees and twitched with what was surely a wonderful dream.

Beverly traced the edge of the mountains with her eyes. "It's really pretty tonight, huh?"

"You know, we've never taken a vacation," Rachel said suddenly. She didn't tear her eyes from the sunset. "I've always wanted to go to Florida. I hear the sunsets there are somethin' else."

A purple cloud was getting pulled apart in the sky, stretching thinner and thinner in tufts like a threadbare cardigan.

"We could visit Scooter, maybe. Last I heard he was in Florida. Santa Rosa Beach."

Rachel reached for Beverly's hand. Her knuckles were like whitish knobs, not the slender pale things they used to be. It was like Rachel's skin had been shrink-wrapped — that was what they called it now — a little tighter around all of the little bones and tendons in her hand. Beverly looked away.

"I don't know where Santa Rosa is. I've never been there."

"We could go," Beverly offered quietly. Rachel squeezed her hand but still didn't turn to look at her. "It's been years since I've seen Scooter. I can hardly remember what he looks like, I guess. Maybe he lost an eye in the Army." She laughed hoarsely.

The edges of Rachel's dark cherry hair were glowing orange in the sunset, highlighting the stray rebels that didn't lie smoothly against her head. A strip of the purple sky traced Rachel's cheekbone and nose. Beverly took a deep breath of September, cinnamon and earth. She let it coat her tongue.

Rachel turned to her, something in her eyes that Beverly couldn't read. "I'm getting cold. Let's go inside." Rachel nodded at the dog, who blinked one bleary eye open and yawned a puppy yawn.

"Come on, girl. Up." Rachel gathered up the blankets and Beverly herded Lucky around in a circle. "I'm thinking tonight of my blue eyes," Beverly sang. She'd been making up songs for the puppy since they'd brought her home, but Gene Autry was always appropriate. "And I wonder if she ever thinks of me?" Rachel never commented, for fear of pointing the phenomenon out, making it cease altogether. She remembered a time when Beverly wouldn't sing at all. Now she was dancing with a dog.

Lucky cocked her head and circled around Beverly's feet as she fumbled a waltz in the grass. "Oh, you told me one time that you loved me. Oh, I'm thinking tonight of my blue eyes."

Beverly almost lost her balance. Rachel grabbed her elbow and steadied her.

"Who is waiting far across the sea." Beverly stopped her waltz, laughing at herself, and turned to find Rachel studying her in the purple twilight. Their eyes met for a moment, then Beverly looked at the grass.

"I missed nights like this." Rachel said, turning to look at the sky. "Like we're just kids again."

"I did too."

Beverly hefted the picnic blankets in her arms. They were heavier than they should've been. She didn't lean around the quilts in her arms, so they might muffle her words. "I know what you did, you know. You used this dog to trick me. I'm not fixating on the politics of the department, or scheming for ways to get them to let me do extra work. I'm just sitting on picnic blankets and watching the sun set." Rachel held her gaze, acknowledging nothing. "And it's enough."

Rachel held the screen door open and Beverly and Lucky went inside, tracking mud across the floor, tiny paw prints following the mud left by Beverly's work boots across the porch.

LENA

2018

. . .

Jolie was on her third coffee of the day, and it showed. Her eyes were darting around faster than her fingers flying on her keyboard. "It's not my fault," she explained after she caught Lena watching her polish off the caramel-drizzled cup. "I missed these lattes all summer. I'm telling you, Len, no one makes them as good as the student center."

"Agreed." Lena took a long slurp of her own coffee. The student center had switched to using paper straws, and hers was starting to dissolve into a pulpy slurry. The sun had melted the ice into a milky layer of water that sat on the top of her latte. She squinted at her laptop screen in the sun. It was the first day of senior year. There wasn't much to do yet, but Jolie had some fellowship applications to finish up, so Lena busied herself refreshing her email.

"Do you have any stuff to do for Bio 101?" Jolie asked without looking up from her screen, like she could tell that Lena was bored.

"Not yet." Lena was the TA for Bio 101. She'd gotten the job over the other applicants because of last summer's stint at her middle school. They'd wanted someone with "teaching experience." Lena had wondered, for a moment, how Peter had gotten the job all those years ago. He'd never taught anyone. "Their first homework assignment is due on Friday, though, so I think this is the calm before the storm."

"Enjoy it. When I TA'ed Spanish 110, I was correcting accent marks until my eyes bled." She went back to her typing.

Early September in New Hampshire is really just the best part of summer. Lena tilted her screen back and looked out across the quad. They were sitting in wrought-iron chairs on the Student Center patio — the black armrests frying in the sun, a fact she learned the hard way — because it had the best view of campus. They'd been too nervous to study there as sophomores, because it was also the most visible spot on campus. It was like you were on stage. Late in their junior year, they'd worked up the courage, and that was when Lena learned how spectacular the view was. The brick buildings framed the expanse of green, and if you sat there long enough, you might actually watch the seasons change. It looked perfect no matter the weather, because if it was overcast, it just seemed all the more mysterious and collegiate. But today it wasn't gray or gloomy. The sun was straight overhead and so bright that your eyes hurt if you looked at the pavement for too long.

"You know, this is our last fall."

"Ever?" Jolie teased. "God, thanks for the warning."

Lena laughed. "Shut up."

"I don't want to think about that, Lena!" Jolie closed the lid of her laptop. She rested her arms on it and leaned across the table, looking out at the trees. They bent slightly in the breeze. "God, nothing beats it, huh?"

The tree directly in front of them, emerging from a mound of fresh mulch, was just starting to turn yellow at the top, like it had been dipped in paint. There was a plaque at the base of the trunk. Everything around here was dedicated to some-body.

A group of boys threw a football around on the quad. They chased each other in wide circles in the grass, shouting at each other, and brought the catcher of the ball down to the ground hard. Jolie and Lena flinched.

Jolie opened her laptop back up and Lena did, too, even though there was still nothing to do. When the screen refreshed, she saw a new email. It was from Kira.

To: L.Rivera.19@marsden.edu
From: kira.riley.33@gmail.com

Hi Lena,

I don't know if you really meant it when you gave us your email and told us to write, but it's my first day of high school and I didn't know who else to talk to. We're taking biology this year, because I guess that's what they teach in 9ᵗʰ grade, and then we're taking chemistry next year. I've been thinking a lot about cells. There's a real science lab here, not just the classroom you taught us in. Do you think maybe they would let me stay after school and use the microscopes? Maybe that's not allowed.

I don't really know why I'm writing. I just thought you'd understand.

I hope college isn't too hard.

Sincerely,
Kira Riley

Lena turned her hands over and let the sun warm the backs of them while she thought of an answer.

"Did you already get a question from one of your students?" Jolie asked.

"Ha. Well. Kind of."

To: kira.riley.33@gmail.com
From: L.Rivera.19@marsden.edu

Hi Kira,

Yes, I did mean it! I'm so glad to hear from you. I know I was very intimidated on my first day of high school (and most of the days after that, if I'm honest) so I think I know what you mean. It's exciting, too! I hope you're excited.

I wish I had thought to ask about using the lab. I just did a lot of reading on my own when I was interested in something, but I think nothing replaces seeing it for yourself. If you think you might have more questions about biology, you should definitely talk to the bio teacher about using the lab. I'm sure everyone will be glad to have you.

Good luck with everything! Please do keep me updated.

Best,
L

She sent it and wondered why she hadn't ever just thought to ask to use the microscopes in her old high school science lab. No one would have cared, probably. It had felt easier to just walk in the woods behind her house, where she didn't have to ask anyone for permission.

The sun sloped lower in the sky. Lena packed up her bag. She'd told Nisha she'd bring takeout home so they could have what Nisha was calling a "Last-First-Day Roommate Dinner." She stopped at the Thai restaurant down the alley behind the student center that was in the basement and always smelled like burnt peanut sauce but had the best — and only — coconut curry in town and got the bags of food.

Nisha smiled when she came in through their graffiti-covered door, laden with to-go containers. "Good to be home."

"I thought you'd never make it."

Nisha and Lena curled up on the rug that had been white when she started at Marsden and was now yellowed with time as Lena unpacked the food. She knew Nisha's usual and hadn't had to call before she'd ordered.

She pulled a soda out of the mini fridge. "You want one?" Nisha shook her head, and the door slammed shut. The fridge was Nisha's, but pretty much everything else in the dorm room was hers. Peter had taken the coffee table with him to Stanford. Nisha had thrown a bit of a fit, saying that the last thing they still needed for the "perfect" room was a place to eat dinner when they ordered pizza on Fridays, but Peter had asked for it. He needed a table for his apartment in California, and she liked the idea of him having something of hers, even if it was just a table. The only thing he'd have of hers now. Nisha had made do; the room was quite cozy. Pictures of the two of them were everywhere, mixed in with a few other friends they'd picked up over the years. George, the aloe plant, still had his place of honor on the windowsill.

"Verdict on the first day?" Nisha asked through a forkful of her Pad Thai.

"All in all? Fine. English is going to be fun, the prof is really funny. We're reading *Pride and Prejudice* and she really said to us, 'You kids study too hard, you could use some romance.'"

Nisha choked on her soda. "Damn, Ghost of Christmas Past." She studied Lena's face, expecting to see signs of the breakup dredged up by a Regency romance. "Speaking of... how is He Who Shall Not Be Named?"

"It's okay. He's good, I'm good."

"But *are* you good? Like, for real?"

Lena twisted the high school class ring on her finger. She took it off and let it roll on the ground. "Honestly? I don't think I've ever been better."

"Good." Nisha hefted their GRE workbooks onto the rug. "Because you're about to get a lot worse!"

Lena shoved her so hard Nisha almost fell off of her elbows where she'd propped herself up. She flipped her book open. "We're taking it *tomorrow*. Is studying for another forty minutes going to do anything?"

"You're not scared? I mean, Len, I will gladly watch *Project Runway* reruns with you instead. Say the word. But I thought your whole schtick was, like, paralyzing fear?" Nisha was joking, probably. She took a sip of her soda, her eyes fixed on Lena's face.

Lena weighed her answer, tested how what she was about to say felt on her tongue. "Actually. I think we've studied enough. I think I'm ready to just... wait? For the future to come to us?"

Nisha nodded, slowly. "Easier said than done." She closed the workbook. The thin pages, grooved from the pressure of a pen tip, slid against each other until it was shut.

BEVERLY

1975

. . .

Rachel had found a radio station that played the hits from their childhood. The antennae were cocked far towards the porch screen and it gurgled static between songs. Lucky barked at the songs she didn't like, the mailman, and the children in the street learning to ride their bikes. It was sunny, and there were more birds and insects flying around than there had been the day before. The world was buzzing, and it was almost hard to hear Rachel over the din.

"I just don't understand why you let them talk to you like that." Rachel tapped her spoon against the side of her teacup and took a long drag like it was a cigarette. Her hands were bonier now, leaner, with raised blue veins.

"To be clear, I don't let them talk to me 'like that.' They don't talk to me at all." Beverly reached under the table and fed Lucky one of Rachel's sandwich crusts. That dog truly believed the world revolved around peanut butter and white bread. "I think that's better," she said with a laugh.

Rachel sighed and looked through the screen window into the front yard. A warm breeze whispered through the porch, end to end. It was almost summertime again. Beverly smiled in the sun, but Rachel didn't seem to feel it. She had an acrylic afghan draped over her legs. She wasn't getting around as well as she had been, and they both pretended not to notice. Lucky nipped at her heels and she barely looked down. "I just want what's best for you, Bev. I just — I just hate to see this. I've hated it for thirty years. You're the best damned scientist in the whole place."

Lucky cocked her head to one side, so her ear flopped over the top of her head. She fixed her one blue eye on Beverly. Sometimes it felt like the dog understood their conversations.

Beverly took another sip of tea. "I'm fine, Rachel. I got a microscope and a desk and a check coming every two weeks. I've got all I need from them."

"What about respect?"

"Mine and yours and —" she reached down to scratch the dog's ears, "Lucky's? I've got all I need." Lucky barked an agreement.

Rachel placed her teacup in its saucer with a dissatisfied clink. "I want more for you."

"And I don't."

Rachel caught Beverly's hand as she started to get up from the table. "Bev. You know I'm just trying to help." Rachel slowly brought Beverly's fingers to her lips and brushed a kiss onto her arthritic knuckles. "And I don't say it, enough, I know that. But I am proud of you." Rachel wasn't scared of *doing things,* but sometimes heavy words caught in her throat. *Saying things.* She held Beverly's gaze for a moment, then her eyes wandered to the screen and looked out towards the trees. "All you're doing, you know. It's a lot."

"What am I doing? I-I'm a good teacher, Rachel. I'm a teacher."

"You're a *professor.* And I'm not just talking about that." Her hand clumsily toppled the stack of letters on the edge of the table. Pale blue, lilac purple, paper folded and stamped with ink from India, Poland, Indonesia. "You're getting letters from all over the world. You're helping a lot more than the 30 boys in your classroom."

Beverly straightened the stack and felt her cheeks burn. "These? They just have questions about my book."

"Yeah, Bev. *Your book*. This guy?" She ripped open the top letter, a purple one with a detailed Indian flag. "He wants your help..." her eyes scanned the scrawled writing, "identifying a species *he thinks you make the first mention of in your book*. Did you discover a new species of algae?"

"Rachel. That's part of the job. It's what all scientists do."

"It's not."

"It's what good ones do."

Rachel was silent for a moment. She picked at her soft hands in her lap. "I can't believe you didn't tell me. That's the kind of thing you should tell me."

Beverly would have told her if it had mattered. But it hadn't.

"How many of those professors in that damn department discovered a new species?"

Beverly folded the letter back up and tucked it into the stack. She would respond tomorrow. Tonight. She'd respond tonight. Her mother always taught her to keep organized correspondence, otherwise the people would stop writing to you. "It doesn't matter."

"My point. Beverly, you deserve so much more than they're giving you."

"So what? I'm getting my work published, I'm doing my job. I put food on my table."

"I'm trying to —"

"What?"

Rachel raked her fingers through her hair. "I just hope you realize the gravity of what you're doing."

Beverly's eyes were somewhere else.

"And what is that?"

"You're the first woman professor, I think. Marsden never had a woman before."

Beverly slammed the heels of her hands down on the railing with more force than she'd meant. When the banister stopped shaking, she looked up. "I don't want to be the first woman anything. I'm the best at my job I can be, woman, man." She laughed. "Child. I never cared about that." A chickadee called from the tree in the yard. "And I wish you didn't either."

"Whether you like it or not, Beverly, you're helping all those girls."

"Which girls?"

"The girls working in the library, the girls they're gonna hire after you." Beverly jerked her head at the thought. Rachel continued. "You think Marsden's only gonna teach boys forever? I think you're helping all those girls, Beverly. The ones now and... I mean, doesn't it make your heart sing a little? Thinking about female students in Carlisle Hall one day?"

Beverly turned around and looked at Rachel. Her eyes flashed. Lucky whimpered in the silence. "You listen to me. I never did anything for those girls except tell them to be quiet and wait."

Lucky whined and laid down on the rug when neither woman turned to look at her. Beverly looked down at the railing. "This needs a coat of paint."

LENA

2018

. . .

Even despite the best efforts of the two energy drinks on her desk, Lena was about to fall asleep in front of her laptop screen when her phone vibrated. *New Message from Nisha: Len!!!! Red alert ... did u see this?* Lena's phone buzzed on the desk next to her. A text from Nisha with a link to an article on the college website. "Marsden Alum Quoted in *Scientific American;* Big Things Ahead for Peter Mitchell '18."

She pulled the article up on her laptop as her phone vibrated again. *New Message from Nisha: Fr he's 1 yr out of school. I hate him!!* It was too late for this. The empty energy drink cans offered gasps of artificial blue raspberry — since raspberries are never blue. The French fries from six hours ago were still in their takeout container on the floor, which dripped with condensation, and the stale French-fry-air was suffocating her. Suddenly the room was too small. She reached for anything to feign stability and all she found was a cup of coffee, now cold, on her desk. But taking a sip of it and pretending that it was still warm was enough to convince herself that she was steeled. Totally ready to read an article about her ex-boyfriend being quoted in *Scientific American* in his first year of grad school.

It was three in the morning and Lena had been studying since dinner, but no amount of exhaustion or screen fatigue could keep her from the article.

Peter Mitchell '18 is making waves out in California working with his Ph.D. advisor Dr. Steven Kemeny. In only his first year of his program, Mitchell and Kemeny were recently featured in Scientific American *for their research on a disease that's killing off the shasta crayfish, an endangered species, work they say has implications for the way we study disease in humans.*

The young alumnus says that "Dr. Kemeny has been an incredible mentor and has kept me involved at every step of the way. I definitely feel a little over my head, but the best way to learn is to surround yourself with the smartest people you can find, so I'm feeling really lucky and excited for the future. Moving to California has always been a dream of mine, and now, to be able to have a real impact in the ecosystem here is a great honor. I don't take it lightly. Now I'm just waiting for Dr. Kemeny to realize that I've got no business being in his lab!"

Mitchell found his new advisor through the networks he made here at Marsden: Kemeny completed his own Ph.D. alongside Mitchell's undergraduate advisor, Professor of Biological Sciences Andrew Ballard. All roads truly do lead to Marsden. We're immensely proud of Peter and cannot wait to see what he does next.

She read it three times. The word "alum" was still odd to see next to Peter's name, since he would always be her Bio TA who stole her oak tree and had never eaten frozen yogurt before. He was always confident, but also young and *just about to start doing things.* "Alum" made him sound like he was an adult, in the real world, *already doing things.* In the handful of quotes, he sounded just as surprised to be in the article as Lena was to be reading it, all humility and self-deprecating humor. Charming, even in a headshot and a 200-word writeup in the alumni magazine.

Lena's phone vibrated again. *New Message from Nisha: Should I come back to Mars and kidnap you? I knew something would happen. This is y I can't leave campus!! Never leaving again!!!*

It was probably a good thing that Nisha was home for the weekend, because if she was here she would've talked Lena out of calling him. But she wasn't here, so that's what Lena did.

New Message from Nisha: Lena!!!! I KNOW YOU'RE GO-ING TO REACH OUT. DO. NOT. CALL. HIM.

Perhaps it was a bad idea for Nisha to talk to her exes. But of course it was, because she dated guys that she met at frat parties or at the local dive bar, and then was disappointed when they didn't want to study for the GRE with her or watch *Doctor Who*. When she finally realized that the guy of the month didn't have anything in common with her, breaking it off was a pretty permanent decision. Lena and Peter had never been like that.

"Lena Rivera. What a surprise." He didn't sound at all surprised. "I'm glad you called." That part, at least, sounded true.

Lena's radiator kicked on. The radiators in the dorms were loud.

"Someone sent me your article." She was practically shouting. "I wanted to call and make sure you'd remember me, now that you're famous."

"Damn. I was hoping maybe they wouldn't run it." Lena was sure he had hoped that. "Do I sound like as much of a dork as I thought I did in the interview?" He laughed. "I still haven't had the nerve to read it."

Lena paced around the room, which was difficult because she could almost touch all the walls from any particular vantage point. She spun on her heels by the door and walked three paces to the window. "Come on, Peter. You sound *much* dorkier than that."

"Oh no! Well then I'll have to read it and demand they retract the piece altogether."

"It's great, Peter. Really." She spun on her heels and walked back to the door. It was like nothing had changed, and also like she was talking to him through a brick wall or maybe a fish tank. "This is a big deal. *Scientific American* today, *National Geographic* tomorrow. A job offer on Friday?"

"It's really not what it sounds like. The *Scientific American* reporter reached out to our lab, because my research advisor is a pretty big deal. When she heard that I was one of his new grad students, she recognized my name because," he sighed with a frustrated laugh, "she went to high school with my dad. She sees the stuff he posts on Facebook or whatever and was like, 'Peter, you should be in this story too.' She got me to do the interview with my advisor, but honestly, it should've just been him."

"You're doing the work, too. It's great. Now shut up and take the compliment." They both laughed.

"So how are you doing then, Len? Senior year everything you hoped it would be?"

"I'm good, actually. I'm applying to grad school. I'm the TA for Bio 101 this year. I'm still getting tea with Knowles sometimes. Oh, I'm living with Nisha this year." She looked around the room and let her eyes dance over the pictures on their wall, her and Nisha in matching Halloween costumes. The plants on their windowsill. "I'm really good, Peter."

"I knew you would be."

They settled into a nostalgic silence, each assuming the other was thinking about the same sepia-toned memories. And neither was, of course.

"Hey," he started, awkwardly. It really wasn't like Peter to stumble over words. "Do you still sit and work at that oak tree outside Carlisle?"

"Of course, Peter. It's my tree."

He laughed. "I mean, I know you've always said that. I still think it was mine first."

She sat down on the floor, then laid down. The concrete floor was hard through the carpet squares. One hand on her stomach, the other holding her phone to her ear. She studied the ceiling tiles. "I think you're wrong. I think it was there for me."

"Like it grew there, just for you?" Peter teased.

"Maybe. There wasn't any place in Carlisle, in all four years, that felt like it was mine. Not Professor Knowles' lab, not the desk I always sat in any classroom. Nowhere. And you wouldn't know what that feels like, Peter. You're at home everywhere." There were thirty-six ceiling tiles. The one next to the window bloomed with a water stain. "I have sat under that tree and gone from highest highs to lowest lows in minutes. Like I'm sure I'm on the right path because a leaf fell into my lap and I got completely distracted by studying the veins in it. And then two minutes later I have an existential crisis because maybe I don't want to be a scientist at all. Maybe I want to teach or write or, I don't know... You know?"

She wondered if Peter knew that she sometimes said things out loud to him that she'd not quite said to herself yet. "You don't want to be a scientist?"

"Of course I do." She hadn't meant to say that.

He was silent, but she could hear him softly breathing.

"And, of course, now I have to be in *Nat Geo* in my first year of grad school. Just because I'm a sore loser," she said. She didn't mean it, though, not at all. It was totally empty. He laughed anyway.

"If anyone can do it, you can."

"Yeah, yeah. Tell me about California, big shot."

"Well, I wake up and run straight into the Pacific Ocean every morning. Then I —"

"Peter! For real!"

"Fine. Honestly, it's amazing. It's terrifying, but amazing. Everyone here is smarter than me. But in the best way."

"But only *you* were in the magazines!"

They talked for an hour. "Lena. It's so late there. You've gotta stop pulling all-nighters, at least on the weekend."

"Hall monitor."

"Delinquent."

"I should go to sleep too."

"Thanks for calling?" He said it like it was a question.

"Thanks for picking up."

"Yeah, well. Goodnight, Lena."

"Night." When she hung up the phone, the article about Peter was still glowing on her laptop.

Lena kept reading it, waiting to feel jealous. Waiting for the nausea clawing at her throat to force her to slam the laptop shut and blast angry music and tell herself she was better than Peter, anyway. But Lena couldn't picture it, she couldn't even find it in her to be jealous. She held up a photo of herself on her phone next to the article. She covered Peter's name with her thumb. And even if she could force herself to visualize it, she wasn't jealous. She just didn't want to be that kind of scientist. And she was waiting to finally understand what that meant.

Lena finally texted Nisha back. *I didn't call him, I'm not an idiot. Hurry back to Mars plz n save me from myself.* She shut the laptop and climbed into bed and stared at the ceiling in the dark, listening to her heartbeat in her ears. She didn't want to be Peter's kind of scientist. It should have been exciting to have this kind of revelation — but knowing what you don't want doesn't always mean you suddenly know what you do. She picked at the hangnails on her fingers until they bled and stained her pillowcase. She didn't realize she'd finally fallen asleep until she woke up the next morning as Nisha came back, rolling her suitcase after her.

"Well, you look like hell," she offered from the doorway.

Lena laughed sadly from her bed and then pulled her comforter up over her head.

BEVERLY

1976

. . .

It had all started with Rachel's knee. Beverly had been busier than ever at work, between the second edition of *Miracles of Biology* — which meant writing letters to England to approve the changes — and the death of a beloved Scandinavian phycologist whose university had requested Beverly's help finalizing and publishing three of his unfinished research papers, and a full teaching load. She hadn't been at the house much, leaving at six in the morning with a thermos of coffee and returning at eight at night, after Rachel had eaten dinner. She hadn't been there when Rachel had fallen on the golf course taking Lucky for a walk, and Rachel hadn't told her about it at first, because she had hoped that if she never told anyone about it, it would go away. Beverly hadn't noticed, at first, that Rachel's knee had been swollen. Sometimes, Rachel was asleep by the time Beverly got home, and she ate her reheated dinner alone. She'd retire soon, though, and all of this work was going to be worth it. She was going to take Rachel to Santa Rosa Beach.

Beverly came home from work that day like it was any other, six in the evening, earlier than Rachel was expecting her. She'd brought the folder of proofs for the textbook home. She could finish her work here tonight. The screen door slammed behind her, and Lucky came running, nails scraping the floor. "Rach?" Beverly set her bag down. The mail was on the kitchen table. Beverly rifled through it. Just bills, most of them torn open already. "Hey, Rachel?" She scratched Lucky, who was staring up at her. One chocolate eye, one blue. "Where's Rachel, Lucky?" Lucky turned and trotted down the hallway.

The bedroom door was cracked open and spilling gold light into the dark hallway. "Rachel?"

Rachel was lying in bed, propped up by pillows. She was wearing the nightgown she'd worn the night before. Perhaps she hadn't taken it off. She'd fallen asleep with a crossword puzzle on her chest. The pencil had rolled onto the floor.

"Rachel, honey, wake up." Beverly sat down on the bed. The sigh from the mattress roused Rachel. Her whole face was pale, except for the shadows around her eyes. "Rachel, why'd you go to sleep so early?"

And Rachel started to sob. It was frightening. Beverly had never seen Rachel do that before.

"My knee." It was all she could muster. Beverly rolled her over and saw the swollen flesh around her joint, stretching up her thigh and down her calf. It was so tender that she screamed when Beverly brushed it.

It hadn't come on suddenly. But Beverly hadn't noticed.

The next day, Beverly took off work and took Rachel to the doctor. She looked small, sitting on the vinyl exam counter on a sheet of paper. She was shaking. Their doctor was a man with a rough bedside manner and a black mustache. He asked where Rachel's husband was and if he should call him to let him know what they would be doing. Beverly interrupted and said no, that would be fine. She counted the cotton balls in the jar on the counter to stop herself from saying anything else.

They ran a lot of tests, did a lot of things to her that made Rachel start to silently cry. It was unnerving to see a grown woman sob like a child. She sat there, full of needles, in her green cardigan. She should've been at the library, shelving books and chatting with her colleagues. She should've been planning their trip to Florida. It was just a few years until retirement. Rachel had already bought the travel books. She was thinking it would be a road trip.

It would take a few days to get the results of the test, the doctor told them, looking more at some spot on the wall than either of the women in his office. The wallpaper once had tiny flowers printed on it. It must have been beautiful when it was new.

Beverly insisted Rachel take a shower that night. For days, Rachel had been afraid, because she was having trouble keeping her balance and was sure she'd slip. Beverly offered to help. Lucky trotted in, nails scratching the tile, because it seemed like something exciting was happening in here. The shower already had a grab bar installed in the wall, for when Beverly's mother had stayed with them after her second hip replacement.

Rachel slowly stripped off her clothes. Her sweater set came off fine, but navigating the waistband of her pants around her swollen knee took the both of them. She sat on the lid of the toilet to reach her socks. Rachel was breathing audible, shallow breaths, the way you do when you have to think very carefully about breathing instead of crying. Beverly folded the sweater and pants so she didn't have to look at her. She wasn't sure why it felt indecent to linger now. She'd seen Rachel naked before.

Beverly helped her into the tub. It was a very pale pastel pink, a choice made by whoever had owned the house before them. Rachel had always liked it. She grabbed the bar on the wall and placed her other hand around Beverly's neck. They didn't close the shower curtain so that Beverly could help her, so as soon as they turned on the shower head, water misted into the bathroom. Beads of water ran down the walls. Lucky barked. Neither of them said anything.

Rachel closed her eyes and tipped her head back towards the popcorn ceiling. Beverly bent down to reach the bar of soap, stiffly, so that Rachel's hand on her shoulder didn't move too much. She lathered the soap in her hands and started to work it down Rachel's pale skin. She remembered, for a moment, the first time she'd seen her. Her cherry hair, now streaked with silver, turned almost black as it soaked up the water. The skin around Rachel's biceps was looser now, and her swollen thigh had straightened its gentle curves. Beverly rinsed the soap off. Rachel sighed.

The water spraying out of the tub had gathered in a pool at Beverly's feet. Her socks were soaked to the ankle. Rachel took her hand from Beverly's neck and shut the water off as Beverly searched for a towel. They listened to each other's breathing and the draining of the tub. Lucky had laid down in the doorway, watching them. Beverly tossed one towel on the floor to soak up the water and wrapped the other around Rachel, who was hanging onto the grab bar with both hands.

"Do you think you can lift me out of the tub?" Rachel asked. Her voice sounded strange.

"I can try."

Rachel shook as she wrapped her arms around Beverly's neck. Beverly bent to wrap her arms around Rachel's dripping legs and slick back. She winced when Beverly brushed her knee, but there was no other way to get her out of the tub. She made it far enough to set her back on the lid of the toilet, where they dried her off in silence.

"I think it's going to be something bad." Rachel tousled her own hair with the towel. Her hair clumped together in curls all on its own, which shook around her and stuck to her forehead.

"What do you mean?" Beverly mopped up the water on the floor and didn't look up at her.

"My leg. I think it's going to be something really bad, Bev."

"Rachel, you don't —"

"No. Don't try to make me feel better. I saw the doctor's face." Beverly gathered the saturated towel in her arms and stood there with it. "I think if I didn't have a reason to worry, he would have told me that." The towel was soaking her shirt, but she couldn't move it. Her jaw was locked shut. Her eyes were fixed on a spot on the floor, the intersection of four tiles where the grout was a little uneven. The grid blurred as her eyes lost focus.

"Come on," Rachel continued. "You're a scientist. You know that inflammation, it's not. I mean it's never... it's not gonna be good."

Beverly wondered if she should have studied something else. Her science couldn't help them now. Algae seemed insignificant. Pond scum.

They stayed there in the bathroom for a long time, Rachel wrapped in a towel on the toilet that she let slip from her shoulders and gather around her waist, Beverly clutching the towels and soaking a wet spot on her shirt. Water dripped slowly down Rachel's legs and traced the bones in her ankle. Neither of them moved, because it was easier that way. It was dark in the hallway, and the darkness came inside in gasps. The bathroom was lit by one bulb in the ceiling — the other had burnt out — and it did its best, glowing an orange halo. It was enough.

The next day, they got the call. Cancer.

LENA

2019

. . .

Lena didn't need to knock on Professor Knowles' door — she had an appointment, and she'd confirmed it again last night — but she knocked anyway. The mahogany door made a hollow sound. "Come in, Lena."

Knowles was already pouring their tea. They'd fallen off their weekly meetings, especially after Knowles had taken her sabbatical to study in the U.K. for Lena's junior spring, but she still made time for Lena when she could. It was always a few degrees warmer in Knowles' office than it was in the hallways of Carlisle. Maybe it was from her tea kettle. The window panes had a touch of fog on them. It was still too early to really be considered spring in New Hampshire, but everyone knew it was coming.

"How are things, Lena?" Knowles set down a mug in front of Lena and clasped both hands around hers. "I imagine you'll start hearing back from grad schools soon? Or is that what you've come here to tell me?"

Lena took a sip, and it scalded her tongue. "No, unfortunately. A lot of my friends have, though. Nisha's going to Duke."

Knowles smiled. "Good for her." It was all she said, like

she was waiting for Lena to add more.

"I'm sure I'll hear soon."

"I'm sure. Did you end up applying to all the schools we discussed?"

Lena picked at a hangnail. Technically, the answer was yes. "Yep."

"We miss you in the lab. I'm told none of this year's hires were as fast to learn the ropes... or as patient with the scales." Lena shuddered and Knowles laughed. "I'm sure you're glad to be moving on to bigger and better things, but my grad students are saying we need someone with Lena's work ethic!"

"Ah, you mean not knowing when to give up," she laughed, and Knowles did, too. The hangnail was starting to bleed. "My ex-boyfriend was quoted in *Scientific American,* so that was fun."

"Oh, I read that article! The chair shared it with all of us. He's very proud of Peter," Knowles smirked into her mug. "Am I sensing some jealousy? Your time will come, Lena."

Lena rubbed at her thumb to stop the bleeding, which made it worse. It spread into all the tiny cracks in her skin, like a fine lace. She set the mug down. "I really felt like I should be jealous, you know? Because that's the goal. Do what he's doing." There were footsteps in the hallway. "But I don't think I want to be that kind of scientist. Maybe."

Knowles nodded and set down her mug, too. "So what kind of scientist do you want to be?" Lena wasn't sure she'd meant anything by it, but Knowles was treating it like a serious thought. As though one could wake up and choose what kind of scientist one wants to be. As though tracks had been picked somewhere along the way, and Lena hadn't noticed.

Lena flexed her fingers. Her nails were cut short, so she wouldn't bite them, and her nail polish had chipped off. She'd stopped wearing her high school class ring, finally. It was almost time to get a new one, in a few weeks.

"I feel like we've been having this conversation for four years, Professor. I still don't know." The books in Professor Knowles' office were colorful. Lena had never stopped to read the spines.

They were all introductory textbooks, undergraduate journals, coffee table books with big illustrations of the universe or fossils. Anyone could have pulled them off the shelf and learned something, with or without a Ph.D. Middle-school-Lena and her maps of the woods would have had a field day. "One of those students I taught, Kira, sent me a note the other day."

"Oh?"

"She got into a science camp this summer. It sounds really cool. She's going to shadow some researchers and take a few classes, and there's a college prep thing, too." Lena flexed her fingers. "I wish I had known about programs like that when I was her age."

Knowles took a sip of tea, considering this. "She was lucky to have met you."

Lena laughed. "So I can pass along my anxieties? Yes, Professor, I made a freshman in high school panicked about college apps; I'm basically Mother Teresa."

"You met her when she was in *summer* school. She was falling behind. And now she's pursuing academic interests in her *free time.*"

Lena shook her head. Her eyes skimmed the rows of books; like she thought she might find some kind of answer there. It was easier than looking at the Professor; she could feel Knowles' gaze on her face without glancing over at her. "So what kind of scientist are you, Professor?"

Knowles followed Lena's eye to the bookshelf. "I'm still figuring that out."

There was one with raised letters on the spine. Metallic foil. Orbiting moons and unfurling leaves and beakers that poured with smoke dotted the white space around the type. It read *Science for You and Me* in big block letters.

Minutes passed, maybe. "Spring will be here soon, Lena."

She nodded. Spring would be here soon, whether it was wanted or not.

BEVERLY

1976

. . .

Rachel hadn't showered in a week when the girls from the library showed up at the house. Even if they had told her they were coming, it might not have made much of a difference. It was that hard for her to get in and out of the tub. But they hadn't called first.

There was a knock at the door and Rachel was propped up on the pillows they had pillaged from the couch. Her cherry and silver hair was greasy and spilled across her nightgown. It stood up at the root. Beverly knew that the bones in Rachel's face hadn't changed, but it seemed like it took more effort for her skin to stretch across them. The neck of Rachel's nightgown was stretched out and had an orange stain on it from last night's soup. Beverly was laying next to her in the bed, over the covers, still wearing what she'd worn to work that morning, her mud-streaked boots by the door. Lucky laid at the foot of the bed, occasionally lifting her head and fixing Beverly with her one-blue-eyed stare. The dog hadn't left Rachel's side since they'd gotten the call from their doctor.

"Were you expecting someone?" Rachel asked after too long, her eyes still closed.

"What?"

"The door."

Beverly had heard the knock, but she hadn't registered that she needed to get up and get it. Everything was moving slower in her head. She had only gone into work in the morning, and had come home at lunch and laid down next to Rachel and had only moved once since then, to bring her some water.

"Beverly, the door," Rachel opened her eyes.

"Right." Beverly stood like she had forgotten how and stumbled down the hall to the front door. Neither of them ever used the front door. It was strange to see silhouettes in the window. Plural. There was a crowd on their porch.

"Hello," she said as she pulled the front door open.

"Beverly! So good to see you my dear!" Beverly registered the face of one of Rachel's coworkers. She'd met her before, at least three times, once in the dairy aisle of the grocery store where Rachel had introduced them, and again at two holiday parties. The woman wrapped Beverly in a hug. She smelled like the perfume her mother had started wearing, the kind that reeked of dead flowers and vanilla and hung in the air even when you left the room.

When she let go of Beverly, she looked around at the other women on the porch. Two were holding aluminum-wrapped casserole dishes in oven-mitt hands. They were all in a variation of the same pastel outfit, high-waisted things that cinched at their middles like their rib cages were unfortunate obstacles to be conquered. Beverly's vision blurred and returned to focus. It had been days since she'd slept. All the women on her porch were looking at her like she was a stray puppy they'd found in a gutter. No one had looked at Beverly with that expression before. And she couldn't remember any of their names.

The women invited themselves in. They were colleagues of Rachel's — that's what they called themselves. Colleagues.

The woman with the perfume was Janice. The women holding the casseroles were Dawn and Marcia, sisters. They took the foil off the casseroles in the kitchen so Beverly could see the tops of them, latticed with slices of American cheese. "Dawn's famous tuna casserole," Janice said proudly, before she swept her eyes around the kitchen. Dirty dishes had piled up in the sink. The counter was covered in bills, some opened and some not. The coffee pot was full and cold. Beverly hadn't remembered making it. "We... figured you two might not be in the mood to cook," she offered, then flattened her mouth into a tight smile.

"Can we see our girl?" Marcia asked. "We brought her a card."

Beverly did not think Rachel was "theirs." It was strange to hear, and it hung in the air between them. "I don't know if that's a good idea. I'm sure she'll be glad to hear you came by. She's... not really ready for visitors. I wish I could have warned you." Beverly steadied herself on the arm of the couch, where Janice and Dawn had already sat down. They noticed the couch cushions were missing, but they did not say anything. They exchanged a nervous glance with each other and then perched at the edge of the couch.

"We sure did miss her at Bridge last month."

They all nodded. Beverly wasn't sure if she knew Rachel played Bridge with them. She must have mentioned it.

Beverly watched as they took in the living room. Her collection equipment, in a heap by the back door, smelled like saltwater and was caked in bright green seaweed, fried in the sun. The room was full of books and was neat, if not clean. Sparse. They all noticed the jar full of change labeled "Santa Rosa Beach" on the mantle and chose not to comment. The silence was oppressive.

"Have you been taking off work to take care of Rachel?"

"Only a little," Beverly sighed. "*We* have everything under control." The women seemed unsure how to react to this word, this "we." Beverly thought she saw Dawn mouthing it under her breath, rolling it around on her tongue. *We have everything under control.*

"How are you two making ends meet?" Marcia asked. "I mean, with you taking off work, and Rachel on leave."

"We have it under control."

"Do you or Rachel have any brothers to come help you here?" Dawn asked, trying to brush off her sweater in a way that did not make it clear she found the room a little disgusting. She failed.

"I have a few brothers, yes. But we don't need any help. I got her."

The women nodded. Beverly realized she'd never turned the lights on in the room. Her fingers hovered over the light switch, then she decided to let them sit in the dark. The sky was growing purple outside. It was nice to have the lights off.

"I'm sure you know to give her bone broth for her strength," Lucia, the smallest one, offered. Beverly nodded like she knew that. She did not. These women all had children to take care of, and pets and husbands. Their lives were filled with things that were fragile, easily injured. They had to know what foods are good for "strength." Lucia and the other women smiled knowingly to themselves, each staring at their folded hands in their laps and each thinking about a person they had nursed. One had a teenager back at home who had just gotten her tonsils out. None, though, had a cancer patient. So they didn't really know.

"Well, thank you all for the casseroles. Really." She wondered how many tuna casseroles you'd have to bake for them to become famous. She wondered if Dawn's tuna casseroles were famous. She wondered if Rachel liked tuna casserole, if she should have been making her tuna casserole. If tuna casserole was good for cancer.

"Of course." They all looked up at her the way they had on the porch. Like she needed their help. It was uncomfortable the way young women get when they think they're not supposed to say something, so it prints itself on their faces instead. "Are you sure we can't see Rachel?"

There was no reason they couldn't, except that they might notice how sick she looked. Rachel might have even liked to see her friends. But she didn't need to see their faces, the expression they'd had on since they appeared on the porch. Rachel didn't need anyone's pity.

"She's asleep," Beverly lied. "I'll let her know you came by."

The women understood. They collected themselves off the couch and shuffled to the door. "We just worry about you, you know," Janice whispered in her ear as she squeezed her in another hug. Vanilla and dead flowers. Like a funeral home. "Two girls all alone."

"We're not alone," Beverly said, louder than she'd meant to.

"Of course," Janice stammered, embarrassed. It was not clear if she was embarrassed for having angered Beverly, or embarrassed on her behalf. She was not sure which was worse. There was lipstick on her teeth. Beverly shut the door quickly, without saying goodbye.

She crept back down the hallway. The whole house was dark now, as the dregs of purple light in the windows slipped quietly away. Orange light spilled from their bedroom, where Rachel had fallen asleep with the lamp on.

Her head had fallen back on the couch cushion, which puckered in the middle. Her mouth was open slightly and her lips would be dry when she woke up. Beverly climbed into the bed next to her and put her head on Rachel's shoulder. Her eyes were only a few inches from Rachel's hair, and she studied the individual fibers. One black one, coarser than the rest, and a few gray hairs that looked like they'd been spun from silver. Occasionally, there was a red hair that was as red as it had been when they were just girls. Beverly smelled her neck, trying to remember every detail, like if she could preserve them all in her head, there would always be a Rachel alive in there with her. She didn't smell like dead flowers or vanilla. She smelled like flesh and earth and dandelions. The powder smell of their soap in the bathroom still lingering. The fresh smell of things that are alive, like when you cut a cucumber and the juice runs down your fingers. She was still alive.

Beverly stared at Rachel for hours until the light started to change in the windows. She slipped towards sleep and would be jerked awake by the twitch of Rachel's fingers or a particularly purposeful exhale. Beverly finally fell asleep wondering if Dawn's tuna casserole was really that good, and if her mother had been right and she should have learned all the things a woman should have learned. Maybe then she would know if a tuna casserole was good for cancer.

LENA

2019

· · ·

The library was incredibly quiet, which made sense for a sunny day in April. Nothing was blooming yet, but it was the promise of blooms that kept everyone going in New Hampshire. The library was empty, except for a few clusters of students who had commandeered white boards and were conjugating verbs or solving equations. That was why Lena had come here, she told herself, to escape from the pop music Nisha was playing in their room and the thumping of the bass from their upstairs neighbor. To really focus. It was not because Nisha had hung her Duke pennant over her bed while on FaceTime with her parents, who asked, not realizing Lena was in the room, if "your roommate finally figured out where she's going after graduation?" Nisha had looked up from her laptop, embarrassed, and quickly said that she was sure Lena would get her acceptances any day now. Lena had come to the library to study, not because her hands had started to shake because even Nisha's parents thought she was taking too long to figure her life out. She was here to focus.

Lena had come to the third floor, which was supposed to be the quietest. She found a stiff armchair that faced a big window. Libraries were full of pieces of furniture that looked more comfortable than they were, upholstered in a kind of slippery fabric that was easy to clean, even though they never really got cleaned. The seam between the armrest and the cushion was full of cracker crumbs.

The view of campus out the window would have been more serene if there wasn't a massive tent pitched on the far lawn between two buildings for the end-of-year performing arts showcase. Stacks of chairs, waiting to be set up, had been left in the grass and were casting long blue shadows. A large banner in front of the tent was almost legible from this window — but Lena had seen it on her walk to the library. It said, "Farewell Class of 2019." Across from that lawn, in the patch of grass in front of another academic building, were three girls stretched out on beach towels. They didn't appear to be working. Some classes were starting to wind down in advance of finals in a few weeks. Maybe they were sophomores and they weren't taking difficult courses. Worse, maybe they were seniors and they'd also already been accepted into their graduate programs, or they'd already been hired. Everyone else, it seemed, had a plan.

The library was incredibly quiet. At the table next to her, a man with a scruffy beard and a Marsden Lacrosse sweatshirt was highlighting a Spanish textbook like he thought someone was going to come and take it away from him. Lena could hear the squeak of the highlighter across the glossy pages. He had headphones in, and she could hear the music leaking out of them. Coldplay. Interesting choice.

Lena's hands were still shaking. She needed to focus. She opened her laptop. There wasn't much to focus on. She suddenly couldn't remember why she'd come to the library. It was a Friday night. She didn't have anything due tomorrow. But Marsden Lacrosse Guy was working. She should be working. She didn't have a job yet, or a grad program lined up, so until then, she should be working. His highlighter squeaked. He burped and he was close enough that Lena could smell the memory of the General Tso's chicken from the dining hall.

Marsden Lacrosse Guy probably had a job already. Maybe he was going to go get his Ph.D. in astrophysics. He bobbed his head to his insufferable music and tapped his foot under the desk. She wondered if he knew she could hear it.

Lena refreshed her email. She wasn't sure what she was expecting to see. Even a rejection would have been helpful, because at least then she'd know. Nothing. Just a coupon from a shoe company she wasn't sure she'd ever purchased from anyways. The air conditioning kicked on and Lena could hear tubes or pipes or whatever they were expanding in the ceiling and walls. Marsden Lacrosse Guy's song changed. His highlighter squeaked. Somewhere, someone moved their chair and it scraped the floor. Lena refreshed her email. Nothing. The sun was starting to dip behind the buildings, casting the tent in shadow. "Farewell Class of 2019." Her hands shook and her leg started to bounce, too. Highlighter squeak. He turned the page. Highlighter squeak. Lena refreshed her email. Nothing. Somewhere, someone coughed. "Farewell Class of 2019."

Lena tugged at a hangnail on her thumb, exposing a strip of dark pink flesh next to her nail. Blood slowly rose between the cracks in her skin. "Farewell Class of 2019." The banner faded into the silhouette of the tent. Her pulse pounded in her temple.

The chair was uncomfortable. She shifted in it, the fabric of her jacket rubbing against the shiny armrest, puckered with buttons. She refreshed her email again. There was still no acceptance, no rejection. But shoes were still on clearance. After an hour, Marsden Lacrosse Guy packed up his books and left. It should have been peaceful without the squeaking of his highlighter and the tinny sound of his headphones. The vacuum he left behind was filled with Lena's own breathing.

Once she became aware of it, she tried to force deep breaths. Consciously breathing is always a little terrifying, because if you forget to breathe, you'll die. Lena closed her eyes.

When she opened them, she wondered if she would ever start breathing automatically again, or if she'd have to remind herself to take deep breaths forever. There were still no new emails. And she had dripped blood on her keyboard.

BEVERLY

1977

. . .

The food on the tray was starting to look appetizing, which must have meant Beverly was really hungry. They'd brought Rachel a Salisbury steak in what the nurse had called "brown sauce," and that was probably the only acceptable term for it. It was brown. And it was sauce. Rachel hadn't touched it, and it was cold now.

Beverly shifted in her chair. It was a dark turquoise vinyl that had stuck to the backs of her legs. She had to peel herself off of it. The sound was just one of the many they'd grown used to here. Rachel had been admitted to Massachusetts General eight days ago, and she'd only moved from that bed a handful of times. There were thin blue curtains between each bed in the ward, connected to the rod overhead with a kind of netting that let air, smells and sounds pass freely. The beeping of the machines attached to Rachel was layered with the beeping from the machines the next bed over, and the next bed over. Rachel hadn't said much since she'd been admitted. Beverly counted the floor tiles when she couldn't bear to keep looking at Rachel's face. The floor was checkered, a pastel peach color and a pale blue. It made Beverly nauseous and she wasn't sure why.

There should have been a window, Beverly decided. That would have helped. A nurse came and took the cold Salisbury steak away. If there was a window, they could watch the sun rise or set the way they could from their porch. Nothing ever seemed so bad when there was a tree line that seemed different every time you looked at it.

Rachel had osteosarcoma. Bone cancer. She'd been right, as she usually was. Sometimes it would have been nice to be wrong — about this, and a few other things.

Someone coughed. Maybe one of the other patients in the ward. It sounded painful. Beverly had been sleeping in this chair, one hand on Rachel's bed.

She hadn't been to work in weeks. The proofs for the next edition of the book were sitting, unopened, on the kitchen table back in Marsden. Lucky was staying with one of Rachel's girlfriends from the library, one of the girls who hadn't been on the expedition to their house. Beverly couldn't have asked Dawn or Janice for help.

There was a card on the small table next to the hospital bed from all the ladies at the library. It had a sketch of a bouquet of flowers on the front, daisies and tulips in colored pencil. It would have been nice to have a real bouquet of flowers, too, and maybe Beverly should have gone and got some. They sold them in the depressing little gift shop, along with sticks of gum and mylar balloons that said, "It's a Boy!" and Beverly had to pass it every time she came and left the hospital. She never stopped to buy any. Flowers are what you bring to funerals. They didn't need flowers.

"Bev," Rachel rasped. She was on a lot of drugs. It was the first time in days that she'd seemed aware that Beverly was in the room. She'd called her "nurse" once before, and otherwise, she'd looked right through her. Like Beverly wasn't even there. The corners of her mouth were dry and cracked.

"I'm here." She reached for Rachel's limp hand, resting on the thin hospital sheets. Her hand was warm. She squeezed it.

Beverly never paid attention to what drugs they had Rachel on, but they were hanging there in a bag, next to the bed, slowly dripping into her system. They weren't treating the cancer; it was too far gone. They were just to keep her comfortable. She should have been more help, should have understood what this medication was or that one. Shouldn't have studied algae.

There were thirteen blue tiles and seventeen peach ones.

"Beverly." Rachel's head rolled over on her pillow, so her glassy eyes found Beverly's face. Something changed in them and came into focus. She was seeing Beverly for the first time in days. "Oh, Bev. There you are."

"I'm right here." Beverly's hands were shaking.

"I thought you were gone."

Somewhere else in the ward, a nurse pulled back a curtain. The metal track was loud.

"I've been right here. I'm always right here."

Rachel swallowed deliberately, like it took some effort. Something that was protruding from the stretched skin on her neck moved up and down when she swallowed. She closed her eyes. "Beverly."

The machine hanging over them beeped. A nurse appeared and switched one bag to another.

"I love you, Rachel. I should've said it more often."

This wasn't how it should've happened. They should have been in Santa Rosa Beach, watching the sunset. That's what she deserved. Not this, one cot in a ward full of beds, indistinguishable from all the others.

"Rachel." Her eyes were closed. Beverly could hear her own heart beating. Maybe if she recounted the tiles on the floor, there would be a different number. More blue tiles this time. Maybe it would help. "Rachel, stay with me. I'm right here."

Her hand twitched in Beverly's. Her face was almost un-recognizable, like the muscles had slipped and moved around, puffed up and then sank back into the bone. Her cheeks were stretched thin over her cheekbones. But it was still Rachel.

"Rachel."

Rachel, whooping in the fire truck as it sped down the street, sirens blaring, red hair fluttering behind her in the wind. Rachel, rattling a handful of Raisinets just to prove she could make Beverly laugh in a silent movie theater. Rachel, dancing in her socks in the kitchen to the radio and grabbing Beverly's hands and making her dance, too. Racing the dog in the grass and getting sad when she lost. Waiting for Beverly outside of Carlisle Hall so they could walk home together. Doing her crossword puzzles before bed with her wet hair dripping onto her nightgown and pillow. She'd gotten Beverly to laugh for some forty years. She'd always been the more emotional one, who thought everything was possible. Why shouldn't they be firewomen? Why couldn't Beverly publish a book? Why couldn't these two old women take a road trip to Florida, get in their old car and just keep driving straight until they saw the ocean? When Beverly hadn't been able to cry, Rachel had cried for her.

"Rachel, please." A tear slipped down Beverly's cheek. It was dark in the ward. She searched Rachel's face. The sun had gone down and some of the patients were trying to sleep. The nurses had slowly turned off all the lights, the way it fades to black in a theater. "Rachel."

Rachel's eyes opened, heavy, and tried to focus on Beverly. "You're here."

She kept her eyes fixed on Beverly until she was gone.

LENA

2019

. . .

It was loud inside Lena Rivera's head. It was spring in New Hampshire, green shoots pushing from the earth and green buds bursting from dormant branches, and Lena didn't see any of them. She was walking quickly, without a purpose or direction, and almost took out a woman with a stroller.

It was like her brain was humming, louder, drowning out thoughts and words with a dull, all-consuming roar. Lena wasn't good at handling Good News, because any news at all was change and that was big and unknown. Her hands were shaking. She needed to tell someone, everyone, the next person she passed on the sidewalk. Her feet were moving, but they weren't taking her anywhere in particular. She was coursing with energy. Grad school. Grad school.

She'd tried Nisha's cell one more time than was appropriate — thirty? Was thirty too many? — and her dad was still at work. The sun beat down on her. Professor Knowles? She'd already passed the Professor's office. Peter's name flashed in her mind. It was odd to see him there.

Lena typed Peter's name into her contacts, and her thumb hovered dangerously over the call button. And she erased it. It had been months, too many months to reach out now. He wasn't going to be the person she called. Lena put her phone back in her pocket with shaking hands, so the phone got caught in the fabric and she had to force it in. Her heart was racing, and she wondered if she might pass out. If she didn't call anyone to tell them, no one would know she'd be lying somewhere, blacked out in the grass, because she wasn't chemically able to handle Good News.

Springtime had exploded in Marsden overnight. Blooms everywhere, choking the air with sweetness and clouds of insects. She wasn't sure who to tell. It wouldn't be as simple as "I got in." None of them knew she'd applied to this program. It had sounded too strange to say out loud.

Lena's palms were sweating. She turned her class ring around her finger — the new one, with the Marsden seal.

And then she saw it. The old oak tree. *Her oak tree,* where she'd sat and eaten lunch freshman year, every day after Bio 101, as long as the weather was warm enough. Where she'd studied for her midterms in the fall and her finals in the spring, as soon as the snow melted. Her feet slowed as she neared the blue ellipse of shadow. In this shade, she'd doubted whether she could be a scientist — whether she even wanted to be one. This was where she'd fallen back in love with biology, lying on her back watching the clouds one day and catching the sunlight streaming through a yellow leaf. She could see every vein, the vascular tissue she'd just learned about in the lecture that morning. An entire universe, nested inside this one, just for her to see and meditate on and hold in her hands. This was where she'd looked out over campus, this was where it had begun to feel like her dominion. And this was where she'd fallen in love for real, for the first time. It was bittersweet to think about, but there it was.

Lena fell to her knees in the grass and pulled out her phone. The email blinked on screen; she read it four or five more times. *Congratulations.*

Leaves fell around her in the breeze like snow, or maybe confetti. This had always been her tree.

Congratulations Lena. On behalf of the faculty of the College of Arts and Sciences, I am pleased to accept you into our Master of Science in Elementary Education program.

Lena laid back into the bed of fresh mulch and let the smell of sweet earth coat her tongue. The people she should be telling were her students, Kira and Liam and Tommy and the rest. Finishing up their first year of high school, somehow.

They would be so excited for her. Lena looked up at the spray of branches over her head, dotted with green buds that would unfurl any day now into leaves. She squinted one eye until the silhouette of the branch above her came into focus. With her heart still racing, she fell asleep in the sun.

She just had to figure out how to tell everyone else that she wouldn't be getting her Ph.D. after all. She was going to be a different kind of scientist.

BEVERLY

1980

. . .

There should've been someone waiting for her when Beverly Conner came home from Marsden College for the last time. Her last day of work, her first day of retirement. There should've been a nice dinner on the table and there should've been someone to dance with, to the radio and in socks on the linoleum floor. But there was no fanfare when she got home, or even a fried chicken.

Beverly retired from the College in relative silence. No one seemed to notice it was her last day. There hadn't even been a card for everyone to sign. She came home that day in creased pants and a white shirt with a red kerchief around her neck, the one that Rachel had always worn in her hair when she was younger. She fumbled for it with her arthritic fingers and smoothed the satin into her collarbone.

Beverly made herself a turkey sandwich and did her crossword puzzle while she ate it. This wasn't the same house, with all of her memories. She looked around her at the porch. After Rachel died, the house burned down. She was still jittery living alone, and a small grease fire in the kitchen had caught. The house had old bones. The boys from Engine 12 tried to take care of it, but the fire had gone up into the walls. They said it burned so hot the brass in the grandfather clock melted. Some of the books and photos had survived. A lot hadn't. She was living close to campus now, a place where she could take the bus to work every day, because she didn't like driving anymore. It was nice enough, but she missed having a garden.

There wasn't really anyone to say goodbye to at the College. All the men who Beverly remembered from the first few decades at Marsden had retired. Dr. Bell, the scientist afraid of scuffed shoes, was twenty years older than her. He'd passed away the previous fall. Dean Peabody, to whom she owed her voice, was long gone, buried in Arlington at a ceremony she'd dragged Rachel to — his wife had been there, and she wasn't sure who cried more. Henry Nightingale had taken a full professorship at Harvard after *Miracles of Biology* had done so well. They didn't speak as often anymore, which was kind of funny, since they were in the same time zone now. The school had grown up right beside her. Within the administration, there were some rumblings of letting women in, perhaps, in a few years. It was a different place, this College of hers. So it wasn't the one she would've wanted to say goodbye to, anyway.

She still had a small porch. It wasn't like the screened-in thing the old house had had — that one had been better, of course, and had listened to fireside chats and to many heated arguments. Her one requirement for this new condo was that she could still sit outside and watch the sunset. Beverly picked up her cane and slowly made her way to the wicker sofa. She was still quite nimble, considering neither of her hips were the ones she'd started life with.

There should've been someone there to look at her. A physicist to study her, a firewoman to give her a boost up the ladder.

They'd never made it to Santa Rosa Beach. The jar full of

spare change they were saving for the trip sat on the mantle inside, half full.

The sofa cracked with a satisfying sound, the way wicker furniture always announces your presence. Lucky curled up on the floor in front of her, studying her with her blue and brown eyes. Beverly always tried to get Lucky to sit up on the sofa with her, but she wouldn't sit in Rachel's spot, as though it needed to be ready in case she walked through the door.

Beverly stared out towards the mountains. The horizon stays pretty much the same, and if all you ever do is look up and out, you can convince yourself that you stay the same, too. Beverly could practically hear the rushing water and peals of laughter from all those summers at Woods Hole. She could close her eyes and feel the sunlight warm her skin and reach out behind her and drag her fingers through the water. Now, her hands shook from arthritis, but her eyes were as clear as the first time they spotted Carlisle Hall in the distance.

Beverly finished the crust of her turkey sandwich and dusted the crumbs off of her lap. She had letters from colleagues and former students to answer. Maybe she'd do that later. She'd started using a typewriter for her correspondence, since holding the pen was exhausting. The pile of letters by the screen door was growing. Last week, she'd gotten one all the way from the Soviet Union, covered with stamps from four countries on its way to her.

She had put a little bookshelf here on the porch, since it was where she'd always liked to read. The first and second editions of *Miracles of Biology* were stacked neatly together. The Green Book she'd kept in her office all those years, even though Rachel had never understood why. The faculty hand-book. Copies of every journal that had published every paper of her career — some forty-five publications in all. They stretched three shelves.

It was fitting that Beverly Conner left Marsden in the

summertime. The ivy that clung to the cracks in the bricks was shrunken, parched. But Beverly knew plants better than she knew anyone alive, and she knew that plants could come back from the dead. In the fall, when students packed the sidewalks and caught up on missed summers, the leaves would be back and they would be green. The mere idea was enough for Beverly, the knowledge that some student might pause outside Carlisle Hall and look up and find that those concrete steps offer a glimpse of an entire universe — a network of veins and cells, lit up and glowing like a private secret between viewer and sun.

Beverly leaned back into the wicker sofa. It stretched behind her. She folded her hands in her lap and watched the sun set. A purple cloud slowly pulled itself apart in front of the rippling red sun. The mountaintops looked like waves.

EPILOGUE

LENA
2019

. . .

June in New Hampshire was bright and hot, even after spring had dragged its feet. The air was heavy with everything in bloom and the dampness that hangs after too many feet have trampled grass. After sitting in a folding chair for two hours, baking in the sun in a black polyester gown and mortarboard lined in now wilting cardboard, Lena was sweating and probably sunburned. All the other graduates were finding their family in the crowd. Lena had told hers to meet her by a tree she'd pointed out earlier. She hadn't spotted them.

Lena unzipped her robe — and thought that the mere presence of the zipper at all made it much less ancient and timeless — and wiped her sweaty palms on the blue sundress her stepmother had loaned her for the ceremony. Her honors cords were damp, and when she reached up to adjust them, she felt heat radiating from the back of her neck. Definitely sunburned. She didn't really care. Lena leaned against the tree and thought this must be one of the few times you could look in any direction you picked and just see smiling faces. She let the hum of competing conversations and the occasional flashes of cameras wash over her. There. Her father making his way through the crowd.

"My graduate." Lena's father flicked the tassel on her mortarboard. "I just can't believe you really did it." He playfully punched her arm.

"Dad." She feigned annoyance, but a part of her lit up at the mention of the word. Graduate.

"My daughter! The graduate!" As his voice climbed higher, Lena's eyes darted around her out of habit. But for perhaps the first time since she'd stepped foot on Marsden's campus, that thing burning within her chest wasn't embarrassment. It was pride.

The graduate.

Her family was just as excited as she was to do the laps. Spilling across every green space, crowded in the blue shade of every tree, families and graduates swarmed. Lena was surprised at how many people recognized her. One girl, whose name Lena could not place, ran up to her and demanded they take a photo. "I'll miss you!" she shouted after Lena as they both melted back into the crowd. Peter's fraternity brothers fist-bumped their congratulations as she walked past, which felt appropriate, since it would have been strange not to acknowledge them but stranger to actually have to say something. They called her "champ" and Lena wondered if they couldn't remember her name. Maybe she should have found that sad, but the whole thing made her want to laugh. Jolie, who had been crying what Lena assumed were happy tears, gave her a shaky hug as they exchanged jokes about not missing that class at all. No more late nights in the library.

Nisha materialized by her side and linked her arm through Lena's, the polyester of their black gowns sliding against each other. They were baking in the June sunshine and beaming exhausted, flushed smiles like runners who had just finished a marathon. And they didn't speak much, as they walked around and waved to professors, librarians, classmates. Members of the junior class who watched the spectacle with envy. It wasn't like Nisha not to speak, but there wasn't much point; everything that she was feeling, Lena was, too. After four years of education, neither had been taught the words to articulate it.

Nisha squeezed her arm as she was called away. "You'll call me tomorrow, right?" She whispered with a laugh, so their onlooking families couldn't hear. "Tomorrow's *Project Runway* night, and a tradition is a tradition."

Lena laughed. She watched Nisha grow smaller through the crowd until she could have covered her black polyester form with her thumb. She wasn't sure if Nisha was serious about their traditions. She wasn't sure if they would last. Nisha had gotten into her program at Duke and made Lena swear she'd come to Durham to visit. Someone bumped into her shoulder and dropped their creased program. When Lena handed it back to them, Nisha was gone.

Professor Knowles caught her eye from across the green expanse. She was talking to two other biology professors and one of their graduate students, who was talking with her hands in a flurry of excitement. The air around them hummed, like it did around Lena as well. At her side, Professor Knowles had a rapt, curly-haired child. She held onto the tips of her mother's fingers and gazed up at the graduate student with her full, wide-eyed attention. Lena recognized the expression. Knowles waved with something more than pride in her eyes and then turned back. The Professor had been the first one Lena had told — she was going to be a science teacher.

They finally made it to the doors of the Student Center, which were propped open with balloon bouquets. The air-conditioned air hit them like a wall. Lena had walked through those doors hundreds of times, dashing in to grab a granola bar between classes, meeting Nisha and her roommate in the basement on Friday nights to study, give up, and complain about their professors over mozzarella sticks and embarrass-ingly awful games of pool in the billiards hall. Lena stopped at the top of the stairs and peered down through the glass windows into the room full of pool tables and wasn't expecting something so silly to catch in her throat.

"I-I'll be right back. I'm going to get some water. Meet you outside." When her family disappeared around the corner, Lena opened the sealed tube with shaking hands and pulled out her diploma like it might dissolve when she held it. It was real, it was here, it had her name on it. Lena carefully sealed the tube up and looked around her at the hallways that felt small now. Bulletin boards with club meetings and a cappella recitals. Old rosters for the squash team from 1935 and an oil painting of the school's president.

There was a silver bowl. They kept it here in the Student Center in a glass case. Lena walked by it every day, one of many plaques now patinated and photos now faded. But if she had ever stopped to read it, which she never did, she would've read something rather special.

The Beverly Thompson Conner Award

Established in 2000 by the First Meeting of Marsden Alumnae, on the fifteenth anniversary of coeducation.

For all she did for Marsden, for Science, and for Women.

She taught us to grow in the most uninhabitable of places.

Lena considered her reflection in the glass and the shapes of her own face, distorted, wrapping around the curves of the silver bowl. Then she walked outside, where her family was waiting with the same smiles that were making their cheeks ache. They were arguing about one of the brick buildings they stood in front of, looking at it for the first time. As Lena approached them, she could almost picture what it was like to look at campus, bathed in sunlight, without painful and beautiful memories.

"Are you ready to go?"

Her father laughed. "We're following you, Lena. It's your school."

The sun glinted in her eyes, and she shielded her face with her hand. "Okay. This way." They stepped out of the shade and into the crowd. Lena looked out from the patio.

The quad seemed to glow in the sunlight, helped by the white buildings that overlooked it. Some brick, as well, for variation. The trees bent and shook their leaves in the breeze so the pale undersides flipped up to the sun. Black caps and gowns grew smaller and smaller as they crossed the quad, like ants. There had always been straight diagonal paths that crossed the quad, but no one really followed them. Graduates and their families cut across the grass in dozens of directions. Some went back towards the road, to their dorms, to doors and windows and shutters. Some were headed towards the mountains. Turquoise shapes on the horizon.

AUTHOR'S NOTE

HANNAH THOMPSON CROASDALE
1905 – 1999

. . .

Hannah Thompson Croasdale was born in Berwyn, Pennsylvania in 1905. She was a freshman in high school when women were granted the right to vote, and she attended the University of Pennsylvania at a time when only three majors were open to women — Hannah chose biology. When she finally left Penn with her Ph.D. and several awards for her research in algae, she spent several years at Woods Hole Marine Laboratory. It was through Woods Hole that Hannah got connected to a job opening at Dartmouth College: a lab technician position, which she was overqualified for, but still took, during the Great Depression.

Though she made herself invaluable at the College, and continued her research and publishing while quietly picking up the slack around the Botany department, it was several decades before Hannah was promoted to a professorship. She was Dartmouth's first woman professor to receive tenure. She was also the first woman to volunteer in Hanover's fire department, during World War II. She taught the first group of Dartmouth women, finally admitted to the College in the

1970s, before she retired.

Dartmouth awards the Hannah Croasdale Award annually to the student who has made the greatest impact on the quality of life for women at the College. When asked in an interview after her retirement how she felt about her impact on the women's liberation movement and the generations of Dartmouth Women she paved the way for, she said simply, "I never did anything for those women except tell them to be quiet and wait."

ACKNOWLEDGMENTS

This work has been around five years in the making, starting my first summer at Dartmouth as Rauner's first Historical Accountability Research Fellow. I fell in love with the story of Hannah Croasdale, Dartmouth's first female professor to receive tenure. Her rich archive — as well as the noticeable gaps in it — haunted me. I came to understand that I knew more about the details of her story than anyone else alive, and if I didn't tell this story, it simply would not get told. I am indebted first and foremost to Hannah, for providing the backbone of what became *Tell Them to Be Quiet and Wait,* as well as Jay Satterfield and everyone at Rauner Library for giving me such support during that time. This novel was sparked by a conversation with Jay, who suggested that I turn her story into a graphic novel. Celia Chen, a student of Hannah's and a professor at Dartmouth herself, gave me great insight that summer that has continued to inform my work.

I would not consider myself a writer were it not for the Introduction to Fiction class I took with Professor Alexander Chee. His guidance, and example, have been incredibly important as I found my voice over the years. This project started as a series of vignettes, which quickly turned into chapters, and was workshopped under Professor Tommy O'Malley my senior fall. His advice, and the patience of the group of peers who became an invaluable workshop — Julia, Madison, Valentina, Nicole, and Daisy — shaped this piece into something that I can be proud of. And Professor Bill Craig, who took over in the last legs of the process during my senior spring, looked upon the project with fresh eyes and a new perspective that asked me questions I didn't yet have answers for. To all of them I am incredibly grateful.

I must thank my parents, whose approach to my brother's and my education in my earliest years allowed me to fall in love with stories and daydream of writing books one day. My father, especially, was one of the first writers I looked up to, and my brother was the first audience I wrote for. The hundreds of stories I subjected him to while we were home-schooled together — full of jokes written just for him — fueled my desire to tell stories. And, of course, I must thank Dhruv Mohnot, who was the only person I would let read my writing for many years and whose opinion, after all these years, is still the most important to me.

Courtney McKee read the very first version of this book, when it was a novella, and the incredible feedback she gave me is present in nearly every chapter of this work. The team of women who believed in me, as well as the mentors who gave me their time and advice, exemplifies what I came to understand in Hannah's story: we are nothing without our community. I cannot express my thanks to everyone who made this work possible, and to the fantastic team at Atmosphere Press, especially Megan Turner and Alex Kale, who took a chance on my debut novel

My grandmother Goldie Cook passed away my sophomore year at Dartmouth. She helped raise me, and was one of the strongest, most talented people I have ever known. She informs Beverly Conner — named for my grandmother's maiden name — as much as Hannah does. But other stories I heard along the way show up in the book as well. Beverly Conner stands for an entire generation of American women who existed in a particular moment in history that asked them to be painfully tolerant in the face of incredible cultural upheaval. To all of them who came before us, we owe everything.

ABOUT ATMOSPHERE PRESS

Atmosphere Press is an independent, full-service publisher for excellent books in all genres and for all audiences. Learn more about what we do at atmospherepress.com. We encourage you to check out some of Atmosphere's latest releases, which are available at Amazon.com and via order from your local bookstore:

Dancing with David, a novel by Siegfried Johnson

The Friendship Quilts, a novel by June Calender

My Significant Nobody, a novel by Stevie D. Parker

Nine Days, a novel by Judy Lannon

Shining New Testament: The Cloning of Jay Christ, a novel by Cliff Williamson

Shadows of Robyst, a novel by K. E. Maroudas

Home Within a Landscape, a novel by Alexey L. Kovalev

Motherhood, a novel by Siamak Vakili

Death, The Pharmacist, a novel by D. Ike Horst

Mystery of the Lost Years, a novel by Bobby J. Bixler

Bone Deep Bonds, a novel by B. G. Arnold

Terriers in the Jungle, a novel by Georja Umano

Into the Emerald Dream, a novel by Autumn Allen

His Name Was Ellis, a novel by Joseph Libonati

The Cup, a novel by D. P. Hardwick

The Empathy Academy, a novel by Dustin Grinnell

Tholocco's Wake, a novel by W. W. VanOverbeke

Dying to Live, a novel by Barbara Macpherson Reyelts

Looking for Lawson, a novel by Mark Kirby

Yosef's Path: Lessons from my Father, a novel by Jane Doyle

Surrogate Colony, a novel by Boshra Rasti

ABOUT THE AUTHOR

Caroline Cook is an artist and writer whose work can be found in *McSweeney's, Ms. Magazine*, and elsewhere. *Tell Them to Be Quiet and Wait* is her first novel, heavily informed by her time at Dartmouth College.

Connect with her on Instagram @obstinateartist, Twitter @caroline_e_cook, or at wwww.caroline-cook.com.

CPSIA information can be obtained
at www.ICGtesting.com
Printed in the USA
LVHW100746251022
731430LV00004B/149